BETWEEN BROTHERS

SACRED HEARTS MC
BOOK 11

A.J. DOWNEY

COPYRIGHT

DEDICATION

To the lovers and supporters. This one is for you.

PROLOGUE

H ayley...

The bell above the door rang and I heard Melody say, "Hey guys!" We had regulars, but none of them brought the level of affection and familiarity that whoever walked through the door did to Mel's voice. It made me turn around. The men who'd walked in belonged to her new husband's motorcycle club which explained it.

I took the plates of food from the warmer and brought them to the table they went to, setting them down for the two older gentlemen who came in occasionally for lunch. They smiled up at me with murmured thanks and I gave them a nod, slipping my hand into my apron pocket for my pad and pen, heading over to the pair who'd seated themselves at one of *my* tables.

Strange, you'd think they'd want to sit in Mel's section...

Cool, liquid gray eyes followed my every movement as I came up the line of booths. I could see the fiery red of the back of his companion's head and when I stopped at their table and smiled, brown eyes with a fire of their own looked up at me. I asked, "You know what you'll have to drink?"

The redhead cocked back his head, those deep brown eyes appraising, and he said, "I'll have a Coke; he'll have water."

Strange that he would order for the other one, but I didn't comment. Instead, I nodded, writing it down and asked, "You know what you want to eat, or do you need a little more time?"

"Give us a minute," the redhead answered, and I nodded and went to get their drinks. He leaned forward and talked to the silent one with the beautiful eyes and I watched them a moment, while they were otherwise engaged.

"I think Blue likes you." I startled and Melody laughed lightly.

"Which is which?" I asked.

"Duracell's the copper top; Blue's the quiet one."

"Don't they have regular names?"

Mel shrugged. "In their world that *is* their regular name."

I pondered that a moment and took them their drinks, setting them down asking, "Know what you'd like?"

The redhead, Duracell, smiled up at me and said, "What'd it take to get your number? Because I think we'd both really like that."

He winked and I blushed and looked away from him, straight into those beautiful, if sad, gray eyes of his *partner? Friend?* I didn't know what they were but the vibe between the two of them was unlike anything I'd ever encountered. Duracell's friend, Blue, smiled at me and my heart fluttered, which only made me color a little more.

"I don't give that out," I murmured to Duracell and asked Blue, "Do you know what you want?" The intensity behind his gray gaze unnerved me, but his smile put me at ease, he pointed to an item on the menu and I looked.

"Do you want ranch, honey mustard, or barbecue sauce with your chicken strips?" He held up a single long elegant finger and I blinked.

"Option one," his friend said. "The ranch."

"Does he not speak?" I asked.

"Only when it matters, and usually only to me."

Curiouser and curiouser, I thought to myself, smiling slightly. I loved Lewis Carroll and a number of other classic authors, and it was rare that a term fit as well as this one did now.

"And what about you? What will you have?" I asked.

"I already said, I'll take your number."

"I don't give that out, and I hardly think it'd be that appetizing," I said.

Duracell tore his eyes from mine and I fought not to shiver, although for a very different reason than what Blue's gaze did to me. I swallowed hard and the two of them stared at one another for a long hard moment, something passing between them, silently.

"Burger and fries," Duracell said, finally. "No onions."

"Cheese?"

"American."

"Fries, onion rings, or chips?"

"If I didn't want onions on the burger why the fuck would I want onion rings?"

I felt the casual smile slide right off my face and I tried not to shake as he turned that burning gaze of his back to my face. I swallowed hard and said, "Just an automatic question, I'm sorry…"

"Chips," he said and I nodded, writing it down.

"I'll be back as soon as that's up."

"Cool."

I went to put their order in and risked a glance at their table, both of them were openly staring at me, Blue murmuring something to the frighteningly intense one, Duracell.

"Hayley, you alright?"

I startled at Mel's voice at my elbow and smoothed my sweating palms over my apron.

"Fine, I'm fine!"

She sighed, her shoulders dropping some and asked, "Duracell being a dick?"

I smiled back and shook my head. "No, it's fine, really... just... is he always that..." I trailed off and Mel smiled, raising her light blonde eyebrows, her blue eyes sparkling.

"Intense?"

"Yeah."

She nodded. "He's being a dick; I'll go talk to him."

"No! No, it's fine, really."

"You sure?"

"I'm sure."

"Okay, but I'd look out for him. Not Blue though, Blue's a total sweetheart."

I turned around as the bell chimed above the door and Melody called out, "Welcome in! Be right with you."

"I've got this one?" she asked and I nodded.

I served the two bikers when their food was up and silently refilled their drinks. Duracell talked at Blue, holding an entire conversation just like the silent man was answering back, and maybe he was but I certainly couldn't tell. I brought them their check at the end of the meal and Duracell handed me a bank card.

"Be right back," I murmured, taking a peek at the name on the card before I swiped it.

Paul Glenn

I took him back his card and handed him the two slips that went with it.

"Got a pen?"

"Sure, here you are, Mr. Glenn." I handed him the pen but he bypassed it, catching my wrist.

"If you're going to call me anything, it's going to be Duracell or just Cell, don't you *ever* say that name again."

"I-I-I'm s-s-sorry," I stuttered and just as fast as he'd caught me by the wrist, around the soft cushion of the white sweatband I wore to protect it from the edges of hot plates, he let me go. *That's not why you wear them,* my traitorous mind whispered. I went to turn and walk away, call my dad from the kitchen but Blue's somber gaze stopped me.

Something silent but meaningful passed between us and my fear evaporated, gone as soon as it'd come. I found myself stumbling a bit as I walked away from their table, tripping over my own feet, transfixed by that somber silvery gaze.

When I turned back, Mel was leaning a hip against their table, her arms crossed, the three of them looking my direction. She said something, and Duracell said something back. I turned away, and a moment later the bell above the door chimed.

"Thanks, Hayley; be seein' you," Duracell called and Blue was heading out the door right behind him. He inclined his head and then the door was closing. Still, I watched through the glass, the retreating colorful patches on their backs as they went down the steps and headed for their bikes in the parking lot.

I blinked and went to bus their table quickly as two more men came through the door. When I stopped to pick things up, there, where Blue had been sitting, was a neatly folded, tiny, paper blossom out of one of their receipts. Delicate, beautiful, far too pretty to throw away. I put it into my apron pocket and quickly went back to work. It was the middle of the lunch rush, after all.

1

Nineteen months later...

B lue...

"Quittin' time, boys!" the foreman called and I shot a look down the road we were working on to Cell. He gave me a chin lift and I nodded. I'd hated this particular job something fierce. We'd been working swing on this project for the last six weeks. We'd still been hitting up the diner, it being open twenty-four hours, but the change in schedule meant Hayley was off shift way before we got there.

I missed her. She was a kindred spirit, I could see it the moment I'd laid eyes on her; that given half a chance, we'd click. I wanted that. Ached for it fiercely, realizing just how much I was missing out by not having a woman in my life. It was a strange sort of relationship I'd found with Cell, but he was hard and the fact he was so closed off and had so many sharp edges meant that I couldn't always get what I needed from him. I needed more, and so he'd reluctantly agreed to let me find a woman to join us.

Being his friend was sometimes difficult, loving him was sometimes impossible. It was like we were missing the piece that went between us. Like we *almost* fit, but we needed that third, and we both knew it.

The only thing I could give Cell was that he had been pretty patient when it came to trying to get Hayley's attention. She was a shy girl, extremely so, and Cell's usual way of doing things wasn't going to work. I'd figured that out the first time we'd met her. So, he'd done the rare thing and had let me take lead in trying to get her to go out with us.

It was a painstaking process because she was so skittish. I started off with just having her get used to seeing us every day. The last six weeks had been hell when it came to that, but this job wasn't going to last forever and we'd be back on days.

Still, I looked forward to dinner tonight. I was hungry, the diner was cheap but with good food, and it meant that even though I couldn't see her, I could still be where she'd been. Sometimes, if I stilled enough, concentrated hard enough, I could almost smell her light perfume. I, of course, didn't tell Cell any of that. He'd call me a pussy and would probably laugh at me. It just was the way he was. Emotions just weren't his thing and he was about as sensitive as bedrock to anything that didn't affect him directly.

"Come on! Quit your fuckin' day dreamin' and get on it," he snapped at me and I realized I'd been staring into space for probably longer than a minute, just thinking about her.

We did that for each other as friends; Cell kept me grounded, while I softened some of his sharper edges. I walked down the road in my reflective, asphalt-stained gear, stinking of the shit and got to Cell and the bikes. He lit up a cigarette, already astride his 2005 Electra Glide.

I threw a leg over my own Harley and dropped onto the seat with a grunt. Cell looked over at me and asked, "You want your colors?" I shook my head, slipping the clear safety glasses onto my face and reaching for my helmet dangling off my handlebar.

"The fuck is that about?" he demanded and I scowled at him.

"I'm sick of the smell," I said and held out my arms so he could take in my road grime stained, and sweaty appearance.

"Home and shower before dinner then?"

I nodded, and we fired up our bikes, pulling up to the edge of the grassy median we parked them on and up onto the shoulder of the highway. We waited for the truck barreling our way to pass before we pulled onto the road to head back to the club which was still home for us for now. The late summer heat dulled from blast furnace to oven temperature; the wind blowing past me drying the sweat to my skin, causing me to itch. I wanted a shower, clean clothes, and to give my cut and colors the respect they deserved by not putting them on over my rank ass.

Duracell rode ahead and to the left of me, the wind lifting the tee off his back, the angry red weal of scar from where he'd taken a shiv for me when we'd been locked up, picked out by my headlight against his pale skin. Thick, raised, and ropy, he'd lost a kidney in that attack and only by the grace of whatever power that be was, I was caught up as one of the aggressors and locked up in solitary the entire time he was in the infirmary recovering.

We'd fucking lucked out. His cellmate had been the one to attack me, and Cell had given as good as he'd gotten. My cellie had been released, and so when I got out of solitary and Cell had gotten out of the hospital, we'd ended up housed together. It'd made the rest of our bid go much, much, smoother.

We pulled up out front of the club and backed our bikes into line, shutting them off. I sat for a moment and listened to the insects. This place was different than where we'd come from. Way more peaceful. I was still torn up on the inside over what happened with our old club. All that time spent behind bars and for what? *Nothing.*

Duracell and I had taken the fall for the lot of them on some pretty fuckin' serious weapons charges. By all rights, we should still be in prison, but the club had tried to help, had gotten the best fuckin' attorney and man... that guy... We'd pled guilty, and it'd been a sweet plea deal. A ten-year sentence each, managed to get out in five. We had to turn state's evidence on our supplier, though. We'd done it with the club's blessing, because fuck them – they weren't club and the chapter could have always found another supplier, but they didn't get the fucking chance.

After release, Cell and I had wanted to relocate, had to go through hell in a handbasket with the state we'd come from, seeing as we had a year of parole left to serve, but we'd been able to make it happen. Still, our old club was in shambles by the time we'd gotten out, most of them dead and when it came to the shambles part of things, so were we. We'd barely survived prison and I do mean barely.

We'd lucked out that Dragon's crew had been in dire need of members and had also been spending a good portion of their time going straight. We needed straight if we wanted to keep out of prison. I sure as fuck never wanted to go back. Cell? He couldn't care less where he ended up, but that was part of why he needed me. To keep him straight out here. To have someone watch his back the way he'd watched mine on the inside.

I dragged my mind back to the here and now and went to my room in the back outbuilding I liked to call the barracks. I picked out some clean clothes; a pair of worn, but comfortable jeans, some fresh boxers and some clean socks out of the dresser before I went to the closet and pulled down a clean black tee shirt. It was a little on the faded side, like the light denim of the Levi's but with no holes. I couldn't say the same about a lot of my wardrobe, I just couldn't be bothered with upgrading anything.

I trekked back down to the bathroom at the end of the hall and went in, dropping my clean clothes and towels on one end of the bench outside the showers. Stripping down quickly and efficiently, I padded across the cold tiles to get the shower started up, waiting for the water to warm up before ducking under the spray.

God, the heat felt good against sore muscles. I put my hands against the tile wall and let the water beat mercilessly between my shoulder blades, the tightness easing some under the punishing spray that just wasn't quite enough for me. It never really was. I needed a good massage but didn't know where to go around here to get one.

I jumped when the door creaked and looked back over my shoulder. Cell dropped his shit on the bench next to where mine lay and dropped the towel off from around his waist. Fuck, he was hard, but I wasn't in the mood. Still, it was Cell, and he typically got what he wanted out of me. It was hard to say no, and the times that I did, he ended up winning me over, anyway.

I thrust my face into the spray, holding my breath, holding it there, until Cell shoved me hard against the wall. He braced an arm across my shoulders and the back of my neck, shoving me forward while his other arm snaked around my waist, hauling me back, setting me up so he could fuck me. Adrenaline coursed through me and I resisted, which only made him laugh a little.

"You know, you fighting me only makes me want it more," he said, and I fucking hated that he was right. It'd come down to this when we'd been in prison, and when we'd gotten out, it'd just sort of kept up. I'd been okay with it, but then again, I'd always been pretty comfortable with what I liked, as in, if I liked it, I liked it… I just rolled with it and I liked Cell… but *just* Cell. I would never let another man do this to me.

Neither I nor Cell considered ourselves gay. We weren't, really. Again, it was just something about it being *Cell*. Any other guy and I don't think it'd be there for me, the attraction, not just the willingness to let a guy fuck me. I liked women, never even considered myself bisexual, or even curious before Cell. Things were just *different* with Duracell. We'd grown close, tight, two pieces of some bigger whole. Like we were some fractured personality or some shit... I don't know how to explain it.

Even though I was a willing participant when it came to sex with Cell, I fought him this time. I wasn't in the fucking mood, but it was useless, per usual, and the more he held me against the wall, the more he laughed about having the upper hand, the more my resolve to resist diminished. My cock stirred a couple seconds into the struggle and when he did me the courtesy of giving me a reach around, which he didn't always do, my resolve crumbled completely and I was all-in.

"Hold still, fucker. I'm not out to fuckin' hurt you," he declared, but it always hurt at first. He fucked my ass, but he so wouldn't let me fuck his. Not Cell's style. I'd brought it up once and he'd grunted and told me to find some pussy or hell, even a chick's ass for that. It was just Cell's way.

He kicked my feet apart and his hand disappeared, I heard him spit in it and he lubed himself up. I braced, relaxed as best I could and hoped he had it in him to go easy this time around. He pressed against my asshole and with a lot of determination worked his way in. I pushed out, and breathed, but it wasn't pleasant, not at first. I could feel my asshole flex and twitch in protest but when Cell's dick didn't go away, my body eventually gave in like I had and let it happen.

"Fuck, I wish you'd keep the fuckin' lube handy," I ground out and Cell laughed.

"Just shut up and take it."

I laughed a little too at his response and groaned, bracing against the wall, letting him fuck my ass. The burning had started to subside, the discomfort of the stretching fading with it until all that was left was the warmth of the friction and stimulation that was hard to describe. He kept one arm braced against my back, shoving me face first into the cool blue tile of the wall and I found my Zen. My own cock was painfully fuckin' hard but it wasn't like Cell to do anything about it. Not usually. I was surprised he'd touched my dick the first time. I dropped an arm and wrapped my fingers around myself, pumping my fist up and down my length as Cell beat the fuck out of my prostate.

"Oh yeah," he moaned and he was close. I could always fucking hear it in his voice when he was going to come and he *always* fuckin' came deep. I braced, and sure enough he shoved in fucking hard and it was the *sound* the soft, "Ughn, ughn, ughn…" that escaped his mouth, punctuated with deep breaths bordering on passionate that sent me over the edge.

Every. Damn. Time.

I swallowed hard, my own chest heaving, the water slicking down my back as he pulled out. His absence uncomfortable for a minute, where his presence had been at the start.

He pushed off of me and started up the shower next to mine, thrusting his face into the spray. I straightened up and he shook his head back and forth, making a stupid noise like he was pumped; which he was. I laughed a little and used the body wash to wash up.

We showered in silence, just a couple of bros in a locker room after that, and that was honestly just how things were. We fucked, then nothing. No feelings, no pillow talk or girly shit. Cell didn't do feelings. Ever. We weren't a couple, more like best friends with benefits. We needed our missing piece… *I* needed our missing piece if I wanted more, which I did. I wanted a lot more. I craved connection on that soul deep level.

Even though Cell knew everything there was to know about me and I knew a fair bit about him, it wasn't like we were open with one another or confidants. It just wasn't like that. I needed a tenderness that he just couldn't or wouldn't provide.

I finished washing up first and went for my towel, drying off; my ass still a little unhappy but I'd live. He'd been downright gentle compared to some of our other fucks. I got dressed, and he eventually walked out of the shower, dragging his towel across his body and eventually up over his hair.

"Gonna ditch that shit so we can get going?" he asked thrusting his chin at the pile of dirty laundry in my hands.

I nodded and went for the bathroom door.

"Cool," he said at my back.

I took my dirty clothes and towel back to my room and dumped them in the canvas laundry bag by the door. I pulled on my jacket and cut from where I'd left them on the bed and sat on the edge of the king-sized mattress in the air conditioned dark of my sanctuary to pull on my motorcycle boots.

I took the time to thread my belt through the loops and buckle up; shoved my wallet in my back pocket and threaded the leather loop around my belt, snapping it closed. One last check of things, and satisfied, I took up my keys off the dresser and went out, locking up behind me, even though I didn't think for a minute one of my club brothers would get into my shit.

It was just a thing some of us had, locking up our shit. Also helped if the cops ever rolled in, which they had just a few weeks ago. Some shit that Cell and some of the other boys had gone to take care of to help out Dragon's niece. They'd stormed in here looking for who knew what the fuck but hadn't found anything. The club's lawyers were now trying to take the pigs apart in court, filing lawsuits and shit about illegal search and seizure.

I'd been kept out of it, and Cell? He just plain didn't give a fuck. It was who he was. Savage, primal, *sociopathic...* I had to admit it to myself. He just didn't *feel* like a normal person, or he had it buried so damn deep it was almost the same thing.

"Let's go, man, I'm fuckin' starving," he called down the hallway and I made strides to catch up to him as he went out the door, slow walking it up to the track and around to the club's back door.

I caught up and we went through the main building and out the front, out to where the bikes were parked. We didn't pass anyone, which wasn't surprising. It was almost midnight and a Thursday night; a lot of us were working stiffs and there were fewer and fewer of us actually living at the club anymore.

We rode out to the diner and went through the door to a pleasant surprise. Hayley was behind the counter, picking up a pair of plates and taking them to a couple of the night-shift guys from around here that were having their lunch. She wasn't in her typical uniform and I had to say, I liked what I was seeing. She wore a pair of comfortable looking jeans, the kind that women wore with the stretch to them that hugged every curve. Up top, she had on a dark gray racerback tank top to beat the heat. A black apron was wound around her lean waist that wasn't much more than a set of pockets in front.

"Hey, look who it is!" Duracell cried amicably and I blinked, surprised at the genuine warmth in his tone. Either that or he was faking it incredibly well to seem normal. I wouldn't put that past him either.

"Hi, guys, I haven't seen you in a while, my section is over here tonight."

She'd warmed to us a little in the last year, but still, the greeting we got just then had me and Cell exchanging a look. He raised his golden-red eyebrows at me and we went over to an empty table in the section she'd indicated. She came by to drop a couple of menus and to take our drink orders.

"Nice uniform," Cell commented dryly as she set down the laminated cards and Hayley tried a smile. She looked a little harried, maybe a little worn around the edges and I studied her face, waiting to see what she'd say.

"Well, you know, I was already here once today but Shirley, our night waitress, called off something like twenty minutes into her shift. I told my dad I'd cover, but I wasn't going to change, so here I am." She held out her hands and looked down at her casual appearance.

"On a date?" Cell asked casually.

She snorted, a self-deprecating sound if I ever heard one. "Hardly, I was in my studio."

"Studio?"

"Stained glass," she said softly. "It's um, sort of a hobby of mine." She rapidly changed the subject. "Do you know what you want to drink?"

Cell smiled at me, giving me a wink while Hayley was overly absorbed in her notepad all of a sudden, a light pink flush creeping across her chest, up her neck and settling across the bridge of her nose. She was fucking adorable when she blushed and it made my heart skip out of rhythm when I saw it.

"Coke," Cell answered her and she looked up over her pad.

"What about him?" she asked.

"Water," I said and she visibly startled.

"More than a year you been coming in here and I think that's the first time I've ever heard you talk," she said. I smiled and kind of ducked my head in a half-assed nod, shy myself when it came to it. She smiled back at me and it was like color was breathed back into my life.

"Water it is," she said softly with a charmed little half-smile and went to go get our drinks.

"Way to go," Cell said dryly. "Only took you something like what? Eighteen *months* to stop bein' a fuckin' retard and actually open your mouth at her?" He shook his head. "Jesus Christ, Blue. You're killin' me." His smile said he was totally making fun of me and I scowled.

"Shut up," I grumbled at him before she could head this way. Duracell just smirked at me and I rolled my eyes. He could be so fucking immature sometimes, but honestly, that could be part of his charm.

"Right, know what you want to eat?" Hayley tapped her pen against her pad.

"Give us another minute, baby," Cell said, but his look was fixed on me.

"Sure thing." She breezed away to see to some of the other guys in the place and I picked up a menu to block Cell's view of me, hiding like a bitch and actually taking my time figuring out what I wanted to put in my face.

I decided on a burger and fries; it just sounded really good for some reason. Hayley came back and I did my usual point at what I wanted and Cell, shaking his head and laughing, finished ordering it for me how I liked with ranch for my fries. For me, that shit was like the new ketchup. I couldn't get enough.

She wrote it all down in her waitressing shorthand like she usually did and took the menus, trailing off to drop them by the register and to put our order in behind the counter. I admired the lean, long line of her body and the perfect curve of her ass in those jeans as she clipped the paper on the carousel on this side and spun it so it faced the kitchen. The night cook plucked it off on his side and squinted, reading it off back to her. They exchanged a nod and he got to work. When I looked back at Cell, he had a soft grin plastered to his face, his eyes sparkling with amusement.

"You finally get up the balls to actually speak to her and the first thing in over a year that you can fuckin' think to say is your *drink order*?" Tears were starting to form in the corners of his eyes as he really started to lose his shit and I just sank down in the booth, feelin' about seven inches tall. *Fuck, I hated when he did this to me.* It wasn't easy for me, talking to people. I got tongue-tied real easy and always said the stupidest shit.

"You're a dick," I said softly and shifted in my booth seat.

"Yeah, and you love it. I do ninety percent of the shit you won't." He had me there. He was also in one of his crueler moods where he wouldn't shut the fuck up and stop making fun of me or reminding me of just how much shit he did for me.

"What're you on your period or some shit?" he demanded when I shifted uneasily again.

I shook my head, scowling darkly while I thought to myself, *maybe.* I didn't know what my problem was. I was on edge, that's for sure. Just every little thing was getting to me right now. I felt agitated and irritated, my knee bouncing up and down under the table at a rapid pace.

We sat in silence, waiting on our food, when Hayley came back with two plates. She set mine down and that's when I noticed it. It was a purely reflexive action, my hand flashing out, coming up under her arm, closing on it to cradle it, my other hand taking hers and uncurling it so I could see better what I thought I'd seen.

A thin, pale indentation ran from the middle of her palm up the inside of her wrist, anywhere from four to six inches long. I blinked and smoothed over it with my thumb. Looking up at her, even if I could speak, I couldn't think of a damn thing to say. She swallowed hard looking scared and I didn't want to do that to her so I immediately let her go with a soft, "Sorry."

She turned on her heel and walked away sharply, but I'd seen it, in her eyes, the darkness there. The same darkness I held in *me.* I cocked my head to the side and watched her ghost around the diner, her walls rising to the occasion, but there was no judgment here, only curiosity.

"Put it in your face," Cell urged and I turned back. He was watching me evenly, that look that said he knew what was up and that I needed to eat. I nodded and picked up a fry, dunking it in my ranch, doing what I was told and putting it in my face, chewing thoughtfully.

"You eat lunch today?" he asked, and I blinked and had to think about it. He shook his head. "You have to think about it, the answer is 'no'. You've gotta eat, man. You can't be forgetting that shit."

I let him lecture me. It was one of the ways I knew that he fuckin' cared. If he didn't care, he wouldn't say anything about it; but on this, he was right. If I forgot to eat, I tended to get the kind of hunger that gave me a harder time keeping certain demons in check. It wasn't considered very 'tough' of a biker to have anxiety, but that was a bullshit citizen stereotype and they didn't know me.

The truth was, I had plenty to be anxious about; prison hadn't helped any on that front, either. While I thrived on structure, that was only half the story on the inside. Sure, your meal times, when you worked, when you slept, where you went, when you showered – all of it was structured, but you also didn't know who you were gonna piss off lookin' at them funny, even if you weren't looking at them at all. You never knew when the next assault from that rival crew or gang was going to come. You never knew who was gonna try and make you their bitch next. There were a lot of variables you didn't know and those were the ones that were important. Constantly looking over your shoulder when you got out? It was a practice you kept on with.

It was easier, being here, with the chapter we were with now. It wasn't just me and Cell against the world anymore. We had a family, men who were with us and who would legit watch our back. That helped, but it wasn't the end-alls and be-alls. Plus, it had been Cell and me against the world for so long, we had a tendency to forget it wasn't just all us all the time and that the club would be there to back us up if we needed it.

"Hey, you listening to me, motherfucker?" Cell demanded and I looked up. I held up a hand flat and waffled it back and forth in that way that said 'kind of, sort of.' Cell shook his head. "I wouldn't ride your ass about this shit if it wasn't important," he said and I softened a little. It was probably the closest thing I would ever hear out of him that even remotely resembled 'I care about you' and it just plain had to be enough. I had to take what I could get where he was concerned.

I met his eyes with mine and gave a grave nod. Leaning back he said, "Good; glad we had this talk," his tone dripping with sarcasm. I huffed a bit of a laugh and finished my food, watching Hayley move around the diner refilling coffee and serving the few patrons present, including a couple of sheriff's deputies that'd come in after us.

They talked to her, a few tables down, and she looked up and our way. She turned back to them and smiled, murmuring something I couldn't hear, the piped-in music and the clatter of utensils drowning out her voice, which was sort of quiet to begin with.

"Jesus Christ, you need to move on this." I blinked and looked back to Cell who was laughing at me again.

I nodded; I had every intention of it. She set down our bill and drifted away and I pushed the receipt paper in his direction with a pointed look. He rolled his eyes and took a pen out of his cut, scribbling whatever it was this time on the back before sliding it back over to me so I could get to work.

I made sure what he'd wrote was suitable and not douchey before I got to work folding it into a delicate and tiny origami orchid, using the paper wrapping from my straw to fashion a vine. I twisted it back on itself and cocked my head, my pulse speeding just a bit. With a hard swallow, I went for it, looping it, and thinking on it a second. I went through my pockets and looked up at Cell.

"I need a piece of tape."

He smirked, hitching back with a laugh making some comment about getting stupid with my paper art. Still, he humored me and went through the pockets of his jacket and cut, coming up with a roll of green electrical tape. Even better! I grinned at him and took it, finishing working my magic with the tiny bits of paper. He shook his head and said, "You're somethin' else, man."

"Go smoke your cigarette," I muttered and his eyebrows shot up.

"Don't mind if I do, pay the bill when you're done with your arts and crafts, fucknugget."

I nodded and handed him his tape. He shoved it back in his pocket, his cigarette already out, tapping the filter against the base of his latest Bic lighter. He liked them better when it came to improvising explosive devices. The plastic melted and didn't leave behind fingerprints. He always said Zippos were too nice to get rid of and were a disaster waiting to happen when it came to trace evidence.

"Hurry it the fuck up," he called over his shoulder and pushed through the diner's door and went outside. He paused just outside the door, smirking through the glass at me, and lit up. I rolled my eyes and shook my head. I mean, did he want me to pull the trigger on this or not?

I finished my handiwork and pleased that it was secure, and wouldn't fall apart easily looked up to Hayley standing by my table with a water pitcher in her hand. She blinked at me with those lovely dark eyes and I smiled up at her crookedly. I took her free hand gently and slid the paper and tape orchid ring on her right ring finger, glad her left was occupied because I didn't want to come across too creepy.

"I see you," I breathed, and her eyes never left mine. I felt it, the moment, falling from a great height, cutting through the tension between us, her body language softened. I stood up, pulling my wallet out blindly, fishing in it for all the cash, knowing there was way more than what was required to pay for the meal. I pressed it all into her hands, and took a moment to brush her cheek with my thumb while she stood there, wide-eyed and motionless.

I winked at her and went out the door and into the night, catching up to Duracell.

2

H ayley...

"They bothering you?"

"What?" I followed the deputy's look, up the line of booths to where Blue was watching. I turned back to refill the second deputy's coffee and shook my head saying to the first, "No, they're actually regulars. Blue, the one facing us, is actually kind of sweet."

"You be careful around those guys, they have a rough reputation."

"I will," I said smiling and moved away from the sheriff deputies' table and on to a different one.

Duracell got up and went outside for his usual after meal cigarette while Blue hunched over their table absorbed in folding their receipt as he usually did... even though they hadn't paid yet. I put the coffee carafe back on the warmer and picked up the water pitcher wandering over to see what he was doing and secretly excited. I loved the little paper creations that he left me, it was one of my favorite parts about them coming in.

I paused quietly by his side. It was fascinating watching him work so finely, his long fingers wrapping a bit of green vinyl tape around a bit of straw wrapper. He looked up and smiled at me and I lost my breath, frozen in place by the look in his eyes. He took my hand gently and slid whatever little trinket he'd created onto my finger like a ring.

"I see you," he breathed, and I believed him. I believed him so hard that my throat closed up and tears very nearly sprang to my eyes. He stood up and I took an automatic step back to let him out of the booth. Still, he was so close, closer than he'd ever been and well within my personal space. I wasn't really too surprised to find that I didn't at all mind. Instead, I held very still and closed my eyes, breathing in the scent of clean man and leather which in turn forced me into the position of trying valiantly not to shiver.

It'd been a *very* long time for me. A little over two years, to be precise. I opened my eyes when his thumb grazed my cheek, the barest whisper of a touch against my skin. He shoved a sheaf of folded bills into my hand and before I could find my voice, he was gone. I looked down at the wad of crisp, twenty-dollar bills in my hand and looked back up and out the dark front window. Just as I made to take a step in the direction of the door, their motorcycles fired up and I jumped slightly.

I looked back down to my hands dumbly. *Too much, he had paid me far too much*, but I think he knew that. I set down the water and blinked. With what was in my hand, he'd left me over a one-hundred-and-twenty-dollar tip. That'd *never* happened to me before. I turned my hand over and looked at the ring he'd put on my finger, a delicate little paper orchid resting just below my knuckle.

I felt my heart give that little flutter and I treasured when it did that. It let me know it wasn't completely frozen or dead. I swallowed hard and put the money in my apron pocket. I went back to work serving my other tables and sighed more than a few times doing it. At least now I knew their disappearing from the diner wasn't me. I mean, they wouldn't have been half so friendly to me if it was, right?

I hadn't had the nerve to ask Melody, what with her just coming back after the awful time she had having Chandler. I was so grateful she'd returned, too. She was good at our job and it'd been a struggle to keep up without her, but I'd managed – just like I was managing now.

It'd been a long, long day and now it was dragging into a deep long night. I drifted between tables refilling coffee between stealing sips of my own from behind the counter. I was half dead on my feet by the time my dad came through the door to cook for the breakfast and lunch crowd.

"That's enough for you, sweetheart. You good to drive home or you need a nap in the corner booth first?"

"I'll be fine, I can make it."

"Get on out of here, then."

I nodded and he wrapped fingers around the back of my neck, dragging my forehead to his lips. He smacked a kiss between my eyebrows, gave me a little shake and let me go. I emptied its pockets and unwound my apron from around my waist and heaved a sigh, folding it up, so I could stash it in a back corner beneath the register.

Straightening, I called out a last goodbye to my dad and smiled when Melody walked through the door. I would have gone regardless, but still, perfect timing.

"What happened to your uniform?" she called out, hanging her coat on the coat-tree by the door. She didn't carry her purse in here, just her ID and a bit of money in her apron. It was a good habit, and one I had adopted, too.

"Night shift called out twenty minutes into her shift with no replacement, so guess what I got to do?"

"Aww, you look half dead."

I chuckled. "Good to know I look how I feel."

"I see Blue was by last night at least."

I startled and held out my hand, unable to resist my charmed little half-smile at the memory.

"Yeah, he and Cell both."

Mel rolled her eyes. "When isn't it Blue and Cell both?"

I shook my head, I mean, it was a valid point. I sighed again, only this time it was in a bid to stifle a yawn.

"I'm sorry, Mel, but it looks like you're on your own today."

"Don't you worry about that, I can handle this hungry horde. You go home and get some sleep and I'll see you when I see you."

We hugged quickly and I smiled. "I'll see you when I see you," I agreed and she let me go. I stepped aside to let a couple of our regulars in the door and ducked out past them as Melody greeted them and led them to a table with a couple of menus she snatched from beside the register. I stood outside watching for a minute and had to smile. She fit seamlessly into the diner and had become a good friend, for all that I didn't see her too much outside of work.

I got into my tired, old Volkswagen Golf and started it up. I carefully drove myself home realizing about halfway there just how tired I really was. I should have gotten a lift, but then again, I *really* didn't want to accept a lift from the night cook. Not that there was anything wrong with him, I just knew that it would have led to small talk, and I just was plain out of any ability to deal with people anymore. At least until after I showered and slept, and not necessarily in that particular order, either.

I pulled into the long driveway and went right past the house around back, parking alongside my studio my dad had built. It was a one-and-a-half story, converted two-car garage, painted yellow with white trim, just like our house. It had a loft with a bed in it for when I worked late nights and was closer than the walk to the house. I'd rather climb the seven rungs or so of the ladder than the twenty steps up to the second floor and my real bedroom.

I dragged butt out of my car and went to the studio's door, unlocking it and letting myself in. I loved it in here. It was full of windows and light. I shut and locked the door behind me and I nearly dropped my keys and purse right there on the floor, I was so tired. However, my mother never would have done that no matter how tired she was after a shift, so I didn't either. I shuffled my aching feet the several feet to my left and hung the purse that'd been stashed under the seat of my car neatly on the coatrack. I pulled my ID and tips from my pockets and stuffed them unceremoniously in the open zippered top of the small black bag as my one concession of wanting to just not care and be messy.

The keys went on the small hook set into a board by the coat rack, well out of the reach of any of the panes of glass set into the door to the outside. Straight ahead of me was a closed, white paneled door that led into the bathroom my dad had put in here for my mom.

This had been her studio for painting long before it'd ever been mine for stained glass. She'd died of breast cancer when I was fifteen; it'd been just Dad and me ever since. When I had said I was ready to use the studio for my passion, my dad had spent every evening and weekend for over a month redoing the interior of this place so it fit me, insisting that mom would have wanted it that way. I knew he was right, still, it would have been nice to keep some of her in here.

I flipped on the bathroom's light switch and half thought about showering or drawing a bath but couldn't bring myself to do it. I barely had it in me to drag a toothbrush across my teeth before hauling myself up out of my hunch over the white porcelain pedestal sink. I stared at myself in the oval mirror on the wall and was almost disappointed to see I didn't look at all how I felt.

I felt like I should have deep, dark, circles under my eyes but nope. Instead, my mother's face, only younger than I remembered it, stared back at me. I pulled the elastic holding the end of my braid together off and set it by the tap handle at the top of the sink. I unwound the thick, dark strands from around each other until I was left with a foaming wavy mass framing my face. My unremarkable brown eyes bounced over my lightly tanned face, picking out slight imperfections and flaws every which way. I sighed and shook my head, closing my eyes for a moment before turning back to the door. I only opened them to see where I was going and once I knew I was well clear of my reflection.

I made beautiful things with glass, but I wasn't what anyone would consider beautiful myself... well, except for my dad, but I was pretty sure he was biased. I kicked out of my shoes at the bottom of the wood ladder set into the wall by the bathroom door and relished the cool, polished concrete floor under my sock covered feet.

Oh God, that felt *so* good against hot, sore feet. I couldn't even begin to tell you. The only thing that felt better was the lovely stretch the round rungs of the ladder pressing into my arches gave them. It felt so good, I simply stood on the bottom rung and bounced, getting in a deep stretch that was to die for.

I climbed the rest of the way up into the loft above my bathroom that had just enough headroom for me to stand up straight and not have to worry about cracking my head on a ceiling beam. There was just enough room up here for a quaint bedroom setup. I had a queen-sized mattress and box spring on the floor, which I had up against the spindled railing overlooking the studio and next to it, I had an old apple crate turned on its side for a nightstand. A corner desk and chair were in the one corner that had just enough room house the desk and chair with the walls on both sides. The entire rest of the one wall opposite the railing was taken up by paned windows and gauzy curtains, facing into tall, thick, lilac bushes that separated our yard from the next-door neighbors.

I crawled out of my pants and just kept on my shirt and panties before crawling into bed. I reached for the bedside apple crate and pulled down the medicine bottle, taking out one of the anti-depressants inside

27

and popping it onto the very center of my tongue. I dragged down the bottle of water I kept beside it and took three giant swigs to make sure I'd washed it down all the way. As soon as I set the water back down, I keeled over; dragging the blankets up over me. I gently pulled the carefully crafted paper orchid from my finger and set it on the edge of the crate so I could stare at it. All of the rest of Blue's creations hung from fishing line, dangling from the beams above my bed so all I had to do was turn onto my back and stare up at them.

Every flower and bird I could imagine hung above me. One for every visit he'd made to the diner, whether he and Cell sat in my section or not. I loved them all, so very much, and still wondered how he had ever learned to fold paper so delicately or beautifully. I was too shy to ask, but it was one of the things I looked forward to the most about going to work. A few had come here and there in the beginning when they stopped showing up to my shift, but then nothing until they'd been there last night.

Doesn't mean he didn't make them for you, it might just mean the night waitress never passed them on, I told myself for the thousandth time.

I closed my eyes and just breathed, Blue's words echoing back to me...

I see you.

I believed him. I also believed that he deserved much better than me with my burden of sadness and low self-esteem. I was damaged goods and no man wanted any part of that. Especially not one as hot as Blue. I sighed and took one last look at the paper creations suspended above me before I closed my eyes for the last time, cuddling down into my bed. I pulled the blankets over my head so I was swallowed by the dark and wished so much that I were a whole person. Normal, like everyone else, but that was likely an impossible goal to reach, even with the medication.

God, I hated being depressed.

3

B lue...

Mid-October sunshine beating down, leaves turning a rich golden red, and a deep sense of fall was riding the air... but it was still over seventy degrees out here. It was officially an Indian summer as far as any of us were concerned, but lacking the haze and conditions to make it a *real* one by Farmer's Almanac standards. Yet another thing I'd learned while locked up. The only other thing besides the art of folding paper to keep me occupied had been the prison library and I'd gone through their selection pretty quick. After the first year, anything that came in that I could use to stave off boredom with, I would... up to and including the shit ton of outdated Reader's Digest and The Farmer's Almanacs that sat dusting in the library's corner.

Cell and I had been back on day shift with the road crew for a little over a month which meant we'd been back at the diner on Haley's shift. Unfortunately, I'd gone and done the one thing I'd never in a million years had wanted to... I'd scared her, and she'd gone back into her shell again. She was quiet, skittish, and yet when I did manage to make eye contact, I could see such a longing in her deep brown eyes. *A chink in her armor, maybe?* I hoped so.

Duracell slapped me in the chest and I startled from my thoughts, shaking myself as if coming awake. We were at the Harvest Days Carnival as a club, but also as a family with all the ol' ladies and kids in tow and we'd been having a blast so far. I scowled at him and he laughed at me, gesturing up the slight incline, we were standing at the bottom of the cotton candy cart at the top.

I followed Duracell's gesture and gaze to a pair of worn cowboy boots, up a pair of gorgeous as fuck legs, over a damn near perfect ass and hourglass figure below a white peasant's blouse. Long dark hair spilled down her back and it was beautiful when it was free like that.

She usually only wore it in a braid with that fringe of bangs kissing her forehead, but not today. Today the top half was pulled up and held by a pewter clip in the shape of an owl. Today she was almost smiling as she took the fluffy blue cloud of candy from the vendor. Today her eyes sparkled as she tore a bit off and licked it off her thumb and oh, God…

I wanted it to be *my* thumb, hell, I wanted her lips, her tongue, on any part of me. I felt it keenly, like a deep, fractured ache in the center of my being. I wanted her so badly between me and Cell while we worshiped and ravaged her body. I wanted to put her squarely between heaven and hell and I just didn't know *how*.

"Hayley!" Melody called and I silently cursed inside my head. I wanted to watch her longer, without her knowing we were here. There was something about seeing her out here, candid, without any of her super self-consciousness that she wore like a cloak when we entered the diner anymore.

"Blue, I'm only gonna fuckin' say this once." I swung my gaze back to Cell's face, already knowing by his tone that I wasn't going to like what I was going to hear. "You make this work your way, now, today, or I'm taking over. You're being a fucking pussy and the case of blue balls with your name on 'em ain't getting any better. You picked her, sure, but I want her, too; and I ain't too keen on waiting much longer."

I scowled at him and dropped a truth, "Your way, you get her once; my way, we could have her forever."

"Fuck you and your logic, man," he said laughing but he was in a good mood and backing off, which is what I needed.

Hayley moved down the little hill toward Mel, giving me a quick sweet smile before shooting a nervous glance Duracell's way. Duracell caught it and looked at me with a shit-eating grin saying, "Do your thing man. I'll fuck off for the moment."

I gave him a nod and he went over near Reaver and Trigger. I drifted up nearer to Hayley while she talked with Mel. She smiled and tore off a hank of her cotton candy for Noah who was reaching for the offered sweet.

"You are gonna be one hell of a mess, little man," his father ground out, but Archer was all rare smiles as he hitched his son further up into his arms. Melody had Chandler in a baby buggy and was rolling her sleeping, second son back and forth over the dry grass absently.

"It's okay," Hayley said to Noah. "Little boys wash, don't they Noah?"

Noah just gave her his wide, dimpled grin and laughed, shoving his little fistful of spun sugar into his mouth, getting most of it smeared in a bright blue stain around it. It was both gross and adorable, but then again, I had a thing about being clean. It was part of why I hated my job so much.

"Hi," I said, pitching my voice low and hoping like hell it didn't come out uncertain, which it probably did. Truth was, every time I saw Hayley I got so damn nervous I almost couldn't stand it. The butterflies launching themselves into a flurry of activity in my stomach to the point I almost felt ill. I swallowed hard and wiped my sweating palms on the seat of my jeans, casually stuffing my hands in my back pockets to disguise what I was actually doing.

Archer and Melody just blinked and stared at me a second, and the attention made my skin grow hot with a blush. This is why I didn't talk to people. Talking led to looking, and the looking meant that I had their attention and I *hated* having people's attention unless I was comfortable enough with them.

I was comfortable enough with Cell because I understood him, for the most part. The only other person I had grown comfortable enough to really talk with since coming to this new chapter was Dani Broussard, Red-Thirteen's ol' lady. If I had to pick a best friend outside of Cell, it'd probably be her. Right now, though, I was trying really hard to expand my tight-as-hell inner circle to include this beautiful creature right here. The one looking at Melody and Archer curiously, the gears spinning behind her deep, soulful brown eyes as she puzzled through their expressions. Her gaze flicked back to mine and she drew a deep, steadying breath before she said so politely, so sweetly, "Hi, Blue, it's good to see you."

I couldn't help but smile and the next words that came out of my mouth came much easier as long as I focused on *her* rather than all of my other club brothers and sisters looking at me like I'd done something utterly mystifying.

"Take a walk with me?"

Hayley smiled, the color intensifying across the bridge of her nose and along her cheeks.

"Oh, my God, girl! Go on!" Melody encouraged, laughing, when Hayley didn't immediately respond.

"Sure," Hayley murmured demurely, and my heart soared; not gracefully either. Instead of an eagle or some shit, that fucker lifted off with all the smoke and fire of a goddamn space launch, the nerves and bile rising with it, scorching my throat something awful as I forced it back down. I forced a smile to my lips even as that voice of derision and doubt screamed in the back of my head, demanding to know, '*What the fuck did I just do?*' and following up with, '*What the fuck was I going to do now?*'

I let my feet carry us away from the prying eyes of my club brothers and felt some of the tension leave my shoulders. Hayley smiled and shyly ate some of the cotton candy she'd bought. All I could do was stare at her mouth as she sucked the sweet confection off her fingers. I was a man transfixed by the smallest thing she did, aroused but also put at peace. Watching her calmed the raging demon of insecurity that pretty much ravaged the hell out of me from the inside out on a daily.

"What's wrong?" she asked softly, her face crumbling and I closed my eyes and shook my head. "Was it something I did?" she asked meekly and I pinned her with a look, scowling.

"Never. The smallest things you do, I just…" I shrugged. "I find them beautiful."

"Oh." Her voice held a bit of a shocked echo, her lovely face, free of makeup, painted instead with surprise.

We'd stopped near one of the rides that had been set up in the field they were holding the festival in, and I turned to look at it rather than face her curious scrutiny right then. It was a Ferris wheel, and I turned back to her and asked, "Go with me?"

She smiled and it was a mixture of shyness and teasing warmth. "Afraid of heights?"

"If I say yes, will you go on it with me?"

"I'd like that," she murmured. "It's always nice to feel needed."

I smiled and felt it, that sense when I'd first seen her, like our pieces just *fit*. I held out my arm and she looped hers through it. We got in line and stood silently when out of nowhere, Cell appeared at the railing and said, "Let me hold that for you so you ain't gotta worry about it." I thought to myself, *So much for fucking off.*

Hayley smiled and handed over her half-eaten cotton candy and when her back was turned, Cell gave me a wink and a slight nod. He was being charming today, which was good. Then again, he'd always been the master hunter. The cool, calculating one. The chameleon, the wolf in sheep's clothing.

I swallowed hard and wrestled with my guilt, and not for the first time when it came to the thought of being with Hayley, of having a woman in our life, I wanted it so badly… Still, when it came to Cell, at what cost? How much would she have to give up?

I was alright giving up what I had for Cell, at first as club brothers, sure, but as lovers? As partners and best friends? It just was, that to be with Cell, you had to give up parts of yourself and be okay with things that put you at serious odds with your maker. I'd been alright damning myself, but was it right to do it to anyone else?

We moved forward in line and Hayley was smiling and talking gently with me.

"It feels strange seeing you guys outside of the diner, I mean, I don't think I ever really have before, you know?"

She was making small talk, and I was doing my best to give her more than one-word answers as was usually my custom when it came to speaking out loud.

"Yeah, I mean, no… I guess I never really thought about it. I'm just glad to see you. In the diner, out of it, it doesn't matter to me." God, I sounded like a rambling idiot.

She searched my face and I wanted so badly to ask questions of my own, to know everything about her, to immerse myself completely in who she was. I'd waited so long out of a combination of fear and a wish to protect her but I was weak, I needed this. I was tired of missing that crucial piece.

She quickly changed the subject, the faint adorable blush painting her cheeks. "So why do they call you Blue, then?"

"Well, when it came time to patch in they said I had a choice, I could either be Blue or I could be Straw."

"Why those choices?"

"Because his last name is Barry," Cell supplied. He'd been keeping a silent pace with us as we waited and moved up the line, was smiling his good ol' boy smile; the one that put everyone at ease and made him the life of the party.

Hayley's brow furrowed in confusion for a moment then smoothed out with her dawning understanding.

"Oh! That's just terrible!" she cried.

Cell and I laughed and nodded. "Most of the time road names are," he said.

"Sometimes they're just funny on the surface."

"I think you picked well with Blueberry over Strawberry," she said gravely and I had to smile.

"Thanks."

"For sure, you ended up on top with that one." Cell sighed. "I fuckin' hate mine some days."

Hayley smiled sweetly. "Don't always want to be known as the coppertop battery?"

"At least they got one thing right," he said, "I have the stamina to come by the name honestly." He winked at her and she covered her mouth with her hands to stifle her shocked giggle. It was both adorable and sad. She hid her beautiful smile far too often.

"See you when you get down," he said with a wink and we began to ascend the steps to the boarding platform.

Hayley took my hand and a thrill went through me. I glanced down at them and she asked me seriously, "Are you afraid of heights?"

I shook my head. "You?"

She rolled her lips and licked them, her tongue tinged blue by the candy and I wanted to taste it; I wanted to kiss her and find out if she was as sweet. I bet that she was. I bet she would be the sweetest thing I ever tasted.

"No, I thought you might be, though," she said seriously.

I squeezed her hand lightly and murmured, "Just because I'm not afraid of heights doesn't mean you're not needed."

She swallowed hard, her eyes a little wide and said softly, "I like them, too. Heights, I mean." The tension in her shoulders told me that she was as nervous as I was. We were being so awkward around each other with how careful we were being while still attempting to remain honest. The line moved up and we were now first, the car gently swinging empty before us. I felt a surge of something, adrenaline maybe, over being so close to her.

I couldn't help but smile and let her get into the car first. I took my seat beside her and the ride was snug, the width of my shoulders making things crowded, so I laid my arm behind her, curving my hand around her shoulder, twining my fingers from my free hand through hers, my palm resting along the back of her hand.

"Thank you," I said suddenly, and Hayley looked at me sharply.

"For what?"

"For walking with me and talking with me... I know I can be awkward in my silence. I'm just not very good at talking with people."

"Is that why you're always with him?" Her voice was timid, uncertain, and I couldn't take offense to the question. I knew how Cell was. It wasn't the first time I'd been asked by someone why I hung with him.

I shook my head. "Cell is my best friend. He's a good man deep down inside despite his outward facing flaws." I didn't want to let on that he and I were much more than just friends, despite his rampant homophobia. I didn't want to scare her away, not yet, that pain could possibly come much later when I'd gotten my hopes up past where they should be.

Her gaze dropped down to him as we moved up some more and she murmured, "Is he always so intense and frightening?"

I smiled then and answered that one truthfully, "Yes, but not so much the more you get to understanding him. Best way I could describe it is yes, he's always that intense, but no, he's not always so scary. I wish you would give us both a chance, get to know us, maybe even date us for a time. I think you'd be surprised."

"Oh, I don't know about *that*. I mean, as friends of course I'd love to get to know you better... but dating two men at once?"

Cell had blown any form of subtly moving into things out of the water one of the first times we'd been around Hayley at the diner. Flirting his best, at his most frank, it had been the wrong approach then and had damaged things pretty much irreparably. Convincing her was going to take far more work. It *was* unconventional, especially here in the land super-judgmental Christians who were pretty much anything but. Still, I could see the curiosity in her deep brown eyes.

"You guys really do *everything* together?"

"Yes."

She shifted against my body and I held very, very still staring at her, memorizing every line of her face, thrilled to just be this close to her. She turned her gaze away from me and out over the fairgrounds which was pretty much a quick setup job in a farmer's vacant field. Her eyes unfocused and she quickly changed the subject.

"This certainly beats the diner, doesn't it?"

I smiled, unable to take my eyes off of her. "It certainly does," I murmured and she turned back to me, tipping her head to the side. The curiosity in her eyes intensified and I wished, so much, that she would ask her questions while simultaneously wishing that she not.

"Why me?" she asked finally and I could appreciate her willingness to cut through the bullshit. It was definitely a quality she shared with Cell.

"Truthfully, a feeling…"

"A feeling?"

"Yeah, I have a feeling, about you, and about us, and I want us to explore it." She stared at me and I grew self-conscious. Finally, I swallowed hard and said, "How long were you planning on being here?"

"I don't have any place to be," she murmured. "If that's what you're asking."

"Sort of… spend some time with us here, and if at the end you want to see us again, we'll make that happen. If you don't…"

She rolled her lips together, her eyes far away and she finally nodded. I would give anything to be inside her head, listening to her thoughts.

"Okay," she reluctantly agreed and I had to smile. I gave her a slight squeeze, a one-armed hug, and she smiled, a genuine smile, and I almost couldn't wait to tell Cell. I also couldn't wait to tell him to behave him-fucking-self.

4

H ayley…
"Help me understand," I said quietly.

We were sitting at a table near the barbecue pits, the spun sugar that had been the dessert to my lunch long since worn off. I had ridden the Ferris Wheel with Blue, watched as Cell tried valiantly, cursing and laughing, to win a stuffed toy from the B.B. gun shooting range. Two of the other Sacred Hearts, Trigger and Ghost, had pretty much mopped up at that game. Blue had murmured in my ear that they had once been sniper partners overseas and I could see their skill.

Now, we were quietly eating what was supposed to be dinner, just the three of us, a large stuffed unicorn sitting at my hip. Cell had redeemed himself at darts after telling Reaver heartily to fuck off before stepping up to do it. He was smiling across the table at me, and it was charming but still it was as if something were missing from it. Everything on the surface polite and super appealing but I'd served these two for over a year now at the diner. I knew that Cell's mood was mercurial at best and that while he was charming now…

"Tell you what," he said leaning back and lifting his plastic cup full of beer to his lips. He washed his food down and let out a satisfied 'ah' before continuing, "Date us one at a time. Let Blue take you out this week, then let me take you out next week. No need to rush into things all at once."

I chewed my bottom lip. Despite the strangeness of it, it was a super appealing offer. I was terribly lonely and a date or two couldn't hurt anything, could it? I looked at Blue who was staring at me intently from across the table next to Cell, chewing thoughtfully, waiting to see what I would say.

I didn't say anything, and neither of them pressed me for an immediate answer, so instead, I took my time and thought about it. I changed the immediate topic to something else to buy myself more time.

"There's supposed to be live music in the next hour over by the beer garden, I was going to go listen…" I hesitated, I wanted to ask Blue to join me but with Blue came Cell and my basic instinct when it came to the man was to avoid him at all costs. I couldn't tell you precisely what it was, but women's intuition, you know?

"Is that an invitation then?" Cell asked, polishing off his beer and pushing his paper plate away from him. I felt myself blush and nodding, I cast my gaze to the tabletop to break away from the penetrating and uncomfortable stare he was giving me. I caught his smile widening when I looked away and I realized that was part of what bothered me about Cell. He *liked* keeping me uncomfortable and off guard and I hated it. The way he looked at me was completely opposite of the way Blue did. When Cell looked at me, it was always with scrutiny, like he was trying to decide if I was worth his time or trouble.

The way Blue looked at me, I don't think I'd ever felt that way before. It was as if he stared at all that was good and beautiful in the world. My heart ached with yearning for so long to have someone look at me the way Blue did, and I wanted it. I wanted to see if he meant it but I was also so very afraid of hurting again – of being little more than a stepping stone, or another notch in someone's bedpost.

My love life had been complicated and messy up to this point. A series of one disaster after the next, each one leaving me a little more heart-sick and a little more broken than the last. The overwhelming sadness and depression I lived with didn't exactly help in that regard. If it weren't for the pills, it'd be a safe bet that I wouldn't even be able to get out of bed, go to work, and be able to function at all.

"We'd like that," Blue said softly and when I glanced up at him, I could see a look of warning in his beautiful gray eyes. The look was directed squarely at Duracell, who barely took it to heart, amusement warping his lips into an almost smug little smile that I couldn't help it... my palm *itched* with the urge to slap it off his face. Only the fact that I honestly wasn't a violent person kept me in check. Well, that and my fear of what he might do.

"What shall we do in the meantime?" Cell asked, giving me a lasciv-ious wink.

I colored deeply and was saved by Melody saying, "Certainly not whatever is on *your* pervy mind!" She said it right behind me without my knowing she was there so it scared the bejesus out of me. I jumped and let out this god-awful, little high-pitched yelp before I clapped both hands over my mouth.

Cell nearly fell off his bench laughing, while Blue, bless his heart, tried in vain to suppress his smile. The difference between the both of them was like night and day. While Cell laughed *at* me, Blue's smile encour-aged me to laugh with him. I dropped my hands from my mouth and let out an explosive breath.

"Melody, you'd like to scare the life out of me!" She dropped onto the bench beside me and knocked her shoulder into mine.

"Had to make sure you were awake and that these guys weren't boring you half to death."

"I am in absolutely no danger of falling asleep when it comes to these two, that's for sure," I said with a smile.

"We were going to head home; the boys are getting fussy. I think they've reached their limit on fun for one day."

"Aw, well give them my love and you guys be safe." I hugged her and she hugged me back hard.

"See you on Monday," she said and got up.

"See you Monday," I agreed.

She left and I turned back to the two men I was keeping company with. Blue stood up and stepped out of the picnic table's bench, gathering up our plates and trash while Duracell slung one leg over the bench and dug into the inside pocket of his jacket beneath his colorfully patched vest that Melody had once told me was called a cut.

He fished out a pack of cigarettes and shook one out putting it between his lips. Replacing the pack, he produced one of those colorful, disposable plastic lighters and flicked it with his thumb. I watched him, and although I wasn't a fan of smokers at all, I had to say, there was something both attractive and appealing about watching Cell light his cigarette. I don't know if it was the surety and confidence, but just watching him go through the motions... despite his attitude, he was one seriously attractive man.

"You won't be sorry if you do it you know." His voice was strained with how he held the smoke in his lungs and he blew up and out toward the sky, letting out a plume of smoke to the free, clean, air.

I twisted my lips and didn't say anything, but I couldn't help but think to myself about how much Cell reminded me of a little boy who ripped the wings off of flies. He held a streak of cruelty. I'd seen it, in the way he talked to and treated Blue... I was afraid of that cruelty turning on me, I knew it would. Knew it down to my very soul that to get involved with Cell meant accepting some measure of pain.

My eyes drifted away from him and back to Blue. He was the real reason I even entertained this foolish notion in the first place. Something about him called to me on a deep level, I was just afraid to pick up the line.

I'd been hurt so many times before, so often. It was true, I made terrible choices when it came to men. Wore my heart on my sleeve and gave of it too freely, receiving nothing in return. I was always some kind of stepping stone for the men in the relationships I'd been in before. Giving my all, only to have them leave and move on to the next big thing. Sometimes moving on to the next big thing before they'd even gotten out my door.

I was so very afraid of the same thing happening here. I mean, what if I fell hopelessly in love with one or the other of them, only to find out I was just another conquest? Another notch on the bedpost? I just didn't know if I could go through that yet again.

I pulled my hands which were resting on the edge of the table self-consciously back into my lap. I usually hid the scars on my wrists with sweatbands that matched my uniform at work, but today, I had my mother's silver and turquoise bangle bracelets stacked on my left wrist and a fashionable leather cuff with an owl on it around the other while I was out here in the world.

"You don't strike me as the type that gets out much," Cell said, taking a long draw off his cigarette.

"I'm not, usually," I confessed. Blue dropped onto the bench next to me, straddling it to listen to what I was going to say. Duracell propped his elbows on the table and leaned in, his cigarette clasped between his index and middle finger, the hand that held it casually holding the other, loosely clasped fist. It was rugged, handsome, the way he held himself. I think the real appealing thing about it was how his deep brown eyes, lightened with hints of caramel, wandered over my face; his own expression passive but interested... he was really *listening*.

I shifted a bit on my own seat and felt compelled to continue, so I did, saying, "My mom and dad would bring me to this fair yearly. Some of the best memories I have of my mom were made here... well, not *here*, the Harvest Festival has moved a few times, but, um... yeah."

"Where is your mom now?" Cell asked taking a drag.

"She died when I was fifteen... breast cancer..."

"Shit, I'm sorry to hear that."

I nodded and didn't say anything. While Cell's words sounded sincere, there was no change to his expression. His face remained thoughtful and listening; only in such a way that I would kill to know just what it was he had going on in there. Something told me that I really didn't want to know.

It was Blue's hand on my knee, giving it a squeeze that made me jump. When I looked into his clear gray eyes, I saw everything that was missing from Duracell's. Sympathy and empathy both radiated from his expression. He took back his hand quickly from my bare skin and I immediately missed its reassurance... keenly.

"Anyway," I murmured after the pregnant pause, "I come every year. I can't help it, it makes me happy."

"You should always do what makes you happy," Cell said.

"Oh yeah?"

"Sure? It ain't exactly living if you don't." He winked at me and got up, stepping out from the picnic table's bench and giving a stretch.

Blue placed his hand on my lower back and smiled saying, "Let's grab a beer and find a good spot."

I smiled and leaned back into the stolen touch saying, "That sounds like a fine idea."

Blue got up and untangled himself from the picnic table and I followed suit, putting my unicorn beneath my arm and accepting his hand to balance better as I stepped over the bench. He let it go, shyly, before I could tighten my grip to let him know I liked it and that it was nice.

"Find a spot, I'll grab the beer," Cell said and left Blue and I to find a table around the edge of the dance floor that'd been laid down. The tables were overturned whiskey barrels with roughhewn barstools. All of them made out of good, old-fashioned and in some cases, reclaimed wood.

We found one of the last tables available that had three stools and took our seats, the band just beginning to warm up, the fiddle player drawing his bow across the strings, fingers dancing along its neck, pausing here and there to adjust tension. A hum of excitement reverberated through my spine as the banjo player joined the fiddler. There were no microphones save for the ones for the singers. There were no electric guitars or amplifiers... this was down-home country bluegrass about to happen and I loved it.

It was generally the only time I listened to it, having always preferred the real thing to a recording. Just something about a recording, even with how clear they were now, didn't do the music any justice. It needed to be raw, be live, with the light autumn breeze and the scent of wood and grass and yes, even beer.

Cell found us, three bottles between his large, scarred and work rough hands. He set them down around the silly rainbow-mained unicorn which I had sat on the center of our barrel top. He parsed them out around the unicorn's butt between the three of us, one to me, one to Blue, and one to himself.

"Cheers," he declared and held his bottle up. I raised mine and Blue did likewise, and we clinked the necks together.

"To new beginnings," Blue murmured and I kind of like that.

He was right, things had turned some kind of invisible corner for the three of us. It wasn't I was just their waitress anymore... I wasn't their girlfriend or lover by any stretch of the imagination, but I definitely felt comfortable with the label of 'friend' and who knew about the rest?

"To new beginnings," I murmured in echo and I drank from the neck of the Budweiser bottle. The crisp, sharp taste of barley and hops flooded my mouth, and I felt myself loosen up just a little without even the benefit of the alcohol hitting my system. Not that I planned on having more than the one.

"Alright, alright!" the singer of the band said into his microphone. "Can y'all hear me?"

A cry went up from the crowd around the floor with some applause, a few sharp whistles split the air and those I could live without. Something about the sharp, high-pitched sound made me tense and grated along my nerves like nails across a blackboard got to most people.

The singer introduced his band and without much further ado, launched into a lively first song. We laughed, dancers took the floor, and we drank our beers and clapped along. Duracell stood, and someone asked if they could take and use his stool. He nodded and said sure and tapped his foot along to the music.

Blue sat back on his stool, one foot planted firmly on the ground, one on the bottom rung between the spindle legs. He tapped an accompanying rhythm against the edge of the seat with his hands and his smile was both perfect and infectious. He turned to look at me and when he saw me smiling too, his grew even wider.

He held out his hand and I took it, letting him pull me to my feet and then we were dancing. Blue spun me around the dance floor and it was as if we were the only two people in the world. The feeling was amazing, and I let the good in. He kept his hands respectful, the weight of his palm against my lower back and just above my hip sending a tingling sensation through my body.

He applied the barest amount of pressure, drawing me closer as we stepped. His other hand, holding mine, was warm, the palm calloused, his grip light and careful. We were a scant few inches apart and I wondered what it would feel like to tuck myself against his chest and to take shelter in the front of his body. I missed closeness. I missed that feeling of being safe and cuddled and cherished.

You could have it times two if you would only give it a try, a voice from inside my own head whispered. It was a tempting offer, one that I didn't want to immediately reject, but one that just felt so outside of the ordinary, so strange… I mean… what would people think? What would my *dad* think?

The song ended and we parted clapping and laughing. The band struck up a slower almost waltz and I felt him before I saw him. A presence at my back, the thrum of almost electricity scattering along my skin, prickling through my clothes. Duracell's presence was electric, no pun intended, but it was the truth. He was like a tempest. One that you watched come up and over the horizon, moving towards you, but you were frozen in its path.

"Can I have the next one?" he asked and I fought down the urge to shiver. His voice was pitched low, velvet and almost seductive. I swallowed and I didn't wish to offend anyone so I nodded. His hands briefly landed on my hips and he dragged fingertips along my lower back as he came around my front.

I placed my hands on his upper arms, the leather of his jacket cooler than I expected it to be. It was moving well into dusk, the sun just a fiery glimmer over the treetops to the west. I swallowed hard and Cell swayed, his hands warm on my hips where my cutoff shorts covered them. I let him coax me down the dance-floor and felt drawn in. As if, he were the spider and I? I were the fly.

"You like to dance?" he asked.

"Not usually, just at things like this."

"What do you like to do then?"

"I um, I like to um…" I felt myself blush. I flustered so easily around Cell. He wasn't easy to talk to like Blue.

"It's okay, you don't have to tell me," he said with a charming smile. I looked around for Blue and he was back at our table, his beer raised to his lips as he watched us warily over the bottle.

"You like my boy, Blue." I looked up at Cell sharply but there was no accusation in his eyes, no jealousy. "It's okay, he's easy to like. Sometimes I have to work a little harder at being likeable… it is what it is." He shrugged nonchalantly and I felt myself relax marginally.

"You… you can be awfully intense," I admitted and he nodded.

"Intense, I like that. Yeah, you're right, that's totally me." He grinned and I felt some more tension ease. I returned the smile.

"What do you like to do?" I asked, trying not to let the conversation turn back to me. I just didn't know if I felt comfortable sharing things with Cell. I didn't get the same feeling from him that I did from Blue.

He laughed a little. "Well, I like to ride and work on my bike, I like to hang with my brothers and see what kind of trouble we can get up to, and I guess I like to dance with pretty girls at county fairs."

I blushed at that last one and looked away. Cell laughed but it wasn't mocking. He asked me, "A little too cheesy; coming on a little strong?"

"No," I answered, shaking my head, blushing like mad. I didn't think I could or would ever be considered *pretty* by anyone.

"You know, I sure would like to meet the man who dulled your sparkle, Hayley." I looked up at him sharply but didn't know what to say. I swallowed hard and he gave me a look that chilled me right down to the center of my being.

"Why?" I managed to croak.

"Because I'd love to break his face for it."

I swallowed hard and felt myself leaning away from him slightly and suddenly Blue was there, at our side. Cell's charming smile was back in place and he spun me back into Blue's arms. I looked up at Blue who smiled down at me and I tried very hard to decide what exactly Cell had meant by what he'd said.

"He likes you," Blue said finally. I looked back at our table where Duracell stood drinking the rest of his beer, arm slung comically over my unicorn's back. He winked at me and I felt fear. I didn't quite resist the urge then. I closed the gap, between me and Blue, and took a little shelter from the chill Cell's gaze sent down my spine.

"I'm not sure how I feel about that," I said honestly and Blue's face lost all humor.

"Trust me, Hayley, you would much rather have him like you than not."

"That's not comforting in the slightest, Blue."

"No, but it's true."

I was silent for a long time while Blue searched my face and I searched his right back. His expression softened and he murmured to me as the song came to a close, "Cell is a hard man to love, Hayley, but if you do and you managed to get him to respect you back, you will never in a million years be safer or want for anything. Once he's committed, he's committed for life. That's just how he is."

The song ended and people stepped away from one another applauding. Blue and I simply stilled. I thought about what he'd just told me and when the next song started we just sort of started moving again, although it wasn't to dance it was to return to our table. The air was cooling and Cell picked up and handed me my half empty beer which was still cold enough to be palatable.

I drank some giving Cell a nod and took my seat, hooking the heel of my boot on one of the bottom rungs of the stool. Blue stood this time,

49

as Cell had taken his seat and we just sort of sat for a moment. The sun had finished its descent beyond the horizon and the evening was rapidly cooling, the weather behaving more like autumn than it had during the day.

"You cold?" Cell asked and I nodded.

"Getting there. I'm also, sad to say, getting tired."

"We all have to be up early," Blue murmured and he was right.

"I keep thinking today is Saturday," I said shaking my head.

Cell barked a laugh. "I like your style of thinking, darling, but nope..." He let out a gusty sigh. "It's Sunday. Back to the grind in the morning."

I let out a harsh sigh of my own and finished off my beer. It was a good half-an-hour walk from where we were to the parking lot and I wasn't even slightly buzzed. I looked around for the trash and spotted someone with one of the heavy-duty gray fifty-five-gallon trash cans on a wheeled platform and a five-gallon bucket.

I watched the young man pour bottles that were barely dregs into the bucket and toss the empties into the trashcan before pulling it along behind him to the next table. It was honest work. Hard, but honest. I smiled at him when he came near and pulled out bottles from the table. I felt the guys' eyes watching me as I smiled at the young man and emptied our own bottles and threw them away. He smiled at me and ducked his head saying, "Thank you; ma'am."

I returned to where Blue and Cell waited and Cell was once again watching me with that calculating look of his.

"Well that was right nice of you," he said in a bit of a mock-country twang.

I didn't take the bait and simply said, "It was nothing." He picked up my stuffed unicorn that he had won me, waved it back and forth making it trot on air and handed it to me. I couldn't help but laugh and took it from him, hugging it to me.

"Thank you for the day, Hayley," Blue said softly. I turned and couldn't not smile wider, hugging the unicorn to my chest tighter, the chill starting to get to me.

"Thank *you* for asking and thank you both for the dances."

I jumped when the warm, heavy leather of Cell's jacket enveloped my shoulders. Blue smiled and Cell said, once again, in that low, sexy growl just beside my ear, "What kind of assholes you take us for, darlin'? You didn't honestly think we'd let you walk to your car alone did you?" He chuckled and straightened up and Blue slung an arm over my shoulders, steering me away from the dancing, music, and the light cast by the naked full-sized bulbs strung back and forth over the plywood dancefloor.

Cell walked on my other side. He'd peeled the vest with colored patches off of his jacket and wore it over his maroon tee shirt, the tail of it hitched up to either side of his hips so he could cram his hands into the pockets of his faded, work-worn Levi's.

"Thank you," I said shyly and he gave me a grin and a wink.

"Don't mention it."

We walked in a comfortable silence for a time before Cell had me stop so he could retrieve a cigarette from his jacket's inside pocket. I turned and stood still while he fished inside the pocket, the back of his hand brushing against my breast. I held my breath. The problem I was having with the contact wasn't that it made me uncomfortable, at least not in the way that he was touching me when I didn't want him to., rather, I found the small touch exciting and that I wanted to explore more.... with both of them... just not maybe at once and maybe not sex. I mean, wouldn't that make me some kind of harlot or slut?

He put the cigarette to his lips and cupped his hands around it, flicking the plastic lighter to life with his thumb. The flame cast his face in high relief and I realized that Cell was handsome in his own way. Angular features, his jawline rugged and strong, dusted with a day or so's growth.

The flame went out, and he tucked the lighter back into the pocket and drew the two sides of his jacket closed, the smoke swirling around us.

"Which way to your car?" he asked in that half growl and I looked out over the fairgrounds, past darkened rides that were all closed down. Goodness, it must be much later than I realized.

"This way." I pointed and he nodded and struck out that direction leaving me and Blue a few paces behind.

Blue's arm returned across my shoulders and he hugged me into his side for warmth. I leaned into him and walked with the two of them out the temporary construction fence that'd been erected around the perimeter of the large field the festival was taking up.

"I had a really good time today," I said, leaning a hip against my tired Golf's dark blue door. Blue stood in front of me while Cell stood somewhere around the front of my car, behind me, finishing off his cigarette.

"You could have more good days," Cell called and I laughed a little.

"It's a lot... I still need to think about that," I called back.

"Take your time," he said but it didn't sound very happy or convincing.

Blue rolled his eyes quickly over his wry smile, his hand drifting up and cupping the side of my neck, his thumb caressing my jaw as he stared at me suddenly serious as if trying to memorize my face.

It was dark and very hard to see by just the light of the half moon, but I was well aware that we were alone out here, even though there was a fair bit of cars still scattered throughout the field that was being used as a parking lot.

"I may never have a chance like this again..." Blue breathed and it sounded agonized. My heart broke a little at his tone, but before the pieces could fall, he bent and his lips were gentle along mine. I gasped, surprised, but then my body took what I so desperately wanted before my mind could resist.

I melted against him, my lips parting for him, inviting him to deepen the kiss and he did. It was as if we were suspended in time; the moment, one of the handful of absolutely perfect moments I had ever experienced in my life.

When he broke the kiss, I stood for a heartbeat, eyes still closed, savoring how gently he'd touched me, how sweetly his mouth had moved against mine.

Hard muscled arms pulled me gently back against an equally hard chest. One of those arms wrapped around my waist holding me back against him.

"My turn," Cell growled into my ear and his other hand gently smoothed up the front of my throat, his fingers pressing into my chin, tipping my head all the way back. His mouth covered mine and it wasn't gentle, it was possessive. Whereas Blue had gently taken my mouth, Cell conquered it, kissing me fiercely; the warmth that Blue had started in my body blossomed into an inferno.

I admit it, I was weak, falling back into Cell's chest, letting him take what he wanted, powerless to do anything but surrender.

He tore his mouth from mine and I stood trembling, chest heaving. He let me go, taking his jacket from my shoulders. Blue stood by my open car door, the dome light spilling weak, watery yellow light onto the dry and brittle grass.

"Think about it," Cell growled.

"Take all the time you need," Blue added gently. I got into my car mechanically and set the stuffed unicorn on my passenger seat. Blue handed me my keys which I had left in the door.

I took them with trembling fingers, and he shut me safely inside. I started up my Volkswagen and turned on the headlights. They stood by and watched me, waiting for me to buckle up and pull out.

I glanced into my rearview and watched them both staring after me and I knew what my answer would be the next time I saw them… I knew it all the way down to my very bones.

5

D uracell...

"I think we got her," I said dryly and glanced over to Blue. He was still staring at the two pinpricks of red that were Hayley's departing taillights. Typical for him, he didn't say shit; not for a long minute.

I was in a good mood and feeling generous, so I waited him out. Finally, when the lights from her cage were gone and the contrails of dust from her tires were nearly settled he turned to me, his face completely neutral.

I knew the look, like he had high hopes that he was struggling with. Trying not to get 'em up too high in case shit went sideways. Dumb fucker. It always went sideways in the end, he knew that, but for now, we had her so it was cool letting his hopes raise a little.

"Did you hear me? I said, I'm pretty sure we got her, dude. So why the long fucking face? It was an awesome day. Fuckin' enjoy it for once. That's your problem, you —"

"I hear you, just shut up about it!" he snapped and he turned his gaze back the way she'd gone.

"Jesus fucking Christ, you're like a goddamned puppy." He was, too, the way he was staring after her after she'd long gone. It was pathetic.

He turned back and glared at me, but I didn't fucking care. I never did, unless it made him pissy enough to resist putting out. Although, to be honest, sometimes that was fun too.

"Come on, we gotta be up in less hours than I'd really like," I reminded him and that spurred him back into action, at least a little bit.

We trekked over to where our bikes were parked under a tree and started them up. He stared off into space while I sorted out my jacket and cut. I could say one thing for the bitch that Blue'd picked. She had good taste in whatever the fuck bitches slathered on their skin or whatever. I could smell it coming off my jacket, floral and sweet.

I was seriously looking forward to utterly destroying that pussy. It would happen, too. We'd hooked her. I knew it down to the bottom of whatever twisted excuse for a soul I owned.

I put on a set of safety glasses and buckled on my helmet. Not because I cared about wearing one, but more so we wouldn't get our asses pulled the fuck over. I didn't need the cops finding the firepower in the back of my waistband that my ass shouldn't be carrying as a felon.

Jail and prison just wasn't as much fun as it was out here, but at the same time, given the opportunity, I could raise just as much hell on the inside as out here. I gave Blue my usual signal that I was taking off. He gave me the hand signal back that he was right behind me and we switched on headlamps and carefully maneuvered over the raw, rough dirt and trampled grass of the field to the dirt and gravel track operating as the road out of here.

I couldn't wait to hit blacktop and traction I could count on. One of the best things about riding was going fast, even if it was a time of night that the only other sons of bitches on the road were sheriffs or stateies out to ruin my ride.

We hit blacktop; I made sure we were clear of any troubles and punched it, getting up to speed. Blue rode with me and I laughed as the cooler autumn evening air washed over me and set me freer than anything else I'd encountered so far, except this life in among the outlaws.

I was disappointed that the rest of these boys had pussed out so hard while Blue and I had been locked up, but I could understand it. None of 'em were like me. It just was what it was. I hadn't found anything better, yet... but I think Blue had just provided a decent change of pace and distraction for the time being.

We'd see if she could hold up or not. She was kind of a timid mouse of a thing. Good thing she had tits and ass for days, some long hair to yoke her with, otherwise I wouldn't have been half as interested. Usually, I wasn't much into banging a chick more than once but Blue made my life a lot easier, caught what I missed and let me know when I was missing emotional or social cues. He apparently needed more than what I was giving him in that department, so I could put up with it... for now.

For the immediate now, we rode back to the club and our beds. I'd pretty much done all of the 'nice' I could manage to fake tonight, but again... he was right. I could stand to have some regular pussy around and Hayley was easier on the eyes and had just about everything I liked. If I wanted to bang her more than once, I would need to do shit Blue's way. Most of all, if I wanted to keep Blue around, I needed to do shit Blue's way...

Decisions, decisions... I guess sometimes there were no shortcuts to take, but fuck I hated doing anything the long way; but, some situations just called for it, I guess.

6

B**lue…**
  Cell and I were both rough around the edges from a lack of sleep the night before. It was still unseasonably warm outside and we'd dressed for the cooler morning. When you worked on a road crew, you dressed for the weather, whatever it was in the morning, but it wasn't until your lunch hour that you could strip any of it off or switch anything out, so we'd been sweating hard for the last few hours. Dragging our asses into the diner for lunch that afternoon almost felt like a chore until I saw her. Just laying eyes on her and I was restored some.

Cell hit the bathroom while I slipped into a free booth. When he reappeared and sat down at the table is when Hayley finally came over. She filled our water glasses and set down some menus. She was solemn today, not talking, lost inside her own head. She turned to leave and get Cell his regular drink order but stopped, back turned. Her shoulders dropped slightly in her cute, bright turquoise, fifties-style waitressing uniform and I wondered what was up while I took her in. That retro dress fit her figure to stunning effect, and Cell and I unabashedly admired the view of the perfect curve of her ass in it for as long as she remained turned around for us to do it.

Finally, she turned back around, stainless-steel water pitcher clutched tightly in one hand, the other buried in her apron. She pulled out a folded piece of paper from that apron pocket and set it between the both of us on top of the menus. It took her a couple of tries but she finally said to us, "Friday, pick me up at eight?"

Cell picked up the paper and unfolded it, his eyes scanning the contents written on it. He handed it across to me and told her, "Blue will. I'll pick you up same time next week."

She nodded rapidly and took off to another table refilling their waters. My eyes fell onto the paper and the address written there. I couldn't help but smile and think to myself that this was going to be one of the longest weeks ever.

I wasn't wrong, and what really sucked was that Hayley had to move back to night waitressing for a while, while they trained a new girl. When Melody got wind of it, she saved the day by switching off with Hayley that Friday night so that Hayley could go on her date with me. Archer wasn't amused when it came to his wife working at night in that neighborhood, but it was only one night and by now, most, if not all of the town knew she was with a Sacred Heart.

Still, I was amused when Nox and Rush showed up at the club in Nox's cage with Archer and Mel's two boys. Why? So Archer could be at the diner while Mel worked the night shift, watching over her.

That was the kind of man I wished I could be for Hayley, but mine and Cell's job sort of prohibited it for the time being.

I was thrilled that she was giving us a chance, body humming with good vibes as I got ready to go get her. Cell watching me from my bed as he thumbed through the channels on my TV, surfing for something good.

I watched him for a second in my mirror as I put my wallet into the back pocket of my best jeans. I wore my newest tee shirt, too. I didn't have much money, I was still paying off debt and other stupid shit from before I went inside. I was almost caught up, but not quite there yet. Another six months or so and I'd probably be able to invest in some nicer clothes. For now, this is what I had and it would have to do.

I went over and pulled my jacket and cut down off of the coat-tree in the corner and looked back at Cell.

"Look at you all dressed to fuckin' impress." His tone dripped with sarcasm and I frowned. He grinned, and gave me a half-assed, mock salute and said, "Good luck, bro."

That part he meant and wasn't entirely being an ass about. I nodded and ducked out into the hallway, not bothering to shut the door.

We'd both ridden by the address she'd given us earlier in the week. It was a nice, small, two-story house painted a bright cheery yellow and trimmed out in white. The front porch was a grand thing, white like the trim with decorative pillars holding up the eaves. The driveway went down along the right side of the house to a spacious side and part of the backyard where a converted garage rested. It was a nice place and easy to find, even in the dark.

I went out into what should have just been a deep dusk and found it darker than it should have been. A quick glance to the sky told me everything I needed to know. The sky was leaden, the clouds hanging low. It was definitely going to rain. *Shit.*

I didn't own a cage. I looked at the sky one more time as I mounted my bike out front of the club and hoped like hell we could get where we were going before the sky decided to open up and that it'd quit before it was time to leave.

I rode over to Hayley's and pulled into the driveway to the back of the house by the outbuilding like she'd written and didn't even have time to shut off the bike before she was out the back door of the house. I smiled and she paused, her big brown eyes wide. My heart sank a bit and then I realized she wasn't looking at *me* with that mixture of doubt and trepidation, but rather my bike.

I smiled and leaned it over onto its kickstand, shutting off the motor. She was dressed for it in form-fitting, dark jeans. She'd paired them with tall, knee-high, brown leather boots that were laced up tight and had a sturdy sole. A soft, but warm looking cream sweater peeked around her dark brown fashionable leather coat that she had belted at the waist and I couldn't have picked better if I wanted to for a first-time ride.

"Come here, get on behind me, and put this on," I said softly and held out my spare helmet that I'd pulled off from around the sissy bar.

Hayley came forward stammering, "I um, I thought between you that one of you might have a car. Do you want to take mine?"

I smiled and asked, "Don't you trust me?"

She looked a little stricken. "Of course I do! I mean, I'm sorry… I didn't mean to –"

I chuckled and covered her hands with mine. "It's fine, you didn't hurt my feelings. I just really want to show you."

"Show me what?" she asked a bit breathlessly.

"The feeling. Can't describe it, but I want to share it. I'd like to share everything with you." I kind of kicked myself at how cheesy that sounded but once it was out of my mouth, it wasn't like I could take it back.

Hayley stared at me, searching my face for several long heartbeats, but then she put the helmet on and clasped it, tightening the chinstrap. I heeled up the kickstand and started it up and she got on behind me. She found the pegs for her feet and I told her to hold on to me. Her arms went tight around my waist, her lush body pressing up against my back and I let out the clutch, shifted, and took us around to head down the driveway the same way I'd come up. I was pleased there was enough room back here to turn the bike around without having to back it up. That was always nice.

I took it slow at first, down her street and stopped at the stop sign at the end of her road.

"Alright?" I called.

"This isn't so bad!" she called back and I smiled to myself. She hadn't ridden with Cell and I needed to both ease her into things and prepare her for that, so I was a little less gentle in my speed when we turned out onto the main thoroughfare.

Hayley gasped, I could tell because she held onto me tighter. I resisted the urge take my hand off the bars just long enough to pat her hands where they rested over my stomach. The wind was biting and smelled of rain and a bit of ozone by the time we pulled into the lot at *Soul Fuel*.

I hadn't had much time to plan for a first date, and it was hard without knowing exactly what she liked, but then I'd overheard Everett telling Dray about the plan at hers and Mandy's coffee shop for this Friday's entertainment. It was too perfect to pass up, and so I brought her here.

The lot was pretty full when we pulled in, but I still managed to find parking about four spaces down next to a scooter occupying a space but courteously pulled to one side of the space to allow for another bike or scooter to pull in. I tapped Hayley's knee and she hesitated, unsure of what I wanted or needed and I said as kindly as I could, "Need you to get off. It's easier to back in."

She startled a bit and jumped down, standing on the sidewalk and taking off her helmet while I backed my bike into the space snuggly next to the mint green Vespa. She quickly checked her long hair in the side mirror of an SUV parked next to us and fixed her windblown bangs, and I smiled and held my hand out. She gave me the helmet I'd lent her and I stowed both of them in one of the hard-sided saddlebags figuring it was definitely going to rain out here before the night was through.

I held out my hand to her and her fingers were frozen. I cursed my damn self for not thinking to give her a pair of gloves and stopped her.

"Sorry, I should have brought you gloves, or had you put your hands in my pockets."

"It's alright."

"No, I should have thought of it."

Taking her other hand and putting both of them, palms together, I raised her joined hands to my lips. I cupped them between my larger ones and blew on them gently; warming them with my breath as best I could.

She smiled and said, "You're sweet."

I didn't say anything back, just smiled at her and turning, tucked her hand in the crook of my arm, an old-fashioned gentlemanly gesture, but one that she surely deserved. I made sure to walk on the outside and we walked up the sidewalk to the lighted entrance of Red and Evy's coffee and chocolate café.

The rain just began to patter down as we stepped inside, and I held the door, guiding Hayley in first.

It was crowded in here, but I'd told Evy we were coming and she'd had a girl put a little reserved sign at a two-seater table for us. It was low and set between two wing-backed chairs. Maren, Nox's sweetheart, gave me a sweet smile and a chin lift from behind the glass case of confections and straightened, leaning in to speak to one of the girls who worked the front.

A few words and the girl came out to make the young couple sitting in the chairs by the fireplace move. They were at least gracious about it, which I could appreciate. I guided Hayley into one of the seats by the fire and the girl, I think her name was Sarah, said "Sorry about that, what can I bring you?"

"No trouble at all," Hayley said brightly and ordered some kind of fancy mocha with more components than I could remember. When Sarah turned to me, my curiosity got the better of me and I held up two fingers to indicate 'make it two.'

"Alright then, coming right up!" she said cheerfully and went back around the counter to the giant coffee machine.

A light pattering of applause drew Hayley's attention from me to the little area set aside with a couple of microphones. Her eyes lit up when the singer from the fair stepped up to it with his guitar. The fiddler was with him, but it was just the two of them this time.

The music was supposed to be a little lower and a little slower tonight, which I could appreciate and I'm sure Hayley could, too.

Maren stopped in front of us blocking the view of the musicians just long enough to set down two plates. She winked at me and said to us both, "Glad you guys came, you get to be my guinea pigs and tell me if this is any good."

"What is it?" Hayley asked curiously.

"White chocolate maple ribbon cheesecake with a regular chocolate ganache finish. I'm trying to come up with a new autumn-themed sweet or two for next year. Mandy wants me to get creative." She made a face like the prospect both excited and scared the hell out of her and I smiled up at her and gave her a nod. Hayley spoke for us without even thinking about it.

"We will definitely let you know, but it sounds absolutely amazing. I'm going to be in sugar overload before we leave here, I can tell."

"You only live once," Maren said and scrunched up her nose in this adorable way that she did before she took off back to the kitchen, just in time for the fiddler to draw his bow across the strings in a slightly mournful tone; the opening notes to their first song.

The blonde girl came by with our coffee and set it on the low table beside our cakes and winked at me and took off before I could pull money out of my jacket. I shook my head slightly and smiled to myself, figuring Evy had something to do with it. Hayley smiled at me and picked up her mug that could double as a soup bowl, sipping at the frothy liquid inside. I smiled back and picked up my own off the saucer.

She wasn't kidding about the impending sugar coma. Between the coffee and the rich cheesecake sitting in front of me, I would be lucky not to get a stomachache. Still, it was something learned about our woman, that she had a sweet tooth. I watched her watch the musicians behind me while I watched her and kept an eye on the door behind her out of habit.

The duo played and sang for around an hour before taking a thirty-minute intermission. My nerves hummed to life when they set down their instruments, knowing that I would have to speak to her, yet having no idea what I was going to say.

She gave me a short reprieve by getting up and going to the restroom before there was too much of a line. When she returned and sat back down, she smiled at me and I couldn't help myself but to sit there and just stare for a long minute. She was so beautiful when she smiled – like some mythical creature from another world and totally out of my league.

"What?" she asked, her smile beginning to die at the expression on my face.

"Just realizing how far out of my league you are," I said.

She blinked and scoffed a laugh. I cocked my head to the side.

"What's funny?"

"You! That whole idea. If anyone is out of anyone's league it's that you are way out of mine."

I blushed then and shook my head rapidly. No, that wasn't how that worked. She laughed again and I looked at her. She was serious... she wasn't just saying it to be nice. I wished I could find the man who shook her self-confidence. I'd make him pay for it. Of course, I wouldn't say such a thing to her. I didn't want to scare her. If anyone was going to do that, it was going to be Cell.

"I'm glad you asked me out, I mean, again... I mean that you were persistent," she said softly blushing as she tripped over her words and I smiled.

"I'm glad you finally said yes."

"Me, too."

Awkward silence.

"So, um, where did you learn to fold the pretty things you do?" she asked.

"I uh, actually taught myself."

"Really?"

"Yeah, I taught myself out of a book, and when I learned all of those, one of the CO's started printing off directions for me and bringing them in with him until I figured out those."

"I'm sorry... I don't know what a CO is."

I swallowed hard. *Crap, I didn't know if she knew Cell and I had been sent up.* I bit the bullet and came clean.

"CO means Correctional Officer... Uh, we moved here after we got out of prison."

"Oh. I um, I think I knew that, actually."

She kind of shrank back, cringing into her seat but I didn't think it was from fear but rather a bit of embarrassment by how she blushed.

"It was stupid. Cell and I took the fall for our entire chapter for running guns; we went up on several weapons charges. We had a good lawyer. He managed to get it down to one charge – possession of an illegal weapon with intent to sell. Carried a ten-year sentence but we were out after a nickel." I shut my mouth, her eyes gone wide at the severity of our transgression.

"Oh... I..."

"We came down to this chapter because they'd cleaned up their act. We don't do any of that shit anymore. I seriously never want to go back to that life. Completely understand if you'd rather not see us anymore."

She sat very still, and I watched the wheels in her head turning. Finally, she said, "You swear to me you don't do anything illegal now?"

"I swear it on my life, on Cell's life and all the lives on the rest of my club. We're out of that life. It was the craziest and stupidest thing I've ever done and I wish I could say I had a noble reason for doing it, but I was in it for the money."

"There's more important things to life than money," she murmured.

"I figured that out the hard way; it's my biggest regret."

She pressed her lips together and nodded. "Thank you for being honest with me."

I could tell she meant that, I could also tell that she wanted to ask me a question, but wasn't sure.

"You can ask me anything," I said and meant it.

She searched my face and asked, "Does Duracell feel the same way that you do about it?"

I didn't want to lie, but I didn't want to frighten her either so I took the easy way out on that one. "I don't know, that's something to ask Cell."

She nodded and said, "Fair enough."

God. Fuck. She's going to bail on us…

The truth fucking hurt, alright. I was living proof right now.

The musicians returned and effectively cut off any more conversation for the time being. I turned to watch them for a moment and a light touch to the back of my hand made me jump.

I turned to look and Hayley held out a hand to me. I took it and she smiled and simply held my hand while we listened. I stopped staring at the duo playing, my eyes suddenly stuck fast to our joined hands.

Maybe I hadn't completely fucked up after all.

7

H ayley...

I studied Blue's profile as he watched the musicians and it was grim, unhappy, as if once again something had been ripped away from him. I thought about what he'd said, about his past, and I knew he'd been to prison – I just hadn't known for what.

I mean, I could easily believe it of Cell, but Blue? I pressed my lips together and thought about myself. While I could never do anything that would send me to prison, I thought about what had led me here, to right now, and I couldn't honestly throw stones. I mean, I'd once tried to kill myself. If ever there was a poor life decision, *that* was certainly a doozy, wasn't it? So who was I to criticize?

So far, even though this was our first date, Blue had treated me so well. I felt like a princess in his presence, a sensation I had never really had before with all the law-abiding men I had ever dated or been with before.

I reached out and touched Blue's hand and he jumped, twisting back around to look at me. I tangled my fingers with his and he reached out his arm so that we were both comfortable and could continue holding hands. He smiled at me and it was almost heartbreaking with how beautiful it was. The rejection he'd been fearing sliding right out of his eyes as if it'd never been.

I hated that my reaction had left him feeling that way, and I wondered how many times before it'd happened. I suddenly thought I may have found something in common with Blue. Rejection was likely something he encountered daily and if it hurt him like it hurt me, then it was any wonder that it took him over a year to finally really ask me to go out with him. While I was sure that really had more to do with the fact that they were asking me to date *both of them*, I would cross that bridge when I came to it.

For now, I just wanted to learn about Blue, and see where things went and not think about Cell too much until I was there... That would be soon enough and something I was uneasy about, but I had a feeling about Blue. A really good feeling, and I didn't want to give up on that too quickly. I feared if I did it would be a great source of regret for years to come, if not the rest of my life.

The music was soothing and we listened, hand in hand, letting it carry most of our concerns away. When the set finally ended, it was with several of us standing and applauding. I laughed lightly, my spirit and heart done good, refreshed by the night out. Honestly, I think that most of that had to do with the company I kept.

We let the café clear out, the parking lot empty some before we got up to leave. Blue saluted the girl who had brought the delicious cakes and she came over to us.

"So what did you think?" she asked.

"Oh, my God... That was one of the best desserts I've ever tasted. You have to keep it. I wouldn't change a thing about it," I gushed, and I couldn't help it, it really had been that good. Blue nodded emphatically in agreement with what I was saying.

"Really? You really think so?"

"Absolutely."

She squealed a bit and bounced on the balls of her feet. "I'm totally going to go ahead and have Mandy and Evy try it then."

Blue patted her on the shoulder and she said, "You guys have a good night. It was nice to see you again, Hayley."

"Nice to see you, too, Maren."

"See you at the club sometime, Blue."

He nodded and placed a hand at my lower back to guide me around the table and to the doors. One of the girls was standing by to lock it behind us.

"Goodnight!" she called as we slipped through and I looked back over my shoulder and called back, "Goodnight!"

It was wet out here. The air humid, but the rain had stopped for now. We went down the sidewalk back to the bike which was beaded with water, small puddles pooling on the leather seat. Blue told me to wait a moment and unlocked his saddlebags with a key. He pulled out a towel and wiped off the seat really well and handed me a helmet. He put the towel back and brought out his own helmet and sat astride his motorcycle. He started it and brought it up out of its lean, putting up the kickstand.

I waited for him to give me a wave before I got on behind him, wrapping my arms tightly around his waist. He took my hands and guided them into his pockets, tucking them down inside.

"Hold on to me, but this will keep your hands warm," he called. I nodded and he took us carefully down the lot and out onto the street.

My heart was in my throat, more so on this ride than the last. The streets slick with rain, I was terrified we would slide but Blue seemed like he was an old hand at this. He piloted the beast of a bike over the wet carefully. The wind damp but fresh until we were probably less than ten minutes from home. That's when the sky totally opened up and it began to *pour*.

I held tightly to him as he cursed and swore in front of me. He took the quickest route to my place but there was really nothing for it. We were soaked inside a minute. It was worse, somehow, for riding into the droplets as they fell. At least that's what I imagined.

When he pulled down the long drive and shut off his bike by the back door, I couldn't let him ride home in this… I mean, I was shivering already and just because he was a man didn't mean he didn't feel cold. That and illnesses didn't care how tough you thought you were.

I jumped off the bike, taking off the helmet and grabbed his hand. The rain was still coming down in sheets, loud and fierce and rather than yell and risk worrying my dad, I gave an insistent little tug on his hand, urging him to come with me. He shut off his bike and leaned it over at the same time he heeled down the kickstand, just like that in one fluid practiced motion and I was captured by how amazing and, well, how *hot* it was to watch. Slinging a leg back over the bike's saddle, he stood and followed me.

I didn't want to take him into the house because, well, my dad was probably asleep – or waiting up for me, and *that* wasn't totally awkward despite the fact that I was a grown woman. It was a good thing I had another option, which is, I think, precisely why my father had helped me rebuild Mom's studio into one of my own. To give me privacy and the ability to have a moment like this, which I was totally grateful for right now, by the way.

I pulled my keys from my pocket and went through them, inserting the proper one into the deadbolt lock on the studio door. Blue was at my back, trying to protect me as well as he could from the rain which was adorable but completely unnecessary. It was already far too late for any of that. I mean, I don't think either of us could get any wetter.

I got the door open and went in, hanging the helmet off to the side on the coat-tree. Blue followed me and I flipped on the studio lights. He paused, letting his eyes adjust as I closed the door on the pounding rain outside and hung my keys on the hook.

"You live out here?" he asked and I shook my head.

"I live in the house, but I have my own space out here. Well, except for the washer and dryer, they're behind the bathroom, here. My dad wanted an office in the house to do the diner's paperwork and deposits, so we converted the original laundry room in the house for him and moved the washer and dryer out here, since I do all the laundry anyway. It's a good thing right now, too. I can dry these wet clothes."

I think I was babbling because it was distracting me from how my teeth were trying to chatter. I shrugged out of my coat and hung it on the coat-tree by the door, over the loaned helmet. Blue shrugged out of his coat and colorfully patched vest and hung it beside mine, his helmet followed by the strap on another branch of the old-fashioned stand.

"Hang on," I said and opened the bathroom door. I snatched the clean, dry towels off of the bar and handed him one. He put it across his shoulders and rubbed it over his hair. I went into the studio space and around to behind the bathroom. I opened up the shutter closet doors on their track by pulling the little knob and they folded, opening quietly, revealing the washer and dryer.

I pulled some clean sleep shorts and a cami of mine out of the dryer and put the rest of my clothes in there into one of the whicker carry baskets on top of the dryer to carry back into the house later. I checked the washer and there was nothing in it. I pursed my lips.

"I don't have anything dry for you, let me grab a blanket from the loft." I turned around, right into Blue's arms. He caught me and stared down at me for a series of heartbeats before his mouth descended to mine.

I was shocked, but the attention wasn't unwelcome. I closed my eyes and turned my face up to his kiss and it was magical. His lips were careful and soft where they moved against mine and I felt the tension leave my body, pouring out of my muscles even as the rain poured outside.

He broke the kiss and leaned back from me murmuring, "I'm fine. Do *you* have something dry to put on?" I nodded and he ordered gently, "Go change."

"Okay, but put your wet things in the dryer," I insisted.

He searched my face and nodded, and I took my dry things up to the loft. I changed quickly and when I turned around, lowering my cami over my stomach, it was to see Blue, frozen down below, watching me. His shirt was off as well as his boots and socks, and he looked absolutely delicious standing barefoot and in only his wet jeans against the polished concrete floor.

I tossed a blanket down over the railing and he dropped his shirt to catch it. He smiled and I smiled back and said, "Let me know when you're covered."

I pointedly turned around, smiling to myself and gathered my wet things off my loft's floor. I waited and heard an almost timid, "Okay." I went down the ladder and found him sitting at my large worktable on my old metal stool, the burgundy chenille throw I'd tossed down to him knotted at his hip and his pile of wet things in his arms.

I took them with mine and padded barefoot across the cold concrete to toss them in and to start the dryer. When I turned around, the rain raged harder, roaring against the roof, and my lights flickered.

"Ooooh, please don't go out!" I pleaded, "I want your clothes dry and warm." I shivered and Blue stood up, coming to me. He wrapped his arms around me and hugged me close, rubbing his hands up and down my arms to generate a warm friction.

"Not how I pictured our evening ending," he said with a wry smirk, "but I'll take it."

I smiled and blushed a little, telling him the honest truth, "I've had fun."

"Yeah?"

"Yeah."

We were quiet a moment and he said, "It's freezing down here."

"Yeah, the concrete's cold. I can turn up the heat, but it takes a while."

"Can we go up there?" he asked and I swallowed hard.

"Sure, but... um..."

"Your virtue's safe until you don't want it to be... I'm not like that."

Hot color flooded my cheeks and I closed my eyes briefly. "I didn't mean it like *that*," I said.

He rubbed my shoulders lightly and said, "I know..."

"I feel like you think that I think the worst of you."

"Citizen's usually do. It's become a habit just thinking everyone thinks the worst. I'm sorry if I made you feel that way, though. I know you're different."

I looked up at him sharply and said, "I am?"

"You are. I think that's what drew me to you in the first place."

I stepped back and took his hand, leading him around to the ladder to my loft. He followed me and I snapped off the track lighting that hung above my work tables, which were empty of any current projects. He let me go first up into the loft and when I reached the top, I flipped the switch on the wall to light the strands of Christmas lights along the beams. I stood by self-consciously while he stood up, head stooped from the low ceiling and took my sleeping arrangements in.

His eyes widened at the little bits of origami of his hanging like a canopy from the ceiling over the bed and I didn't say anything. I was waiting for *him* to say something first.

"You kept all of them?"

"Of course, I did."

"They mean this much to you?"

"Of course, they do."

I went to the bed and dropped onto the corner. Blue came over and dropped down beside me, staring up at the dangling bits of folded paper almost awestruck.

"I love them," I confessed, hugging my knees. "I love all of them. They're beautiful and the highlight of my day."

8

B lue...

"So, did you hit it?" were the first words out of Cell's mouth when I walked through my hou- bedroom's door. *It's not a cell, it's not a house, you're not in prison,* I reminded myself for the thousandth time.

I scowled at him and he raised an eyebrow. "Seriously, *did you hit it?*"

"On the first date?"

"Why the fuck not, you puss?"

I shook my head. "You really have no idea how regular people work, do you?"

It was his turn to scowl. "I'm not regular fuckin' people." That was the truth. "Well that's fuckin' irritating as shit. I was hoping to hit that come my turn."

"Slow," I reminded him, and he rolled his eyes.

"So, what did you do? You at least round second base, Junior? Seriously. Give it up!" I shook my head and turned around, irritated with him. "Aw, come on!" he cried after me but I shut the door on his smug look and went out back, trudging across the wet grass to the one person I found I could talk to that would actually give a damn about how I felt, who would listen and be happy with me.

I tried the smaller side door into Dani's shop and found it unlocked, which it always was. When I opened it up, hot air wafted out to greet me. Red looked up from his phone from the small table and two chairs set up in the corner for visitors. He had a six-pack of beer next to him, the amber glass sweating, one of the bottles open and three-quarters empty by his elbow.

Dani looked up from her workbench and over, her eyes magnified comically behind a pair of those square jewelers' goggles. She set down her tools and pulled the apparatus off, cocking her head word-lessly to the side, communicating with a look, asking what was wrong.

I smiled and shook my head slightly and her smile lit up the world. I turned back to Thirteen who was grinning.

"Heard you had a hot date with that little waitress you been pining over. I take it by the smile it went well?" I nodded and blushed slightly and Thirteen plucked a beer out of the six-pack and held it out to me. "Congratulations, brother!"

I took the offered beer and twisted off the cap. He kicked the chair opposite him out from the table and I dropped into it, the buckle on my jacket rattling and clacking against the arm of it.

Dani stood and gracefully stepped across the cracked concrete floor, lowering herself into Thirteen's lap. His arms wound protectively around her trim waist and I smiled a little bigger. I was happy for her, and for him, but I had to admit it to myself… before Hayley and even still, I held a little bit of a torch for Dani Broussard. If the stars aligned and I were allowed, I would go there.

Dani put her hands over Thirteen's and smiled before saying, "Tell me *everything*," and I shifted a bit uncomfortably. She raised an eyebrow and gave me a secret little smile and I huffed a laugh. She was going to make me do it. She was going to make me talk in front of Thirteen.

Thirteen laughed a little and said, "'S'all right, man. Your secrets are safe with me. That's how this brotherhood and club business is supposed to go."

I nodded. Things hadn't exactly worked that way at the old chapter and this chapter, it still took some getting used to that it worked exactly how I imagined these things were supposed to work when I first went in to prospect with that first chapter. They'd talked a good game, but they hadn't exactly walked the walk. Not like these guys did.

"I took her to *Soul Fuel* for that live music thing that Red and Em started up –"

"And?"

And I told them, all of it… I even told them about how she'd saved every bit of origami I'd ever folded for her. They celebrated with me, and I felt good about the time I'd spent with her. By the time I finished a couple of the beers and the conversation, I felt good, relaxed and ready to take on the ration of shit that Cell was likely going to have waiting for me for walking out on him.

I went back to my room and sure enough, Cell was waiting, the blue light of my flickering TV casting shadows and highlights across his face. The expression he wore gauging and calculating. He raised his eyebrows and said nothing, and the worry and apprehension evaporated. He genuinely wanted to hear how the night had gone. No more jibes, no more fucking around.

"Seriously, you gonna make me ask?"

I nodded, and he rolled his eyes but moved over so I could drop onto the edge of the bed and get out of my still-damp boots.

"Fine, this is me being totally serious. How'd it go and how far did it go?"

I leaned back against the headboard and put my feet up before I answered him, then I thought about how to answer, seeing as I just gave the full story to Dani and Thirteen. Still, spin was important when it came to Cell, mostly to make sure he kept himself reined in.

"It fucking dumped on us on the ride back to her place."

"Nice, that lead to some hot and heavy?"

"Some, but honestly, it didn't go any further than making out like a couple of teenagers for a few hours."

Actually, what it'd led to was one of the deepest, most perfect moments of sharing I'd ever experienced. It'd led to us lying in her bed, the blankets up around us, getting warm again and being close; talking into the night. It'd led to her fingertips tracing over my skin in these light, torturous touches. Picking out the scar along my ribs that I'd earned in a fight with a couple of the Suicide Kings, a rival club that'd caused trouble for this chapter and one of the reasons Cell and I had relocated here.

It'd needed stitches, and Cell had done a pretty decent job of 'em. We'd taken care of ourselves back then. Still new to this chapter, our old chapter gone to hell and gone – wiped out by their own greed and dirty dealings. Crossing the mob was a bad idea, but they'd done it, hell, *we'd done it*. It was why we'd barely survived being on the inside. Our colors having made us a target.

There was no such thing as a small crime family, we'd all learned the hard way that small meant doubly or triply as ruthless. We'd been the lucky ones locked up. By the time we got out, the rest of our chapter and the next furthest one north had been wiped out. Facing that reality, it was clear that we sure as fuck couldn't stick around the area.

We'd reached out to the next nearest chapter and had been told the call had gone out for aide from the mother chapter, that they needed guys. So, we'd gotten our bikes out of storage, got them back up and running, and had ridden out here. Right into the middle of another kind of war… but one we had a distinct advantage in. The Suicide Kings hadn't required near the level of skill surviving the mob had.

I still couldn't be sure we were totally free and clear on that front, but these guys out here… they had it on lock. We'd left the Bianchi family's territory; had effectively disappeared and hadn't looked back. I think it had been enough. We hadn't heard or had to deal with anything since, and honestly, didn't want to have anything to do with it either. Enough time had passed to make us feel secure. That was part of what had taken so long for me to make a move on Hayley.

"So, you mean to tell me after all of that, you barely edged down the line toward second base? Jesus fucking Christ, you didn't give me shit to work with, did you?" he complained.

"Sorry, but getting your dick wet on the first date doesn't exactly scream longevity to a woman."

"Yeah, fuck you and your logic," he said grumpily.

"So, you decided where you're going to take her, or what you're going to do for your date?"

"I have some ideas," he said honestly.

"Like what?"

"That's for me to know and you to find out, you closed mouthed bastard." He grinned. "Two can play at this game."

I smiled and shook my head. "She's the one, Cell. I know it."

"Yeah, yeah, we'll see."

I wasn't a praying man, but I sent one up right then that Cell wouldn't blow this for us. I guess in the long run, it was up to Hayley not to blow it with Cell but there was no way to tell her. I sighed and settled back, focusing on the TV screen.

"Just don't fuck this up, please?"

I didn't make it a habit of asking Cell of anything, so I think I got his attention. He searched my profile even though I kept my eyes riveted to the TV screen. His went cold and his jaw clenched, like mine was.

"I fuck this up and you're gonna make my life hell, ain't yah?"

I turned and looked him in the eye and nodded once. He sighed and shook his head and that was the end of the conversation. We both turned our attention back to the TV and dropped the subject for now.

9

H ayley...
I was nervous. It was Saturday and a week and a day since my date with Blue; and I was waiting at the curb in front of my house for Duracell's arrival. It was nine o'clock in the morning, on the dot, the time he'd asked me to be ready and waiting, and I could hear him coming.

It was at least sunny between spates of clouds today and the temperature was more autumn-like than it had been. He pulled up to the curb in front of me and shut off the bike. He crossed his arms and leaned forward against its gas tank, his eyes unreadable behind his sunglasses. He pulled them off and his eyes were smiling. Some of the apprehension drained from my body and he reached out, smoothing a thumb along my cheek.

It was the most Blue-like thing he'd ever done, and for a moment, it was like he really saw me.

"Really want to kiss you hello," he said and I blushed faintly and smiled, nodding.

I leaned in and he pressed his lips to mine, warm, and chaste by his standards. Just once, twice, a third time, barely sucking on my bottom lip with absolutely no tongue. It surprised me. He was being very respectful of my boundaries with that one kiss, which knowing him the little bit that I did, respecting boundaries wasn't exactly Cell's thing.

"Hi," I murmured lamely when he broke the kiss, settling back down onto the seat of his motorcycle.

He smiled and said, "Been looking forward to this for almost two weeks, you ready?"

I nodded. "Yeah, I think I am."

He grinned, pleased and said, "Good deal. You ride before?"

"Once, with Blue."

"Alright, look at you! Gotta be brave to get on the back of my bike. No joke, I like to go fast and we're going to have to hit the freeway to get where I want to take you."

I nodded and said, "Thanks for the warning." He dug into the saddlebag on one side of his bike and came up with a helmet.

"You look good, darlin'," he said smiling. "I like the pigtails."

They weren't exactly pigtails, but I did have my hair braided on either side of my head to keep my hair from tangling in the wind. Cell had warned me ahead of time that he 'didn't do cages.' I'd had to ask him what a cage was, and he'd laughed and said, "A cage is a car in biker speak."

He'd also said that he would make an exception if rain were in the forecast, but lucky him, there was only a thirty-percent chance, and when I'd gotten up to get ready there hadn't been a gray cloud in the sky.

I'd dressed warm, per his request, and climbed onto the back of his motorcycle in sturdy ankle-high brown boots with thick, warm, gray wool socks rolled at the top. My jeans fit close to my legs, and I wore a satin and lace camisole against my skin, underneath the heather gray faux angora sweater – I could never afford the real thing. The sweater was long sleeved and long in the torso, coming down over my hips to peek out beneath my leather jacket.

I'd remembered the close-fitting leather driving gloves that had come as a match to my coat and wore a decorative darker gray scarf around my neck. I'd even added some light makeup to my appearance, a natural look, as I had on my date with Blue.

I wanted to impress them, and to be honest, I liked dressing well; I just didn't often have an excuse to do it.

Cell was dressed much as Blue had been. Comfortable, worn-in jeans over much-used motorcycle boots. He wore a somewhat faded, but comfortable looking maroon tee shirt beneath his equally well-worn leather jacket and cut. His one concession to the chill in the air, a light gray hooded sweatshirt between his jacket and tee.

He looked good, and when I got onto the motorcycle behind him and wrapped my arms around his waist, I could smell him. Clean man with a light, crisp cologne that I would be lying if I said it didn't rouse my senses.

"You settled? You good?" he asked and I nodded. "Okay, hold on tight, here we go!" He fired up the bike and I jumped.

He eased onto my street, but wasn't joking about going fast, making it to the stop sign at the end of the road in half the time that Blue had. By the time we reached the freeway to go wherever it was he was taking us, I could already tell I much preferred riding with Blue. His handling left me feeling as safe as you could feel on the back of a motorcycle with the pavement rushing past beneath you, but Cell? Cell's driving made me feel like we were tempting fate to intervene just a little too much.

I buried my face against the back of his shoulder and held on for dear life when he switched lanes to take the exit he wanted. He cut between cars with precision, but far too close for comfort and I would be glad when this ride was over. I felt his body shake with laughter at my discomfort, but it didn't strike me as malicious.

"Trust me, baby! We're good!" he called back, and I believed him, I really did, but riding with him, I felt, would always be an adventure and not necessarily the good kind.

He took it easier on the country roads and I had an inkling that I knew where we were headed when the signs leading to the haunted corn maze and u-pick pumpkin patch grew in frequency. He turned down a long dirt track and was very careful by comparison when it came to navigating the blacktop. He found a space for us and parked in the dried grass, tapping my leg as Blue had, to let me know I needed to get off.

I hopped down and immediately went for the chinstrap holding my helmet on, suddenly finding it restrictive. Duracell took the helmet from my hands and stowed it back in his saddlebag, stashing his own next to it. He got up and kneeled, strapping the bag closed and then stood with a satisfied 'ah.'

"That wasn't so bad, was it?" he asked.

I lied; I smiled as best I could and shook my head as in *no, it wasn't that bad.*

He laughed at me and stepped forward, putting an arm around my shoulders and pulling me in, pressing his lips to my temple and smacking a kiss there. "You're a terrible liar," he said next to my ear, following it up with, "I like that."

I sort of liked how freely and casually he touched me. As if it were comfortable and as easy as breathing. He walked with me, arm around me toward the entrance lined in hay bales, and the ticket booth beside it.

"Put your money away," he said, "I've got this." He winked at me and I inclined my head, slipping my little wallet back into my pocket, stripping off my gloves and shoving them into the other. He pulled his wallet out of his back pocket and paid the lady at the folding table under the easy up awning. She stamped our hands with a jack-o-lantern stamp and said, "Have fun!"

"Thanks," Cell said and led me into the tall stalks of corn.

"Doesn't really seem like much," I said apprehensive, of course, just in time for a chainsaw wielding Jason Voorhees to jump out of the stalks, revving the machine. I jumped and screamed and, predictably, leaped right into Cell's arms who was laughing.

I blushed furiously and climbed back down off his body, which was very nice, laughing nervously myself.

"Scariest corn maze in three counties," he said. "Four-and-a-half-star rating."

"It's the middle of the day!" I burst out. "It can't be that bad!"

"Eh, guess we'll see. We have to find our way through, out the back to get to the other fun in store."

"I can hardly wait," I said rolling my eyes.

He laughed again, and it was a good sound. I started to relax, his hand warm and solid in mine.

We wound our way through the wide cut paths in the stalks. Clowns and creepy dead ghost children jumping out at us. Scary tableaus set into the dead ends with mad scientists, and serial killer's burial grounds.

I laughed and ran my hand along the dry stalks, the whisper they made at our passing a light, airy sound that lifted my spirits even more. I turned around saying, "How much further do you think it is to the end?" but Duracell was gone. I was alone. I turned, my heart leaping in my chest. I turned, and spun, and looked this way and that, but nothing…

"Cell?" I called out. Several heartbeats and nothing.

"Cell?" I tried again, and same result. My shoulders dropped and I tried again.

"Cell, come on this isn't – Ah!" I let out a girly scream as he lunged out of the corn behind me with a cry. He scooped me up, arms around my waist and spun me while I laughed.

He set me down, one of my hands in his and spun me like a dancer so I faced him, his other arm hauling me up against his body. He laughed too and I shook my head.

"Alright, okay, you got me."

"Yeah, yeah I did. I couldn't resist."

I giggled, both of us a bit breathless. "Pretty sure the exit is just up here," he said and his voice was dusky, the moment hanging between us, just waiting for one or the other of us to capitalize on it. I thought for sure he would, but he smiled and stepped back, giving me a bit of room. I was half disappointed.

"Right! What's at the end?"

"Ah, ah, ah… you just have to wait and see," he teased. He took my hand and we plunged back into the maze. Three frights and one dead end later we burst free, into a clearing with food tents and market stalls, beyond them a great wide field full of pumpkins just waiting to be picked and carved.

"Hey! There they are," I heard a woman call and I looked up. Several of the other Sacred Hearts' members stood around with their women. Melody was the one who'd called out and I laughed.

"We're about to go out there and pick pumpkins and take them back to the club and carve them. You coming?" she asked.

"We're coming," Duracell assured her. "I just want to grab her some hot cider first. It was a cold ride and it's chilly out here."

"Already done, I have it right here." I turned at Blue's soft voice and took the steaming paper cup from his fingers that he offered me.

I smiled up at him and said, "Thank you." He nodded and took another from the drink carrier he was holding and handed it to Cell.

"Good lookin' out, man."

He took the last and ditched the paper drink holder in one of the fifty-five-gallon drums with the giant black trash bag flowing out of it, the recycling emblem spray painted on the side. He came back and joined us, putting me between them and I blushed, glancing quickly around at the rest of the club members to gauge their reactions.

None of them paid us any mind, there wasn't any judgement on any of their faces, nor were any of them trying overly hard to *not* look at us. It put me at ease.

"Okay, go, go, go, go, go!" Mel encouraged and turned both Noah and Eden loose, toddling through the pumpkin patch. Melody took pictures while the fathers looked on, laughing and talking about it.

I hid behind the rim of my mulled cider cup, drinking the sweet and perfectly spiced liquid, laughing at some of the antics of the adults as much as the babies. I roused myself from staring at their angelic chubby cheeks and from indulging in their high-pitched squeals of laugher and delight to find both Cell and Blue staring at me.

"I'm sorry, did I miss something?" I asked, but they both shook their heads.

"No, we were just watching you, watch them," Cell said casually, taking a sip of his own cider.

"Sorry, I know it's silly, but I always wanted kids someday…"

"Why is that silly?" Blue asked, frowning.

I closed my mouth and shook my head and hoped that they would just let it go. Cell actually came to the rescue then, saying, "You gonna pick your pumpkin?" It was a blatant change of subject, but a welcome one.

"What?" I asked laughing.

"Club tradition; the weekend before Halloween, we pick our pumpkins and carve them back at the house." I looked over at the person who'd spoken and smiled, nodding.

"I see," I told Dragon, the club president. He smiled and gave me a wink and went out into the field near Dray and Everett, who was showing. Hitting his son in the shoulder who was bent over moving pumpkins around for Everett to inspect and decide on.

"Get off my ass, Pops! Jesus!" Dray cried to Everett and Dragon's laughter.

"Come on, babes. Your turn." Cell took my empty cup from my hands and stacked his in it, passing it off to Blue who raised his in salute. Taking my hand, Cell dragged me gently out into the pumpkin patch mayhem.

"What shape you like?" he asked.

I looked around and told the truth, "I like the round squat pumpkins. The ones you always see in cartoons and mass produced."

"You should find one with a flat side, though," Trigger said, overhearing me. "It's easier to carve the image and they come out better."

"I didn't think about that," I said honestly.

"We're pumpkin-carving pros! We get all fancy and shit, tryin' to outdo each other each year," Reaver called over.

Hayden gave him a shove and said, "I make him carve mine." She made a face. "I just scoop the guts."

"A master is nothing without his assistant!" Reaver cried and his son, Connor, called out, "Dad! Come look at this one!"

Reaver went over to where his teenager was with Maren's little brother, Sage, while Maren and Nox looked on a little ways away, choosing their own pumpkin. A good portion of the club I knew, but the ones I didn't, I had learned about through Melody and her pictures. She would bring them to work sometimes and show me when it got slow. She'd told me she wanted to come photograph some of my windows, but I hadn't worked up the courage to invite her to my studio.

"Everybody pick two!" Dragon bellowed and I jumped.

Cell winked at me and said, "You heard the man." He straightened up and called out over the field, "Hey Blue! C'mere!"

I smiled, amazed at how comfortable I was feeling around Cell, and super pleased that I got to see Blue today, too. We picked our pumpkins and loaded them onto the floor of the hayride tractor after buying them. The patch then took us for a ride around the corn maze and back to where we parked. The guys were really good about tagging the stems with everyone's names, to make sure there were no pumpkin mix-ups. It was clear that they had done this before, long before any kids and that it was one of those grown-up traditions that had been tempered down for the little one's enjoyment. Some of these guys were really just big kids themselves.

"You want to ride with Blue?" Cell offered after lifting me down from the back of the wagon and I thought about it for a long moment. As much as I would rather ride with Blue because Blue wasn't insane on the road, I decided that wouldn't be fair. This was Cell's date, and as Cell's date, I should really stay with him… especially if this was going to work the way they seemed to want it to.

I shook my head and he smiled, saying, "I won't tell him so, might break his heart." Blue's hands landed on my shoulders and he pressed his thumbs, kneading between them. I jumped and whirled, and he smiled down at me. I scoffed, incredulous and swung back in Cell's direction lightly slapping him in the chest for not telling me Blue was behind me.

Cell cringed back at my pathetic assault and laughed. "Hey! Easy, tiger."

"It's your date," I said, then turned back to Blue whose smile lit up his eyes. "You understand, right?" He nodded happily and bent down, placing a kiss against my forehead. He let my shoulders go and Cell smiled at him and winked.

"We parked over here, I didn't want to give away the surprise," Cell told him. Blue nodded and gave us a wave, drifting back over to the rest of the club where the pumpkins were almost finished being loaded into the back of a box truck, full of what looked like shelves of parts and tools on either side.

"Come on, darlin'." Cell held out his hand to me and I took it, and let him draw me along, back in the direction of his bike.

"You having a good time so far?" he asked and I nodded.

"The best, thank you."

He stopped me and looked me over, studying my face and gauging me. I waited patiently, wondering just what it was he was looking for when he silently answered my question by lowering his lips to mine. He kissed me, gently at first, but all too quickly it was as if a fire had been ignited, and he devoured my mouth. I couldn't say I didn't like it, but that intensity was back, there, in his kiss, in the way he drew my body tightly into his own.

I felt my arms go around his neck and shoulders and I pulled myself closer. He smiled against my mouth and drew back slightly, kissing the tip of my nose.

"That's what I like," he murmured and I felt myself flush.

The ride to the club was far less exhilarating after that earth-shaking kiss.

10

D uracell...

I was almost disappointed. She was proving to be far easier to win over than I thought she would be. She just needed a firm hand. I kind of hated it when they gave it up that easy. Of course, I was pouring on the charm.

I'd specifically engineered our date to have Blue as a backup, in case I just couldn't read her right. I was thinking that maybe she wasn't as deep as what Blue claimed but when I cornered her again, coming out of the bathroom, and got my hand up her sweater, I didn't get any further than a caress against her ribs before she pulled my hand away, forcing it down.

"I'm not ready for that," she breathed. "Not on the first date."

"I can respect that," I said automatically, but the fuck I could. Looked like I'd be hitting one of the whores at *Sugar's* later tonight. I didn't give a fuck, I wanted to fuck, and I was in the mood for real pussy, not Blue's man-pussy.

I gave Hayley some space, still pretending, cursing in my head that I'd given my word to Blue that I would see this through, do this his way. She went back out to the common room and I went to deal with my own need to hit the head.

When I went back out, Blue was with her, smiling, talking softly, and my frustration cooled some. I played my role the rest of the day, did what needed doing until I could take her home. When I stopped at the curb in front of her place, she got off the bike hastily and I had to smirk. She hated my driving. That screamed she was boring, but at the same time, my initial assessment of her may have been wrong. She was going to be a tougher nut to crack than I'd thought.

I kissed her goodbye, because it was expected and part of the long-con to get her in my bed. Then I left, hit the strip club and got my freak on.

When I got back to the club, Blue was waiting.

"*Sugar's?*" he asked with a disappointed expression.

"Yeah."

"Hayley?"

"She was alright." I lifted my shoulder in a shrug. "Wasn't going to give it to me though, so I had to get it somewhere else."

He nodded, and went back into his room, shutting the door. He knew better than to argue by now. He also knew the only reason I was in this at all was for his punk ass.

Hoped he fuckin' appreciated it.

11

B lue...

I sat near Hayley and watched her. She was sitting on a metal stool, staring down at her large worktable covered in white butcher paper, a pencil in her hand and a worn-down gum eraser, yardstick, and ruler nearby. She was staring at the blank paper as if waiting for it to speak to her.

She hadn't even noticed me yet, she was so inside her own head, and I simply sat a ways away, watching, waiting, wanting to see what she did and how she worked. It was the week before Thanksgiving and our third date, and we'd agreed on a quiet evening in her studio. She wanted to work on a project for a local bookstore.

I'd arrived and found the lights on in the converted garage. I'd knocked but no answer. I'd seen her through one of the many panes of the window set in the door and had tried the handle and found it unlocked. So, I'd quietly let myself in and had taken the empty stool she had set out.

She was lovely, dressed comfortably in black yoga pants and thick white athletic socks. A gray college sweatshirt with the neck artfully cut away hanging from one shoulder, the racerback of her sports bra peeking at the back. Her hair she'd clipped up, but stray tendrils escaped, framing her face, tickling the side of her neck which was long and graceful, begging for my lips to trace the sensitive places and make her shiver.

We'd been growing closer, more intimate, but we hadn't gone much past kissing and heavy petting. I'd just barely managed to keep my hands out of her panties and off her breasts – the struggle was real. I wanted her. I wanted her badly.

Cell had been growing irritable with the lack of progress and was losing interest in the chase, but for once I couldn't care. This was at Hayley's pace and I, for one, was enjoying the slow burn.

She took a deep long breath, let it out, and dropped her pencil, pressing her hands to her face and her fingertips into her eyes, rubbing them. I got up and the stool I was sitting on creaked. She jumped and let out a little scream, nearly falling off of her own seat.

"How long have you been there?" she cried, and I smiled and went to her, folding her into my arms. I kissed the top of her head and massaged the back of her neck. She looked up at me, her wide brown eyes just slaying me.

"Long enough... what's wrong?"

"Just frustrated, I guess."

"Yeah? With what?"

She looked off to the side, and for the very first time ever, she lied to me and it was adorable.

"I just can't think of something to do for this window. I just don't know what to draw. Not that I'm very good at the whole drawing part anyway."

I smiled, knowing full well that wasn't it, that something else, something far more important was bothering her, but like with everything else, my Hayley required patience.

"Sounds to me like you could use something to eat. Let me take you out for a quick bite and we can brainstorm."

"Really?" she asked, swallowing hard.

"Really. It's too cold out there for you for the bike, can we take your cage?"

She visibly relaxed a little more and said, "Yeah, absolutely."

"Okay, find some shoes and a coat and let me take you out."

"Sounds good."

She went up to her loft and came back down in some sturdy running shoes. I got up and went over to her as she lifted a knitted scarf off of the coat-tree. I plucked down a down jacket and held it out for her to shrug into, which she did, and handed her down her purse. She plucked her keys off the hook and smiled at me and it held an edge of tiredness.

I took them from her and asked, "Mind if I drive?"

"Not at all."

It felt good. It felt normal, like we were a couple, and I'd be lying if I said that I wasn't fully indulging in the sensation.

I placed my hand lightly on her lower back and led her outside, turning only to lock up her space, the one I was honored she let me into. She hadn't brought Cell back here yet, and that wasn't lost on me.

I held the passenger door to her cage open for her and closed it for her. Doing everything a gentleman was supposed to do, not because I was a gentleman, that was laughable, but because she deserved it. She deserved to be treated well, because everything about her behavior screamed long and loud that she really hadn't been up until now.

"Is diner food okay as long as it's not your diner?" I asked.

"Sounds great," she said. "I could really use a good milkshake."

I smiled and drove us in silence, waiting to see if she opened up, growing concerned when she didn't. I took us out to another diner Cell and I frequented when we were just too far from Hayley's to make it, which was honestly just a handful of times.

It was a little flashier, but the food wasn't quite as good. I wondered if it would improve with the company. I held the door for her, and the waitress seated us in a booth by one of the front windows. When we'd ordered our drinks and then our food, I decided that I was going to have to pry if I was going to get to the bottom of what was wrong.

"Hayley," I said and she looked at me, her face falling when she got a look at my expression.

"Do you like me?" she asked and I tipped my head to the side. I loved her. I loved being around her and exploring this new thing. I loved going out and learning about her and what she liked, and I tried to tell her as much with my eyes while keeping it careful with my mouth.

"I adore you. I love every minute of the time we spend together. What's *wrong?*"

"If... if you like me as much as you say..." she shifted uncomfortably and a fiery blush overtook her, and the lightbulb went off.

"Then why haven't I made more of a move?" I asked. She nodded mutely and burned with shame. I chuckled, I couldn't help it. "Because I've been waiting on you."

She blinked at me and swallowed hard. "I... I don't know what to say..."

"Then don't say anything. Just nod if I have your permission, and I'll do the rest."

She nodded emphatically and I laughed, reaching across the table, my hand palm up. She put her hand in mine and I curved my fingers and she curved hers and we just sort of held on to each other. Her lips pursed and she ducked her head between her shoulders slightly, her cheeks still flaming, and I couldn't help myself.

I got up from my seat, still holding her hand, and rounded the end of the table, sliding into the booth beside her. She blinked up at me in surprise, and I caressed the side of her face. No walls, no lies, nothing standing between us.

I kissed her and the tension drained from her body and she leaned into me. I put my arms around her and gathered her close and did everything I could to steal her breath away. I was blocking anyone's view from the aisle, and the windows were shoulder height and so I tore a page out of Cell's playbook. Placing my hand on the top of her leg and boldly sliding it up to the juncture of her thighs. I pressed lightly over her clit with my fingertips and rubbed her until she squirmed in her seat. Half pressing against me harder and half trying to get away. Conflicted, confused, and I knew why.

Dating was one thing for a girl-next-door type like her, but sex? Sex was a whole new bag of bricks and sex with me would mean sex with Duracell, and her inhibitions were stopping her. Keeping her from having sex with each of us, let alone both of us together. She wanted us but feared judgment. I totally got that.

One roadblock at a time, I thought to myself.

She pulled back, breathless and I backed away just enough to see her face. She looked up at me, eyes dilated with desire and taking back my hand, I whispered, "Don't ever have any doubt about my feelings for you."

She sucked in a breath and the waitress set our food in front of us. I kept one hand on her knee under the table as much as I could while we ate, the topic of conversation shifting to something normal and safe; what she would do for her window she had to craft.

"What's the place called?" I asked.

"Twice Sold Tales."

"What about a cat with two tails sleeping between books on a shelf?"

She froze and looked at me, searching my face, her mind working on the problem and finally she said, "I actually really like that."

I lifted a shoulder in a shrug and said, "Does that mean we're going back to your place so you can work, or am I taking you back to mine to finish what I started?"

She nearly choked on her milkshake, coughing violently until her airway cleared. I pounded on her back until she eked out that she was fine and blushing furiously, tears from her coughing fit in her eyes, rasped out, "Your place."

"You're sure?"

She nodded. "I'm sure."

I nodded and gave her knee a squeeze under the table, while we finished up our meal. On the outside, I was calm, cool, and collected but on the inside? I was a bundle of some seriously pissed off anxiety screaming '*why!?*' at me, but also, I felt like I was seventeen all over again. Seventeen, with my first crush and about to hit a home-fucking-run.

I felt like I was on the top of Everest, standing on the roof of the world, while simultaneously about to be pitched off that very same roof. My palms were sweating, my heart pounding, and my mouth suddenly dry, and just once in my life I wished I had Cell's fucking calm – even if it did mean I didn't feel a goddamn thing to go with it.

Hayley was still a little quiet while we finished our meal and I think I knew what about, but the middle of the diner, out in public, was neither the time, nor the place to talk about it. I took her back out to the car, nervous, but still excited… trying to crush down my rapidly inflating hopes.

"I need to make one stop," I said as I pulled out onto the street. It felt weird to drive a cage after not for so long. Cumbersome and unwieldy, closed off and, well, *caged in*. I hated it, but it was worth it to hold her hand and know that she was warm enough... comfortable enough.

"Okay, what for?"

My turn to blush. "Ah, fresh supply of condoms..."

"Oh! Um, good idea."

"Not offended?"

"No! I mean, why would I be?"

I gave her hand a squeeze and pulled into an open grocery store's lot. I parked and pulled the emergency brake, turning to look at her.

"Be real with me?"

She stared at me and said, "I can't imagine being anything else."

"Do you think that by having sex with me, that it automatically requires you to have sex with Cell?"

"No," she said firmly. "No, I want you... what scares me is I want Cell, too... I don't know what to do with that. I mean, I wasn't raised that way."

I knew just what Cell would say to that, and I said as much. "You know, if Cell were sitting here with us, he would ask you, 'Your parents coming to bed with us?'" I smiled as she predictably colored and cried, "No!"

"Would you lose your home?"

"No... I don't think my dad would be very happy about it if he found out but..."

"But you're curious?"

She turned to face out the window, as if not seeing me right then would be easier and I understood that. Her breath fogged the window when she spoke, and I watched her face, as best I could, by her reflection in the glass. The only reason I could was from the night pressing in from the outside.

"I dream about it."

"About what?"

"You… mostly. I have for a long time. About what it would be like, to be with you, but lately, I find I'm dreaming just as much about Cell and about…" her voice faltered and I helped her.

"About what it would be like, the both of us together with you?"

"Yes."

"Do you want it?"

She shifted pressing her knees together, trapping her hands between her thighs. Nervous, afraid of being judged I'd imagine. She was with the wrong crowd when it came to hanging around the club if she expected judgment. That wasn't how we rolled.

"I… I think I do, but really, I just want *you* tonight if that's alright."

"More than alright. This is all at your pace, baby."

She bowed her head, a wry smile on her lips. "Duracell seems to be in a big hurry."

I smiled wryly too. "Patience was never his thing." Going fast, stirring shit up, and instant gratification was more his speed.

"No, no it isn't," she agreed laughing.

The mood lightened, the tension in the small space lessening and I felt like I could breathe again.

"Want to come in with me, or just want me to run in?"

"I'll come in," she murmured and reached for the door handle.

I liked that. That she was willing to be brave, with me… for me… *I knew she was the one.*

12

H ayley…

It began to rain, the swish-shush of the windshield wipers in the close dark of my car a soothing sound. Blue's hand was warm and heavy in mine. A paper bag with lube and condoms sitting between us on top of the emergency brake handle.

I deferred to him when it came to the purchase. While I wasn't a virgin, I couldn't exactly claim to be experienced either. There was history there. History and reasons behind my choice to abstain for much of my twenties, so it'd been quite a while, jeez, I think a year and a half – maybe two? Since I'd last been with anyone and maybe five or six years before him.

Painful memories, for sure.

I knew I had hang-ups about sex and relationships, but I couldn't help them. Of course, I wasn't a teenager anymore. I wasn't naïve. *I just wish I could go back there. I wish I could do it all again.* Blue didn't deserve the neurotic girl sitting beside him. He deserved a confident woman, a fierce one, like Melody or Everett… like Hayden or Shelly.

But oh, God… How I wanted him.

I was torn, afraid he would be like the two I'd had before.

I know, pathetic right? Twenty-eight, going on twenty-nine and only ever been with two men… *and about to be with two more.*

"We don't have to right now… tonight…" he said and I startled, realizing we were stopped. I blinked and focused outside the window, realizing we were behind the club, parked on the asphalt track, off to one side by the squat outbuilding next to the big shop building.

I'd been here a few times before. The first time for Melody's wedding. A few other times to help her with taking photos of Rush's furniture.

"I'll take you home –"

"No! No, don't do that. I'm just nervous… I guess."

"I think it's more than that."

For a long moment the only sound inside the car was the rain drumming down on the roof. I turned and looked at Blue whose beautiful gray eyes were leeched colorless by the blueish lights on the back of the shop building. He silently searched my face, concern his paramount expression.

"No," I shook my head, he didn't deserve to be lied to again, even if it had been a white one, so I changed tact. "You're right… It is but it's not you, not at all, it's really me." He leaned back, the leather of his coat creaking, rasping against the upholstery of my car's seat and I squeezed my eyes shut and rubbed my forehead. I shook my head and let out a frustrated sigh.

I said, "That came out all wrong, but it didn't, but it did… Um, God, why can't I do this right?" I laughed but it was an anxious thing and Blue took my hands away from my face, taking both of them into his and rubbing across the backs of my fingers gently with his thumbs.

"Hush, no need to be anxious. It's just you and me in here with the dark and the rain. Just listen to it for a minute. Close your eyes…"

I didn't want to close my eyes now. I just wanted to look at him. His gaze gently urged me to do what he asked and so I did. I closed my eyes and listened.

"That's it," he soothed when the tension and anxiety began to drain from my muscles. I breathed and listened to the wild thrum of the rain on the roof and window and just soaked in Blue's calming presence. "When you're ready, just talk to me."

I licked my lips. "Isn't there some kind of rule about talking about your exes when you're on a date with a man?"

"We aren't normal people, me and mine. Pretty sure you've noticed by now."

"Maybe that's what drew me to you in the first place?"

"Maybe. I know what drew me to you."

"What?"

"Well, I'd be lying if I didn't say you were beautiful and that was the first thing I noticed, but really what caught my eye was your spirit. Like calls to like and I don't know, I guess I recognized a certain amount of beautifully broken in you."

It was an ugly truth, but he made it sound so pretty; poetic almost. I nodded, an incredible sadness washing over me, then fading. Like a wave crashing onto the shore before receding back out into the dark.

"What broke you, Hayley?"

"I've only been with two people," I confessed and swallowed hard. He was silent, patiently waiting me out and I somehow found the courage to go on, despite the humiliation of it.

"My mom died when I was fifteen, and I started working at the diner after school to help my dad. It, um, didn't leave a lot of time for dating and I've always been shy. So when T.J., one of the cutest boys in school, started to pay attention to me I was kind of smitten, you know?"

Blue remained silent, and though I couldn't look him in the eyes, I could feel him watching me. His thumbs never stopped making those soothing motions, lightly encouraging me across the backs of my fingers, back and forth, back and forth, back and forth.

"I wasn't popular, so we had to keep it a secret... or so he said and I believed him. You know? I didn't want to cause him trouble and I certainly didn't want the wrath of the mean girls. I was seventeen, and high school was everything back then."

I pursed my lips and closed my eyes and took a deep breath. I let the breath out slowly and bucked up, this was so painful. "He was my first and it was all a trick to get me into bed with him. There was a bet going around inside his circle of friends that he couldn't get me to put out and..." Tears sprang to my eyes. I hated this part. I hated even more what I'd done because of it.

"We used his room, his parents were out of town and I thought it was beautiful, right? It only hurt for a minute, but I bled, you know, and it got on the sheets and when I went to school on Monday," the tears fell, I couldn't stop them, "the sheet was flying from the top of the flagpole and everyone was laughing at me and calling me a slut."

I pulled my hands from his and pressed them to my face which was burning with fresh shame. The horror and embarrassment were unreal. I missed my mom; my dad wasn't doing the best and was all about the diner. I fell into a deeper darker depression that I couldn't get out of on my own. I was alone, and lonely, and two months before my eighteenth birthday, I slit my wrists in a hot bath and tried to make it all disappear.

Blue held me to him, his arms around me, hand in the back of my hair kneading my scalp as I wept bitterly into the front of his leather jacket. It'd been years before I let another man in, and the results then weren't pretty either. I'd loved him. We'd even been engaged... until I found out that he had been cheating. His excuse? I was perfect wife material, good breeding stock, but I was *boring* and didn't make him happy. I made his parents happy though, so I guess there was that.

My dad had gone after him with a knife from the kitchen and had chased him all the way up the street. He'd spent the night in jail for it, but I'd never seen Beauregard again.

Blue weathered the storm of my past beautifully and dried my tears. The look on his face and in his eyes – one of admiration. I didn't understand that.

"Let's go inside," he murmured. "We don't need to do anything tonight, but I would really like to hold you, and I'd really like to have you in my bed regardless of how many clothes we do or don't have on."

13

B**lue...**
  I got out of the cage and went into the back to pick up my cut
where I'd laid it across the backseat. I swung into it as I went around to
get Hayley's door for her. I'd been honored that she'd opened up to me
about something so painful and really glad she'd opened up to me and
not Cell. Still, it didn't stop me from being angry on her behalf. It also
didn't stop me from wanting to bring it to Cell.

He could be creative in his cruelty and while he was no caped crusader,
any excuse would do to rain misery on a son of a bitch. Cell had some
methods to his madness. One of them was to work inside the system.
The system being the club's system – not the legal one. He did what
the fuck he wanted, got off on not getting caught by the 'man' but used
the club as a sort of measuring stick so he didn't go too far. He was as
useful to the club as they were to him, so it proved to be a pretty mutu-
ally beneficial relationship.

I opened up Hayley's door and held out a hand to her. She took it and
stood, the rustle of paper in her other hand causing my heart to skip a
beat before racing to catch up. I took the bag with the condoms and

lube and led her to the door at the end of the building that would let us into what I called the barracks.

"Bathroom is here," I said touching the door. "There's another one just like it at that end of the hall on the other side."

"Which one is yours?" she asked softly.

I drew her down the hallway nearly to the opposite end and stopped at my door. I unclipped my keys from where they hung near my wallet chain and stuck the right one into the lock, giving it a twist.

The door swung inward with a slight groan. I could have oiled the hinges, but why? Noisy hinges were an early warning system. Sure to wake me up if anyone came in here. Being an ex-con had left me a light sleeper out of necessity. Before prison, I'd like to sleep like the dead. After? I was still lucky to sleep the whole night through even though we'd been out a couple of years and more now.

My room was pretty simple. A king-sized bed, a dresser, and a couple of nightstands. The TV mounted to the wall next to the closet, a small cabinet under it to hold the Blu-ray player and the wireless speakers I had for my phone so I could play music.

The furniture all matched and was all made by Rush when he'd seen that I just had the mattress and box spring on the floor. It was all nice stuff. Old, weathered, distressed gray wood that'd been reclaimed from somewhere. I stepped aside and let Hayley in the door, watching her as she stepped into the center of the room and turned, taking it all in, in the soft glow of the beside lamp.

I tossed the bag and its contents from the grocery store onto that bedside table before I let my jacket and cut slide from my shoulders. Closing the door, I twisted to hang them up on one of the three hooks set into the back of it. When I turned back, Hayley was holding out her coat, scarf, and purse. I hung them up for her and she tucked her hands into the slightly oversized sleeves of her sweatshirt, slightly hunching her shoulders. It was chilly in here, so I chose to think it was that and not fear or unease that caused the left of center body language.

"Cold?" I asked her. The doubts eating away at my edges.

She gave me a half-charmed smile and nodded. "Yeah, and still nervous. I suffer from depression and anxiety. I kind of can't help it."

I went to her and folded my arms around her, holding her close and sighed, the feeling of her in my arms a balm to the soul. She laid her head on my chest, and didn't push away, but rather leaned into me, melting into me in a way that made my heart take off like a rocket ship.

I kneaded her back through her sweatshirt, starting low by her hips, working my way up on either side of her spine, my heart leaping again when my fingers found the end of the material and touched against her petal soft skin.

She rested her forehead against me and let out a pent-up breath and I wanted her with a deep, longing ache. I smoothed my hands slowly up the sides of her neck, her pulse thundering against my palm as I tilted her face up to look at me. I covered her mouth with my own as soon as I could and drank her in.

She was as sweet as pie and I was hard to the point of pain. Her lifting my shirt, placing her cool, satin palms against my heated skin did nothing to quench my desire and everything to fuel it. I devoured her, pulling her tight against me, and I couldn't help myself, gripping her ass to do it.

She gave a little leap, wrapping her legs around my hips and I groaned, turning to lay her on the neatly made bed. I ground my raging hard-on into her out of that sheer animal need to just –God!

I tore my mouth from hers.

"What?" she gasped. "What is it?"

"Are you sure? Because if you're not sure, I gotta stop now."

She stared up at me, chest heaving for several breaths. One breath, two breaths; three breaths – I was just about to lift myself off of her when she committed.

"Yes! Yes, I'm sure."

"Hayley…" My voice held a warning. "No going back, Little One."

"No going back. I want this."

I stripped my shirt off over my head and groaned, "Touch me," before returning my mouth to hers. She kissed me, her hands smoothing along my ribs, along my back, delving beneath the waistband of my jeans and shorts to grip my ass and pull me into her body harder. I heard a thump and then another as she toed off her sneakers behind my back.

I followed her lead, but rather than going down, I went up. Sticking my hands beneath the hem of her sweatshirt and touching more of her skin, warm against my hands and so soft it nearly drove me mad. I backed off of her and went to my knees beside the bed. Pushing her shirt up out of the way so I could put my mouth on her skin. Tasting, sucking; kissing along her stomach while I toed out of my own boots, glad they were cooperating.

"More skin," she gasped, begging me, and I was on the same page. I helped her sit up and lifted the sweatshirt over her head, tossing it onto my floor. It looked better there, anyway.

My mouth, I returned to her skin while her fingers threaded into my hair, pressing me to her body. My hands, I blindly used to strip off her socks so I could get to her pants. I slid my fingertips along the soft material of her yoga pants, up the outsides of her legs while I kissed the side of her throat and practically dry humped her. The heat between us was explosive, and I needed inside of her, but I wanted to give her time. Enough to make sure she was absolutely sure.

Her hands working my belt's tongue free of its buckle answered that. She was as desperate to have me inside of her as I was to be there. Jesus, the amount of self-control it took to fish the box of condoms out of the bag and rip it open; the speed with which I gloved my cock in latex set some kind of new record.

Hayley had crawled up onto the bed properly while I'd rolled the condom down my length, my fingertips where I pinched the reservoir at the top slipping against the pre-cum seeping from its head. I'd gotten it started down my length and rolled it down completely, watching her, watching me.

She still had on her sports bra and panties, her fingertips dipping into the front of the waistband of the simple black cotton bikini-briefs. She teased herself, eyes aglow with the dark light of passion and I felt myself twitch. I reached for her bra and lifted it up over her head. She raised her arms and I tossed it aside, letting it hit the floor with the rest.

I stood and pushed my boxers and jeans off the rest of the way while she skimmed her panties down her legs. I got up onto the bed and wrapped my arms around her thighs, pulling her down the bed, settling between her legs. She watched me, face impassive, yet accepting. She arched her hips – offering herself – and that was definitely one offer that I couldn't refuse. I climbed up her body and settled over her, my face hovering over hers, my eyes staring into hers as she wrapped her arms around my neck.

"Please," she whimpered, and I lined myself up at her opening, pressing into her wet heat slowly. God, *agonizingly* slowly, letting her adjust to me, making sure that it wasn't too much all at once.

She whimpered and writhed underneath me, and it was the sexiest damn thing I'd had a woman do. Her hands on my shoulders as her body gripped me, milked me; tried to pull me in deeper.

My body met hers flush and I bowed my head, kissing her for all I was worth. Working myself in and out of her in tight short strokes that stimulated us both and kept us on the very edge of things.

"Blue," she murmured, her voice begging me.

"What you need, baby? Just tell me what you need." She gasped, breath coming in sweet little pants.

"Harder, faster!"

I did as she asked, stroking long and deep, striking a fulfilling rhythm for the both of us. I twined my fingers with hers and rocked in and out of her, pressing her hands to the pillows on either side of her head, stretching her arms above her head, grinding a bit, changing pace and angle, looking for what was a hit and what was a miss.

I finally let her go, getting up on my knees; an arm beneath her lower back to support her. I was in deep, but our bodies separate, holding her so I had the room to use my other hand, drifting it over her body, teasing the planes and valleys with light fingertips. She moaned and arched back, giving herself up to me and I promised her, silently, she wouldn't be disappointed.

I pressed my fingers against her body and slid my thumb between us, slicking the pad through her wetness and teasing her clit. She let out a deep, throaty moan and arched harder, riding me.

Her pussy tightened around me and I gritted my teeth, determined to make her come before me.

"That's it, baby, tighter. There you go," I encouraged, and she cried out. She was wound up so tight, I knew it was only a matter of time, I just had to hold out a little bit longer which was easier said than done. My balls were drawing tight, that telltale tingling at the base of my spine starting. I was shaking with the effort to hold her up and hold back. Her body flared around mine and I knew it – she crashed, the tension falling out of her body as if her strings were cut. Her pussy tightened up and throbbed around my dick pulsating in that way that was a siren's call. I couldn't hold back. I couldn't help myself, I came with her in one of the most perfect unions between two people that the universe could witness.

14

H ayley...
I lay at peace, content in the circle of Blue's arms and drowsed with my cheek against the swell of his chest. He held me, stroking his fingertips lightly across my skin as if he needed to keep touching me to assure himself that I was really real, and that I was really here.

It was perfect. Almost too perfect, but I wasn't willing to let the feeling go.

"What's your name?" I asked quietly.

"Blue," he answered automatically.

I giggled and looked up at him. "No, your *real* name."

"That is my real name now, you want to know my birth name, but my road name is and always will be more important to me."

"Fair enough," I murmured, nodding.

We were silent for a long, long time and his arm tightened around me, pressing me into a one-armed hug around my shoulders, his lips descending onto the top of my hair.

"Joseph," he said. "My birth name is Joseph Barry."

"That's not bad at all, why do you hate it?" I said it before I could really think about the consequence of asking. He stilled under me and sighed slightly.

"It was my grandfather's name on my father's side. A mean, drunk son of a bitch. He made my father into the same. I came from a long line of drunk, abusive assholes on my pop's side."

"Oh, I'm sorry…"

"Not your fault." He paused then went on, surprising me, "Kicked out when I was seventeen, hooked up with the club by the time I was twenty-two. In and out for petty crimes. No felonies, just a bunch of misdemeanor possession charges. Weed, mostly."

He swallowed audibly and I stared at our hands where they rested on his stomach, fingers twined.

"I'm sorry," I whispered, and I felt his pain keenly. The pain of having nowhere to belong, and no family.

"Hey…" He took his hand from mine and cupped my cheek. I craned my head back to look at him. "It's okay. I found the club, and Cell. Yeah, I made mistakes but I'm right where I'm supposed to be… I found you."

I pushed myself up and climbed his strong body, straddling his hips over the sheet and kissed him. I could feel him grow firm against me and I broke the kiss long enough to draw back and see the desire in his eyes.

I reached for the condom this time and stood up on my knees so he could move the sheet. He did, with one hand, the other he played against my body, sliding a finger then two inside me. I paused and closed my eyes, my hips jerking.

He played my body expertly, the music he made with my sighing breath, whining, begging moans for more was incredible. I gripped him in my hand and stroked him, the condom temporarily forgotten in my other hand.

"Tear it open, put it on, or I might not be able to contain myself." His words were honest and sent a shiver of anticipation through me. I did as he bid, tearing open the wrapper, rolling it onto his length slowly with both hands. He was long without being overly thick. Somewhere between seven and nine inches, I'd imagine. I was never really good at measuring things by eye.

I felt every single hot inch of him as I eased down onto him. His hands gripped my hips, kneading my ass, his eyes staring deep into my soul. His body and mind touching every vulnerable and intimate part of me with a satisfying caress. I rolled my hips, and his eyes slipped shut. He groaned and I couldn't help but smile, my confidence boosted by the fact that I could do that to him. Me, make him moan, like that.

"Oh, baby…" he breathed, and I closed my eyes and tipped my head back, moving over him slowly, riding him gently. The passion building between us a slow burn. Heating up slowly to a rolling boil, the plea-sure effervescing up from my core and out along every nerve ending.

"Tell me what you want," he demanded.

"I want you."

"Tell me something dark, something sweet; something you've never told anyone else."

I swallowed hard and wracked my brain, wondering what deep and dark desire of mine that I had to impart, wondering what I could tell him that would satisfy him.

"I've never tried it any other way but this way, and the way we were before. I… I want to try something new."

"Arms around my neck," he instructed gently and sat up. I wrapped them around his shoulders and neck, my legs slightly uncomfortable with the added pressure but it wasn't for long. He put his hands under my ass and twisted so he sat on the edge of the bed, bending forward and standing in one fluid motion as if I barely weighed anything at all.

"Hold on to me," he urged, his strained voice the only giveaway that this was tough for him. He backed me against the wall, and I crossed my ankles behind his back. I couldn't believe how deep this forced him into my body. I thought riding him had felt deep, but this?

He drove up into me and slid his hands along the outsides of my thighs, hitching me up higher.

"Uncross your ankles."

I did and he changed the position of his arms, winding them from the insides of my thighs until my legs were draped over them. He lifted me then, moving me up and down on his dick, penetrating me deeply, the sensation incredible. I felt weak but held on strong, trusting that he wouldn't drop me.

"Oh, my God," I gasped and he grunted, and it sounded suspiciously like agreement.

Pleasure swirled tight in my belly, and I tightened up around him.

"Oh, baby, like that. Just like that."

I bit my lower lip and tried harder, gripping around him until he had a hard time thrusting. The head of his cock touching deep, teasing and torturing that secret place inside me. I closed my eyes, concentrating on the sensation of him and tried to warn him.

"Blue, I'm going to come…"

He turned me from the wall and walked me back to the bed, letting me fall back onto it. He stood by it, lifting my hips bodily and moving me up and down on him. I sucked in a sharp breath and fell anyway, out of my body, down, down, down, into a pool of standing pleasure as warm as bathwater.

He grunted, thrusting sharply but without synch into me, bottoming out. Every time he touched my cervix, goosebumps flowed over my skin until I shuddered and gasped with another orgasm, only slightly less intense than the one he'd just given me.

He reached between us and I shivered as he withdrew from me, holding the full condom on himself. He closed his eyes, the beatific expression on his face as he pulled from me, overly sensitive himself. He stripped the condom from his still hard, but flagging, cock and threw it in the little trashcan by the bed.

He held out a hand and helped me up, lifting the blankets for me to get back into the bed. I did and he climbed in after me, immediately pulling me into the protective barrier of his body which he'd insisted on keeping between me and the door.

We lay together, panting, coming down together. I rested my head against his shoulder, and he pressed it to him and his lips to my hair. This was bliss. This is what I had always wanted on the surface, and for the first time that I could recall, I didn't feel deep down inside, that it was a lie. There was something in his eyes when he looked at me that gave me no doubt that he felt for me as I did him and I think that is what bothered me about Cell.

I pulled myself closer into Blue's side and let my leg drift over his. He put a hand on my thigh and didn't hesitate to haul my leg up his body, over him more, so that there was more of me in contact with his skin, draped along his body.

"I hope that one day, Cell will be on the other side of you," he muttered and his voice was rough with raw emotion.

"I don't understand him," I confessed. "I also don't understand why you're with him."

"I'm not honestly sure I could explain it, Hayley."

"I mean, I know I haven't asked but are you two..." I drifted off and groped for the right word.

"Lovers? No. Not like you and I are now... Cell fucks me, but I don't fuck him. He's not into that."

I frowned. "But you are?"

"Not when it first started, no. I don't think I'd let any other man near me like that. It started in prison as a sort of necessity... but then things changed. My feelings about it, and about *him* changed."

"It's a little overwhelming, I mean –"

"It's not normal?" he asked, plucking the thought from my head as if out of thin air. He huffed a bit of a bitter laugh and asked the all too important question, "What *is* normal?"

I swallowed hard and said, "Good question."

"All I can tell you is what I know, and how I deal with it and that is, I just go with it. If it feels right, I do it. If it feels good, I do it a lot more. If it doesn't, I fight it and I stop it... but I don't not *try*."

"Otherwise, how would you know if you liked it or not?" I asked.

"Hmm, smart and pretty," he said and I could hear the smile in his voice.

I laughed lightly and murmured, "I know I like this... I like it a lot." I cuddled into his side and he sighed contentedly.

"Then please tell me you'll keep doing it, and that you'll try new things."

"I think that sounds reasonable."

"I'm glad, because I really, *really* like you Hayley. I have for a long, long time."

There was a solid foundation of truth to his words, the sound of it a comforting thing, soothing, and I felt some tension bleed from my muscles as if I had set a heavy burden I hadn't even realized I'd been carrying, down.

"You're a lot braver and stronger than you give yourself credit for."

"How do you figure?"

"To be willing to trust me, to do this with me after the things that have happened to you… to be willing to explore your sexuality with us… that's kind of incredible, babe."

I didn't have the heart to tell him I'd thought of that and had already come to the conclusion that if things went badly, that the most likely outcome would be that I was just hurt again. I was sick to death of feeling so lonely and none of the guys who had hit on me at the diner were like Blue… none of them had ever given me the feeling that they could and would care back and I honestly didn't want *just sex*. I wanted it all… a relationship and unconventional as it may be, Blue and Cell had offered me just that.

Well, at least Blue had. Cell was still a mystery. I couldn't ever tell one way or the other just how he felt. He was hard to understand but I was betting that like Blue, and like even me, he had a history behind that.

"Turn out the light?" I asked.

"Sure, anything else?"

"Yeah, don't let me go…"

"Hm," the sound was amused. "Never gonna happen."

I really, *really*, liked the sound of that.

15

D uracell...

They were both in a sexed-out bliss coma. Blue was out so hard he hadn't even heard me open the door.

I stood by the bed, the blue, indirect light from the shop falling across them through the high window of Blue's room, falling across them in bars from the open slats of the venetian blinds.

A slight smile curved her lips and Blue looked probably as contented as I'd ever seen him.

Well, it was time to fuck that up. I nudged him and he jumped, immediately looking down at her where she rested against his chest to make sure she was still asleep. She was out like a fucking traffic light. Nothing short of a full-frontal assault was gonna wake her up and don't think I hadn't thought of that.

I took a certain perverse pleasure in defiling pure things. I was just kind of an evil son of a bitch like that by conventional standards.

"Congrats on sealing the deal," I said low and soft.

Blue glared at me and let out a breath. His eyes communicated daggers of annoyance which just fed my amusement.

"What's the word? Can I get in there?"

"Carefully, and quietly. Don't wake her up."

"Seriously?" I asked, a little surprised. I hadn't expected that answer.

He nodded and jerked his chin to the other side of the bed, indicating I should get in behind her.

"Just sleep," he warned.

"Don't worry about it. I'm too tired to fuck." I gripped my dick through my jeans and was already starting to get a semi. Yeah, fuck it... I really was too tired to fuck right now, but that didn't negate any first thing in the morning action.

"Shh!" Blue hissed at me and I froze from where I was hanging up my jacket and cut. I whipped my head around and scowled but damage was done. Looked like she was stirring.

"Blue?" she murmured sleepily.

"Shh, 'sokay, Little One, go back to sleep," he murmured and she nodded against his chest. She was draped artfully along one half of my boy's body and it was hot.

"Is that Cell?" she asked.

"Yeah, darlin', it's me," I said quietly.

"Come to bed," she muttered and I grinned.

Nice work! I mouthed to Blue. He frowned at me and mouthed back, *Hurry up!*

I pulled my shirt over my head and dropped it among the wreckage of their clothes. I ditched the rest of my shit until I was nude and went around to the other side of the bed, lifting the blankets and scooting across until I was up against Hayley's back.

I wasn't usually into cuddling and shit, but I'd been out at the bar and the ride back had been cold as fuck. She was warm and when my skin came in contact with hers, she jumped and let out a petulant moan, writhing against me in a way that made me instantly hard.

"Condom," I ordered, even though I hated the things.

Blue hesitated and Hayley murmured, "Give him one."

She'd gone very still between us both and I could see the pulse nearly jumping out of her skin at the base of her throat.

Blue groped at the pile I'd seen at the bedside table and I could only assume that it was our primary form of birth control, which sucked, but knocking a bitch up would suck even more, so I could deal.

I tore open the packet with my teeth and lifted the covers to roll it on. I looked at Blue over Hayley's shoulder and he gave me a murderous look that said one thing… *I'd better go fuckin' easy or he'd be a pissy little bitch for the rest of the week.*

Hayley lucked out that I was tired, easy was all I had in me. I thrust a chin at Blue, and he moved her leg a little higher up on his body. I rubbed my dick against her hot pussy, and she gasped lightly.

Sinking into her was hot. It was even hotter that she gave a little wiggle to get me in as deep as I could go. I put my hand on her shoulder and pressed her down to the root, shoving myself into her as savagely as I could muster from this awkward angle.

She gave a throaty gasp and I thought to myself, *Hot damn… she's gonna be a good lay.*

I pulled back and surged forward and she moaned. Her pussy was slick with want and I liked that. It was hot. Made it easier for me to get what I wanted. Blue had done a good job priming her up and he gave me another assist, reaching between them to play with her clit, which I couldn't reach. Not that I really cared if she got off, but it was always nice when a bitch came all over my dick – added a new sensation.

Bitches didn't always come with me, but that was alright as long as they either sucked good dick or cried when I fucked them. If I couldn't get either one of those, usually I did when I ass fucked them, and Hayley had a really nice fucking ass.

I'd be tapping that later. I even saw that Blue had grabbed more lube. The other bottle was in my room.

I pumped in and out of Hayley, her breath coming ragged and uneven. Blue held her to him, an arm around her back, between us, which I didn't care. I was here to get my rocks off, not cuddle. Would be bad enough I'd have to after I nutted up in the condom.

I gripped her shoulder hard and thrust up into her harder to the point she cried out, half in pleasure, half in worry or fear. That sound was music to my ears. She tightened up harder around me and I grunted. It was getting harder to push my way into her, but she was close. Blue and I made eye contact over her head and I nodded. He teased her clit and she fucking jerked against my body. I put an arm around her, across her chest, and pinched down on her nipple. A lot of bitches really fucking liked that when they were coming on me like Hayley was. Made their cooch do great things. Hayley wasn't any exception to that rule.

She gave a throaty, guttural moan and pressed her pussy down on my dick even more and I jerked, spilling deep inside her. I gave a satisfied grunt or two and let out a satisfied sigh.

I was going to have fun testing her limits. A lot of fun. I smirked at Blue over her shoulder and he stared back at me.

I told you so, he mouthed, followed by, *You better be careful.*

Yeah, yeah... or what?

16

B lue...
Hayley was asleep, her back rising and falling gently in the morning light. Cell was awake on the other side of her, looking at her, the calculation back on his face and I was nervous. It was like he was on the fence and I was waiting for a final decision. Did he like it enough last night to want to keep her, or was he of the opinion to throw her back, like some fish he'd caught that wasn't satisfying enough?

"She's got a pussy with a GI-Joe Kung-Fu grip," he muttered and I tried not to laugh. She was lying on me and laughing would wake her. Shit! I lost the battle and she stirred.

"Morning," Cell grated and Hayley inhaled sharply.

She cuddled into my side a little more and I felt her lips curl into a smile against my skin. She kissed my chest and looked up, looking like the cat who'd gotten the cream and said, "Good morning." I could tell that Cell was pleased with Hayley and wanted to do more with her by what he said next.

"Look at you, shattering all those inhibitions." He even sounded complimentary.

I smiled to myself, the happiest I'd been for a while, and hugged Hayley against me, pleased when Cell grinned and nipped her shoulder before springing up into a sitting position. He scooted to the end of the bed and stood up. Lean muscles stretched and showed off to a spectacular effect, leaving Hayley and me both staring with admiration. Cell had a great body, and one that he didn't have to particularly work for outside of our day job.

"You both want we should go again right now?" he asked, and Hayley blushed but didn't look away.

"I'm starving," she said and Cell gave a crooked grin.

"Well, get dressed. Sunday breakfast is probably still going on out there and we can spend the day together – maybe go for a ride or something."

"My bike is back at Hayley's," I said.

"Shit, yeah, I saw her cage out there when I came in last night."

"That's okay," Hayley piped up. "I mean, we can go get it. I can dress warmer…"

"Yeah?" Cell asked, making sure.

"Yeah."

He nodded and smiled. "Alright then."

We got dressed, and Hayley looked beautiful with her hair tousled by sleep and sex. I handed her a comb after running it through my own short hair and apologized that I didn't have anything better. She smiled and laughed slightly.

"It's fine," she said and went to her down jacket, getting her hair clip out of her pocket. She stood in front of the dresser mirror and combed through her long hair patiently, before gathering it into a ponytail. I watched her, fixated, the way her sweatshirt hung artfully off one shoulder, the way she swept up her hair, the elegant line of her neck revealed.

We'd shared something last night. Something deep and personal and I cherished it. I cherished her. I never wanted to let her go. I knew what this was. I'd felt it once before and I looked at Cell, the only other person I'd felt it for. He lifted one side of his mouth in a sardonic smile and shook his head at me. He knew. He knew, too, but he also was letting me have this.

Gratitude swamped me and I felt the urge to go to him and kiss him. I'd had that urge a time or two in the past when it'd come to him. Only tried the one time, the first time, and had had my ass beat for the trouble. Instead, I pulled the treasure that was Hayley into my arms. She looked up at me and smiled, a light of happiness in her eyes.

I bent and kissed her, putting everything into it that I was feeling at that moment, pleased that I completely stole her breath away.

I raised up so that I could see her face, and her eyes were closed, her body relaxed, and her expression one of concentration. As if she were committing the feel of my lips, this moment, to memory.

She was so the right girl...

"Hey, no way I can top that... I'll get mine later," Cell said, holding up his hands when Hayley turned to him. She smiled and picked up her shoes, going to the bed to sit on its edge to put them on.

I looked at Cell and he gave me a still look back. He wasn't in the mood for contact that wasn't on his terms today. I could respect that. Hayley, I worried, wouldn't understand it. So, we had to work together to strike a balance, for now.

Cell pulled his shirt over his head and down over his beltline and sat down to pull on his boots. I pulled on mine and we were just about out of here. I held out Hayley's coat for her and she shrugged into it. I looped her scarf around her neck and pulled her in, pecking her on the nose and she laughed.

"Come on you two, I believe the lady mentioned she was starving and I'm not far behind her." Cell tossed me my jacket and cut, his already on, and opened my door, ushering us out into the hall with a wave of his hand. Hayley paused before going through and reached out, laying a hand along Cell's face. He flinched slightly, but she didn't take notice. I saw it though, a slight movement, a tightening of the muscles around his eyes, his jaw clenching slightly.

"Thank you," she murmured and he smiled, all charm and turned his face, pressing his mouth to the center of her palm and giving it a quick peck.

"No problem," he said and Hayley stepped past him the rest of the way. I gave him a nod and he gave one back and we went to breakfast. He even sucked it up and held her other hand as we walked from the barracks to the back door of the club.

17

H ayley...

When we stepped through the back door of the club, a peal of masculine laughter filtered down the hall from the front of the club-house and I froze. It was one thing to be with the two men I'd just been intimate with... safe and cared for in their presence. It was another to face the potential judgment of their peers.

"You're cool, darlin', just keep walking," Cell urged.

"There's history here," Blue murmured before coming around to face me.

"What history?"

I pursed my lips together and shook my head. I didn't want to think about that now. Blue touched the side of my face, drawing his thumb down in a light caress and asked, "Do I have your permission to fill him in later?"

I nodded. *Yes, I would like that. Spare me from having to say it again.* I knew it was a coward's way, but sometimes it was better – a small act of cowardice now than a larger act of cowardice when it really counted

– so I allowed myself this small indulgence so that I could go in there with all those people looking at us and paste on a smile while the panic seized my guts and tried to steal my appetite.

I took a deep breath and put my feet into motion and when I cleared the archway and the curtained glassed-in room, it was to find a full house. Just about the entire club plus babies and children were here.

"Hey!" Reaver crowed. "Was wondering when y'all were going to get out of bed."

I swallowed hard and pasted on a smile, quickly scanning the room for any looks of reproach or stares but all I found were legitimately care-free and friendly faces.

"Get you some breakfast, boys and girl," Dragon grunted and stabbed his fork at the bar which was laid out with a veritable buffet of all things breakfast.

Cell stepped around me and went up to it, handing me back a plate. I went the rest of the way into the room and took it, handing it to Blue behind me and taking the next one that Cell handed me.

"Thank you," I murmured.

"You bet," he said and started down the line, loading up his plate.

We filled our plates with what we wanted to eat, and I felt some of the unease and tension leave me with having a task in front of me to do. When I turned back around to follow Cell to a seat, no one was looking at us, all of them involved with their food and individual conversations.

There were three seats open at a table with Dray and Everett and Cell took one. I went over and sat next to Everett and Blue pulled out a chair across from me. Everett was smiling and rubbing her baby bump and I couldn't help myself.

"When are you due?" I asked.

"March, but I'm hoping he'll take his sweet time coming out. I'm kind of crossing my fingers for a St. Patty's day baby."

"He?" I asked and she grinned and moved a shiny piece of paper over to me to have a look, I could see a baby on the scan, but there was truthfully no telling what sex – at least not to my untrained eye.

"Aww!"

"I know! We're so excited."

"I'm so happy for you!" I cried and dug into my food, cutting my syrup-soaked pancakes with a fork.

"You riding with us?" Dray asked and I pursed my lips.

"Um, I don't know… We hadn't talked about it."

"Blue left his bike at Hayley's last night like a dumbass."

"Mandatory ride."

"It's only nine, and we don't leave until eleven, right?" Cell asked.

"Right."

"Then don't worry about it, we'll be here."

"Where are you going?"

"It's a charity run, getting toys and –" Everett glared at Dray and he ducked his head. "Stuff together for charity for kids at Christmas. We go, we pick up, bring all of it back here and the ol' ladies have a wrapping party. Wrapping all the gifts that were donated while some of the guys go buy more with the raised funds to bring back," Dray finished.

"So we can wrap some more. We could really use another gift-wrapping hand around here," Everett said with a smile.

"Is there coffee involved?" I asked.

"For you, absolutely. I still am off it. In fact, will you drink a cup for me and tell me how amazing it is? Mandy won't."

I laughed. "Sure."

"Right, so food, back to your place for a change of clothes and Blue's bike, and I guess our day is pretty much decided for us."

"You knew it was coming," Dray said and Cell shrugged a shoulder.

Blue blushed and said, "Kind of let myself get distracted and forgot all about it."

"That I believe," Dray said with a wink.

I blushed, but it wasn't judgy or super uncomfortable. Just my usual shyness at work.

I went home with Blue, Cell opting to stay behind and not cause any kind of awkward if my dad happened to be out and about, which he was when we pulled into the driveway. He was out back at the wood-pile, chopping wood for the woodstove in the house. His typical autumn-time chore before it got too miserably cold out to do it or started snowing.

"Hi, pumpkin!" he called out and raised an eyebrow at me. He knew I was dating, but I hadn't told him who. Now that he saw, I could see that he was less than happy, just as I suspected he would be.

Thank God he didn't know it was the both of them...

"Hello Mr. Vannerly," Blue said, marching forward with his hand out to shake it. I blinked in surprise at Blue for being so forward. I mean, that had never been his style before.

"Hello there..."

"Blue, they call me Blue."

"Got a real name, Blue?"

"Joseph, sir. Joseph Barry."

"Ah huh, I see."

"Daddy!" I admonished at his unenthusiastic tone.

"Hayley," he drawled evenly.

"All due respect, sir. I wanted to say I appreciate you letting me see your daughter. She's a fantastic human being and I respect her very much," Blue said before my father could further embarrass me.

My dad jiggled his axe in his hand and looked Blue over. My dad was *not* a small man. Wide in breadth of shoulders, he'd been a big, hard-working man my entire life and I loved him for it. He was also protective, which I couldn't blame him for... he'd lost his wife, my mother, and had already nearly lost me once... those aren't things a man like my father got over quickly.

"Ah, as much as I hate to admit it, my little girl is her own woman and does what she wants... she takes after her mother that way."

"Speaking of doing what I want," I said with a wry twist of lips, "I need to grab a shower and a change of clothes. I'm helping do some charity work today."

"Sounds like something you would do." My dad leaned his axe against the stump he used as a chopping block and came over hugging me and kissing the top of my head.

Blue explained the charity work while I slipped away and went up to deal with things. I quickly showered and went to my room to dress, checking on them both outside my second-floor window overlooking the backyard.

My dad and Blue both stood, arms crossed, breaths pluming in the cold talking back and forth. Blue leaned forward and laughed a little and nodded. I ducked back and pulled on a complete outfit that was both warm and comfortable enough for my Sunday that would be spent wrapping presents.

I pulled my wet hair into a tight bun to avoid having to dry it and blew some quick hot air onto my bangs just so I could style them before I went back downstairs, bursting out the back door with a, "There, sorry! I didn't mean to take so long."

"Not at all, I'll follow you back to the club on the bike?"

I nodded and went to my dad, putting a hand on his forearm and raising on tiptoe. He bent so I could kiss him on the cheek and grudgingly said, "Should have brought him around sooner to meet me."

"Dad!" I scoffed. "It's only been a few weeks!"

"Right, well, it was nice to meet you Joseph. You take care of my little girl."

"Likewise, sir, and I wouldn't have it any other way."

I felt like I'd missed something, like some sort of esoteric caveman conversation had happened in the twenty minutes I'd been away to shower and dress. I rolled my eyes, and Blue followed me back to my car and insisted on opening the door for me, handing me the keys he'd hung onto. I adjusted the seat and mirrors while he fired up his motorcycle and put on his helmet and protective eyewear.

He followed me back to the club and when we got there, had me park over with a bunch of other cars, pointing where he needed me to go. I pulled in and he backed his motorcycle into line with the rest in front of the club.

He met me halfway across the lot with Cell at his side. Kissing me quickly, he said, "Back in a few hours."

Cell leaned down and kissed me much the same and winked at me. "Go on inside where it's warm."

I smiled at them and called lightly, "Be careful," before I went inside.

"Oh, my God, she's here! Hayley!" Melody called and it was all excitement. I laughed and smiled as she came running up and hugged me tight, dragging me along to the circle of women sitting around in chairs that had been moved to form one in front of the air hockey table against the wall.

The toddlers and babies played on blankets on the floor or napped, and I was a bit taken aback when Mel pressed a glass of wine into my hand.

"It's eleven o'clock in the morning!" I cried.

"It's noon somewhere, and for those of you that can drink, please do!" Everett said.

I looked across at Shelly who held her new baby boy and said, "And you?"

She shook her head and wrinkled her nose. "Pregnant again."

"What!?" You *just* had him!"

"Big families require commitment, a lot of fucking, and sometimes getting pregnant back to back," she said but she glowed with happiness.

"Aww, he's so beautiful," I said when she leaned forward so I could see him. Eldritch James Pauley was barely ten weeks old.

"My doctor told me to wait at least eighteen months before getting pregnant again," Mandy said and Shelly sighed.

"Believe me, I wanted to, this wasn't planned at all. Neither was Eldritch," Shelly said with a gusty sigh.

"At least you waited longer between Harmony and Eldritch," Everett said.

"That was a birth control failure, this was a total *we didn't use any because we were too drunk* failure." Shelly looked up at me and said, "Harmony had some kind of allergy to breastmilk and was a formula baby. We went straight formula with Eldritch, we didn't want to risk it, so please don't think I was drinking and breastfeeding!"

I shook my head and took a sip of the blush in my glass and asked, "Why would that be any of my business?"

"Oh, girl!" Everett said, rolling her eyes. "Women are so out of bounds when you're pregnant or have a new born. Always getting into your business trying to touch your stomach –"

"Always with the unsolicited advice," Mandy agreed. "I was once standing in the aisle comparing diapers and a woman walked up and told me that I was basically doing it wrong by even considering store-bought diapers. That I should be using cloth and a laundry service."

"I remember that! That was with Eden, wasn't it?" Shelly asked.

"Yes!"

I listened politely and waited for the inevitable question of when *I* was planning on having kids, but surprisingly it never came. They traded funny and sometimes horrifying stories of people's rudeness and laughed about much of it, but not one asked about it.

Hayden and Ashton both expressed their desire for children, though while Hayden had pretty much come to grips with not having any children of her own and just having her stepson Connor to dote on, Ashton still seemed deeply saddened by the prospect of never having one of her own.

The topics shifted after that and within the hour, Aaron, Disney's boyfriend came through the door with an armload of gifts.

"Truck's here!" Shelly declared and the women rose. I pitched in and helped, bringing packages and gifts in from the back of the box truck to those with children nearby so they could keep an eye on their kids while things moved to-and-fro.

I helped wrap the first wave, but being around so many people, while it was nice, I needed time to myself before my shift the next morning. That, and, I wanted to spend some time in my studio; at least begin the drawing for the latest window I was supposed to be doing.

I looked up into a pair of sparkling blue eyes framed by jet black hair when I went to call to Mel that I should get going. I stopped and kind of shyly smiled back at Dani.

"Hi," she said and I licked my lips.

"Hi."

"I just wanted to tell you that I think he's the happiest I've ever seen him."

"Which one," I asked quietly, blushing furiously.

"Blue, but Cell too, in a way." Her words were frank, no judgment and no recriminations. I looked up sharply from organizing the table I had been wrapping at.

"Thanks."

"Don't mention it," she said and then, "I totally get the over stimulation... I'll totally let Blue know they were taking too long and that you had to go."

"Oh, no, it's not that," I said, lying through my teeth, sure, but it sounded so *rude* to bail out before my boyfriends got back. "I just have a side job that I need to work on a little bit tonight, and I have a really early morning."

Dani smiled brightly and said, "Sure, we'll go with that, but Hayley, you don't have to explain anything to us or worry that we're judging you for anything or anything like that. We're a family, and you being with Blue... and Cell, makes you part of that family."

"Um, thank you..." I didn't know how to feel about that. I really didn't.

"I can see that right this second, I'm just making things worse."

"Oh, no! I don't want you to feel that way at all!"

"That's no reflection on you," she said with a wink and touched my arm over my sweater.

"I just really wanted to say thank you for making Blue happy. He's like my best friend and he deserves it."

"I didn't really do anything, though…"

"You did enough by just being you."

With that she smiled, turned, and stepped back through the chaos of gifts being wrapped and those wrapped packages going back into the club somewhere to be stored. I couldn't help but smile, too.

Blue had said she was insightful on one of our dates and he hadn't been lying. I went and found Melody and told her I needed to go. She was gracious about it, as were the rest of the wives and girlfriends of the club members. Thanking me and hugging me with cheerful and glad cries of 'see you later.'

I slipped out into the gathering dusk and took a deep, cleansing breath letting it plume the air. I zipped up my coat and went to my car and made a clean getaway after that, though I was a little sad that I didn't get to see them or say a proper goodbye for the night.

I went home and up to my room, hanging up my clothes and changing into some comfy sweats. I took my phone with me, which also doubled as my alarm clock for the morning, to the studio with me and about a half hour to forty-five minutes after my arrival home, and a good ways into my drawing for this latest window, it rang.

'Blue' flashed across the screen and I swiped where indicated to answer, excited.

I put the phone to my ear and said, "Hello?"

"Hey, Little One."

"Hi."

"I am so sorry it took us so long to get back."

"It's no problem. What happened, though?"

"One of the bikes broke down and it took longer than we expected to do the shopping. Cell's disappointed, too."

"Aw, well tell him I miss you both."

"I heard that!" Cell called out in the background and I laughed. The phone changed hands and he said, "Sucks you aren't here, darlin'. I could really use a round like last night."

"Yeah, me too."

"I gotta grab a shower so I'll give you back to Blue. See you tomorrow, maybe?"

"First day back on days... hopefully the new night girl works out. If she doesn't, my dad is switching shifts with me for a while."

"Okay, well, sleep well."

"Thanks."

The phone changed hands again and Blue came back on. "I know I won't. Not without you here."

"Friday can't come soon enough."

"It's Cell's week this week," he reminded me and I giggled.

"Mm, so it is."

"How are you feeling about things? Still good?"

"Yeah. Yeah, I think so."

"Good. Like Cell said, sleep well... I'm glad I get to see you tomorrow at least."

"Me, too."

"G'night."

"Goodnight, Blue."

The line went dead, and my music resumed through the wireless speakers. I worked for a while longer before climbing up into the loft, plugging in my phone, and lying down.

Friday really couldn't come soon enough. I was curious about Cell and what things would be like, just me and him. The ice had been broken, but he was still who he was. An unknown quantity in a lot of ways. Closed off, mysterious, and unreadable.

I stared up at the dangling, folded works of paper art and smiled. Blue was right about one thing when it came to Cell – I felt safe around him, and he felt like a man that God help you if you ever crossed him. I knew I never would.

18

B lue…

I ended the call with Hayley and felt a little hollow; a little empty. The room was a little sadder without her in it. I missed her. Didn't help that the bedsheets still smelled like her. I set the phone on the bedside table with the condoms and lube and dragged my shirt over my head. I'd stripped down to boxers when Cell came back into the room with just the towel around his waist.

"Lose those, too. I feel like fuckin'." He shut the door behind him and twisted the lock and when he turned around, he wasn't joking, towel tenting out in front.

"Miss her?" I asked.

"Kind of do. She had some grade 'A' pussy. I ain't been gripped like that in a while."

I stood up and lost the boxers, my own cock starting to get hard. I wrapped it in my fist and stroked.

"How do you want me?"

"Silent and on your fuckin' knees, how do you think?"

I got up onto the bed and got on my knees. I heard the towel drop and Cell stood behind me. He at least had the courtesy to use the fuckin' lube, opening the top with that flip top plastic creak and crack.

"Face down, ass up, that's the way I like to fuck," he recited, and he teased my asshole with a finger full of lube.

"Being gentle for you," I remarked.

"Yeah, well, practice makes perfect. Pretty sure she's never been fucked in the ass and I totally plan on popping that cherry."

Him and his damn thing for defiling the innocent. Well, not so much defiling as corrupting. He loved that. I think he got off on the fact that I took his cock where I never would have before. Wasn't my thing back then, as much as it wasn't his… It was an acquired taste, for sure.

"Here we go," he warned, and I liked him when he was like this. When he wasn't being a total asshole.

He pushed in, pressing carefully and I groaned, burying my face in the pillow I dragged from the top of the bed, biting it as he eased all the way in.

I pushed one of my hands down so I could grip my own dick again, the grunts and sounds of pleasure he was making turning me on. He fucked me, working his way in and out of my body in a pace that was sedate for him and I could tell, this was going to be one of those long-haul fucks. One that took a couple of hours rather than a couple of minutes, which if I were being honest, he never really went that fast.

I let him have me, concentrating on the feeling of his hands gripping my hips, on the sounds he made, and the impassioned panting.

"Oh, God, yeah…" I uttered and he punched me in the back.

"Shut up."

I sometimes wondered if he imagined he were fucking a woman when he did this, and that he didn't want any reminders it was me. Then he would say shit like he did then, in the heat of the moment, an hour or more into this when both of us were flying high.

"Oh, fuck, Blue... I'm gonna."

I closed my eyes, and relaxed, my own release happening into the palm of my hand which I was trying to keep off the damn bedding. I didn't want to wash anything that smelled like her. I pressed back onto Cell's dick and he groaned, grunting, and shoved in deeper. I felt him twitching inside as he blew his load and as soon as he pulled out, I stood up. Grabbing my discarded shirt that needed to be washed to clean up and checking the bed. I hadn't fucked it up... *good*.

"I'm sleepin' in here tonight," he said and I nodded.

"I'm grabbing a shower."

"Bring me a wet washcloth and turn out the light," he grunted, settling into my bed and I nodded, switching out the lamp on the bedside table as he tried to clean himself up with the towel he'd worn in.

"Bring one back with me."

And that was the extent of our pillow talk.

I really missed Hayley.

19

Hayley...

Cell looked at me from across the table, back against the window, ankle perched on one knee, foot bouncing impatiently. I smiled and shook my head, blushing furiously at what he'd just asked me. He grinned and asked, "What?"

I picked up my drink and sipped, hiding behind my glass. It was a simple question, but one I didn't really have an answer for.

"I wish I could tell you, but I... I'm afraid I'm not experienced enough to answer."

"You don't know what you like?"

I pursed my lips and shook my head and he shook his incredulously.

"Does this mean I can take you back to my place and educate you?"

I laughed. "That's an interesting way of putting it."

"Yeah?"

"Yeah. I mean, do *you* know what I like?"

He raised an eyebrow and looked me over intently saying, "I have a few ideas, and the rest we can probably explore some."

"Yeah?"

"Yeah."

"Why does that prospect, coming from you, scare me a little?"

"Well, if you were a smart girl, it would scare you a lot." He winked at me despite how serious his expression and I scoffed and threw a fry at him. He laughed and put up his hands in defense.

"Seriously, though… what is there to be afraid of?" I asked and he sat up and faced me, suddenly very serious.

"I'm not always gentle like Blue. I like it rough, and I like some kinky shit." I sobered some and paid attention, licking my suddenly dry lips.

"Rough like how?"

"Like hold you down, pound the shit out of that hot little pussy and no skin off my nose if you start to cry or anything."

"That sounds like rape…"

"Not quite. We'll pick a word other than 'no' if you need to tap out, you use that word and it stops. The club frowns on rape."

I swallowed hard, suitably unnerved. *The club frowns on rape…* not *I'm not into rape* but *the club frowns on it.* The choice of words wasn't lost on me, but then again, Blue had talked with me the middle of this week about some of the things that Cell did. Warning me, after a fashion. I was actually a bit surprised by how open and upfront he was being. Blue had opened up, had been afraid that he would surprise me with his proclivities and that it would scare me away from both of them.

"So, um, what word would we use?"

"I'll leave that up to you, just don't pick something stupid like 'lollipop' or some shit."

I laughed, again, and shook my head. "So something not absurd, even though it's totally absurd I have to pick something more…" I trailed off looking for the right word and he accidentally supplied one for me.

"Badass?"

"Sure, we'll go with that."

He shrugged and then blinked and caught on. "Oh! Oh, shit. You mean 'badass' is what you're going with."

I stuck out my tongue and said, "Who's the dumb one now?" in a teasing tone.

He grinned and said, "Oh, I'm definitely taking you back to my place now."

I smiled around my straw and sipped some more of my cocktail. He finished off his beer and he paid our tab.

He'd taken me out to a bar to play darts and have a drink to loosen me up. It was a Friday night, and had been a long week and I, admittedly, was somewhat of a lightweight. One drink had been all it'd taken to loosen me up. The second drink had put me into the land of drunk, but the fries had been perfect to bring me back squarely into the middle of a pleasant buzz.

It was cold out there, and we'd ridden here. Cell staunchly against anything that rolled that wasn't a motorcycle. My car remained at home.

Blue had picked me up to cover me with my dad and had dropped me off safely with Cell here at the bar, but I would be riding back to the club with Cell which I was certain would sober me up completely. Duracell rode like a maniac on a good day, and it wasn't a good day out there. It was icy, winter setting in, and Thanksgiving was just next week.

Cell and I stood by the bike and pulled on gloves and helmets. He'd brought me a pair of the clear safety glasses as a present today, to keep the wind out of my eyes and I thought it'd been sweet. He eyed me over the sleek machine and asked me, "So, am I taking you home or back to my place?"

"I believe I am willing to take the chance... Your place, if you please."

He got onto the bike and turned the key, starting it up. I got on behind him and held onto him for dear life and he took us out of the back-angle park job he'd done against the curb and into the flow of traffic.

It was bitterly cold, and I cuddled against his back, huddling down as much as I could to block the wind. He reached behind him and squeezed my knee and I could already feel myself getting aroused, wondering exactly what he might do when we got back to the club.

The party was in full swing when we pulled up. Music bumping out of the common room, the glass in the window in front with the Sacred Hearts' flag in it rattling in its pane. Duracell had me hop down and backed his bike into the line of them out front. When he came and captured my hand, though? He took us through the parking lot and the long way around the building.

We followed the blacktop track toward the outbuilding, silently passing below the rise where a fire was going on in the firepit and several brothers were smoking and talking, making use of the benches on chains surrounding it.

He let us into the same building that housed Blue's room but took me to a different door. I slipped inside and he shut it behind me, taking my coat and hanging it on the back of the door.

I turned around and he stepped into my personal space, hauling my body against his. He bowed his head and claimed my mouth and it was nothing like when Blue kissed me. Duracell didn't give, he *took*, and he was going to take *everything* if I let him.

Was it wrong of me to be curious? Was it wrong of me to want this? I didn't think so anymore. I felt a sense of excitement thrum through me as he slid a hand under my shirt and massaged my breast through my bra.

I pushed his coat and colorfully patched vest off his shoulders, and he let them fall to the floor. It was a frenzy of getting the clothes off and once they were, Duracell picked me up and tossed me on the bed, laughing. He got between my thighs and rubbed against me, staring into my eyes. I swallowed hard and the smile disappeared from my face.

He was so serious, something primal, dark, and deep radiating from him like summer heat from a sidewalk and I'd let him snare me. My heart climbed up into my throat and Cell covered my mouth with his again, determined to get to it and devour it.

I put my arms around him and pulled my body up off the mattress, closer to him and he groped off to the side for the condoms waiting on the bedside table. He broke the kiss and stood up saying, "Get on the bed, in the middle, on your fucking knees."

I swallowed hard and did what he asked, not sure what he had in mind. He rolled the condom down his length and said, "Play with your pussy. Touch yourself, tease your clit."

I did what he asked as he got up onto the bed behind me. He braced an arm against my back and slammed me face first into the pillows. I gasped and tried to push myself back up, but it wasn't about to happen. Then he was inside me, and he wasn't gentle or careful the way he had been the first time, when Blue had held me while Cell had taken me.

"You touching that pussy?" he demanded sharply and I nodded. He spanked my right butt cheek. Laying a hand on it in a rough, stinging slap that made me cry out but also did some *really* nice things. I writhed where I was impaled on his cock and cried out, "Yes!"

He was fast, and brutal and I admit, frightening but I didn't cry out. I didn't use the word to make it stop because *it felt good* and *I liked it*. Confusion and turmoil tried to bubble to the surface because of that but I forced all those things back into their lair, determined to enjoy this, giving myself over and letting *go*.

His body met mine with the sharp sound of slapping skin and I jumped, startled when he put his finger against my anus.

"What are you doing!?" I cried and he laughed.

"What I want; now relax; whether this feels good or not is going to be totally up to you."

He slowed down and reached over to the bedside table and I bit my bottom lip. I considering calling out and stopping this, but I was also curious. He hadn't hurt me, or insisted on doing anything I overtly didn't like and *how would I know I didn't like it if I didn't at least try it once?*

"Cold," he warned, and I jumped when he teased me with the lubricant. He started moving again and I arched low to the mattress, his presence inside me stretching and filling me. Sparks and flits of pleasure moving down every nerve ending, building, the sensations not unpleasant at all, in fact, they were surprisingly just the opposite.

"Touch that clit, baby," he ordered, and pressed what I assumed was his thumb into my ass. I rubbed my fingers at the top of my sex and whined. It felt so good, so different, and I decided I *really* liked this for several reasons.

"Yeah, that's it," he encouraged and I felt myself tighten around him. He pressed his fingers in and out of me, stroking in counter rhythm to his penis and I moaned. My body was awash in the most amazing and indescribable sensations, sweeping through me, building into a crescendo, until with a final thrust, a final swipe of my fingers, I came.

I came hard, face planting into the pillows, my voice muffled by them as Cell worked himself in and out of me, playing my body to his own ends. He pulled from my pussy but kept playing with my ass and I honestly couldn't get enough of the sensation, that is, until he pressed his cock there.

"Push out, it helps. It's only uncomfortable for a moment."

It *was* uncomfortable. He was too big. A moment of panic, the word to stop everything on the tip of my tongue, and he stopped moving. His voice pleased and filled with ecstasy as he said, "Aw, yeah, baby. That's it. I'm all the way in. Just stop, relax… that's it."

We were still for a minute, my chest heaving, and then he began to move, slowly at first, and *oh, my, God…* I gripped the sheets in my fists and held still, letting him do whatever he wanted because this? As taboo as it might be, *this was amazing.*

"Oh, God, oh yeah, oh yeah, oh fuck yeah!" he panted, stroking in and out of me at an even and regular pace. The slight burning from the unfamiliar stretching swamped by the pulsing and twitching deep inside my vagina that I could only label as an orgasm, although quite different from the ones I was becoming accustomed to.

He jerked and thrust deep and the suddenness of it made me jump and was slightly uncomfortable, but his grinding against me felt so damn good, his twitching deep inside the unfamiliar channel felt unreal and I almost, *almost* didn't want it to end.

When he pulled out, I just naturally folded down to the mattress. My body trembling, skin dewed with sweat but strangely chilled. The after-glow strong and the euphoria bearing me away. Cell stood up and got rid of the condom, vaulting my body to lay on his back on the other side of me, but not touching.

"How long were we like that?" I asked, panting lying on my back. My knees ached and my wrists were sore from having been in the same position holding most of my weight for so long.

He glanced at the bedside clock and said, "Shit, a couple of hours at least."

I laughed a bit and sighed, saying, "Wow."

"Yeah, that about sums it up," he agreed. I rolled onto my side in his direction and moved my hair, tucking myself into his side.

Just before I laid my head on his shoulder he asked, "What are you doing?"

I froze. "Um, getting close to you?" I pushed myself up more onto my hands and he was laying, half holding himself up by his core alone, his hands up and out to the side as if avoiding something unpleasant.

"Yeah, I'm not like Blue when it comes to that, you want cuddles and shit, you go down the hall to his room."

"What?" I asked, voice hollow and uneven, not believing what I'd just heard.

"Did I stutter?"

I pushed back and sat up completely. He was dead serious. I swallowed hard and got off the bed.

"You're serious."

"Always."

"But I –"

"But nothing, throw on some clothes and head that way, because you're not going to get it from me; that's totally Blue's department."

I was shocked. I couldn't believe this was happening. Humiliation burned my face and tears pressed at the backs of my eyes. I gathered up my clothes and put them on and he flipped on the TV, completely unconcerned. I pulled my coat down from the hook and he hadn't even said a word. I opened the door, and he raised a hand in a half-assed wave goodbye and the tears that'd until now just pricked the backs of my eyes, spilled out. A maelstrom of emotion took over, too many to count. Confusion, hurt, anger, heartbreak, humiliation, embarrassment... so many all at once, overwhelming me, swamping me, the sadness dragging me under and rolling me.

I stumbled out the door furthest from the back door of the club and sucked in a deep breath of frigid air. I didn't want anyone seeing me make this walk of shame, which is precisely what it was, and so I took the long way around the track and down the driveway. I looked both ways. I wasn't thinking, I mean, I should have driven but my car was at home. I struggled into my purse, crossways over my chest, my bulky coat and scarf not exactly conducive to getting it on and struck out in the direction of home. I would walk. It might take me all night, but it was better than the alternative.

I stayed on the shoulder, as close to the grass and as far from the lane of traffic as possible, even though it was quiet out here. Not a soul traveling in either direction. I wiped at my eyes and sniffed, keeping my hands buried in my pockets for the most part when the sound of a bike reached my ears.

I didn't want to face anyone, I really didn't, so the sound made me cringe. Blue pulled up beside me and yelled over the motor, "Hayley, what are you doing!?"

"I'm going home!" I cried.

I think he swore, reaching out and grabbing my arm I turned, and his face was barely suppressed rage.

"What did he do?" he demanded, and I realized he wasn't angry with me.

"I just want to go home," I moaned and he nodded.

"Come on, get on. I'll take you straight there."

I crumbled a bit, wanting desperately to be left alone but at the same time desperately wanting to go home to my studio, my own space where it was safe, and I could go back to being unrecognizable by the world at large.

How could I have been so stupid?

"Come on, my little one… get on. Let me take you home," Blue begged.

I hated what it did to me, when he called me that. I hated how it made my insides turn liquid with relief. I hated how it made me want to believe…

I got on the bike and held onto him, not even caring that neither he nor I wore a helmet. He took me home and I was grateful that it was without incident. He pulled up alongside my studio and I immediately jumped down and went to the door, digging for my keys in my purse. My hands were shaking, my vision blurred by tears and Blue reached out with frozen fingers, plucking the ring from my hands. He unlocked the door for me and I went in, the warm air from my studio puffing out at us. I ripped my purse off from over my head and hung it up and Blue stood by, passive, waiting, but not leaving.

"What happened?" he asked.

"I don't want to talk about it. I just want a shower."

He nodded and said, "I'm not leaving you like this, without knowing what went on. Go get under the water. I'll find you clothes and clean towels."

I didn't argue, his presence always having been a soothing thing… plus, he wasn't Cell. He was Blue.

I threw what I was wearing down on my bathroom floor and turned on the water, getting under before it fully had the opportunity to heat up. I felt awful, dirty, but certainly not in a good way, and worst of all taken advantage of. I scrubbed and finally overcome, just sat down in the bathtub and cried.

It was like high school all over again and I hated that. I hated that I let myself believe that I could do this, that this was even a good idea. I should have just stuck to my damn self, making my windows and wishing for something more.

I huddled miserably in the bottom of my shower and let the warm water wash only the surface dirt away. I don't know how long I was there, or how long I'd cried but I was all cried out when Blue came in.

He had towels hung over his shoulder and moved the curtain aside to turn off the tap. He kneeled by my tub and wrapped one of the towels around my shoulders, helping me to cover up. The towel was warm, fresh from the dryer.

"Hey," he murmured, and smoothed some of my wet hair out of my face.

"Hey," I whimpered back miserably.

He gathered me close and held me, rocking me while I went through a fresh spate of tears.

"Come on, my little one. Let's get you up and get you dressed."

We stood and he handed me the other towel for my hair. I wound it up and he was gone when I straightened. I made sure the rest of me was dry and he met me at the bathroom door with a sleep set, also warm and fresh from the dryer.

"Thank you."

"Just get comfortable. We don't even have to talk right now, but please... don't send me away."

I froze and looked up at him. He leaned a shoulder into the doorframe and looked down at me, waiting.

"I don't want you to go anywhere," I said and it surprised me that I *wasn't* surprised. He nodded and turned his back, waiting for me to get dressed. I went to him when I was clothed and wound my arms around his waist, resting my head against his back and murmuring, "You don't have to do that. I mean, you didn't do anything, and you've already seen everything, so…"

"So, nothing. I don't want you to be unhappy. I don't want you to be uncomfortable. Not around me, not ever."

I nodded and stepped back enough for him to turn around and hold me back. We stood like that for I don't know how long, until I shivered a bit, the cold creeping up through my feet where they rested against the frigid polished concrete floor.

"Go on up, I'm right behind you," he whispered into my hair and kissed the top of my head. I turned and he worked at shutting off lights and locking things up down below while I climbed the ladder up into my loft.

He followed me up quickly, just as I'd finished plugging my phone in. He looked at me and motioned for me to get into bed.

I lifted the blankets and climbed in; Blue sitting down on the edge and tucking me in. I felt myself laid low, still miserable from Cell's treatment of me, but closed mouths didn't get fed and so I asked, "Stay with me?"

He smiled and looked relieved, nodding his head. He pulled off his boots and stood, ditching his pants but leaving his boxers on. He pulled his shirt off over his head and I lifted the covers, scooting over. He lay down on his back and lifted his arm closest to me, inviting me to get close. I cuddled into his side and laid my head on his shoulder.

Silence. Sweet, calming, silence, comfort, and grace.

"I hate seeing you hurt," he murmured and pressed his lips to my forehead.

"I should have seen it coming."

"Why do you say that?"

"Because I'm not blind, Blue. I watch the way he treats you. The way he treats *everybody,* and something has always felt a little off about him." I was silent for a time, just enjoying the warmth and feel of his hard body against mine.

"I don't know what's worse," I said. "Letting myself believe... or the fact that I genuinely *liked* everything he did to me up until the end."

"What did he do?"

I swallowed hard and because it was Blue, I told him. All of it.

"Shit," he sighed and held me close. "Fuck, would it really have been so hard for him to give you ten fucking minutes?"

"I don't want him to do anything that he's not comfortable doing."

"Hayley, no... that's honestly not how things work."

"Well then help me understand, Blue! How is this supposed to work?"

"We should all be getting what we need."

"And what do *you* need?"

"You. I need you, I need this, and I don't want to lose you, or Cell, but I don't want any of us to get hurt in the process. Dammit."

A long time later, each of us having been lost in our thoughts, I said, "This is some kind of a mess isn't it?"

"Yeah, and it's my fault. I shouldn't have –"

"Oh, hush. I'm hurting right now, but I'm glad you did. I needed you two as much as I think you needed me."

"Yeah?"

"Yes. I never would have rejoined the land of the living and regular people if it hadn't been for you. Just... I guess, I knew this wouldn't be easy, but I didn't anticipate *this* being the problem. I expected it to come from the outside, you know?"

"Yeah, I know."

"Has he always been like that?"

"Yes."

I pulled myself closer to Blue and sighed. "Why? Do you know?"

"Yes."

"Can you fill me in?"

"I would love to, but I'm not sure that's my story to tell."

"I can understand that, but it doesn't make it any easier to swallow." In fact, it was a pretty bitter pill, but I didn't want Blue to feel any worse than I already could tell he did. We talked more, but eventually lapsed back into a comfortable silence.

I woke up in the middle of the night, Blue sleeping soundly beside me, still wrapped up warm in his embrace and it gave me some more time to think about things, alone and without distractions.

I believed it was too late for me, when it came to Blue. I was already past the point of no return when it came to falling in love with him. I could tell by how he was still here, taking care of me and making sure I was okay, that he loved me, too.

That was worth putting up with a certain amount of, excuse my French, but bullshit from Cell. I could tell they were inextricably linked by something. Past experiences, bonded through events I couldn't begin to understand. I also couldn't deny that Cell could be charming and that he was far more charming than not when it came to me.

That didn't mean he was going to get a free pass on his behavior and that also didn't mean I would excuse any future bad behavior from him toward either me, or Blue. There needed to be some form of compromise and some way to achieve that compromise. I didn't and couldn't expect them to bend around me and me alone. I needed to understand and do some bending of my own. *Fair is fair in such an unfair world.*

I sighed and it must have been too heavy, because Blue jolted awake. He looked down at me and I looked up at him, his hand automatically coming up and leaving a light caress alongside my face. I pushed up and leaned forward, putting my mouth to his. He held me, hand holding my face, tucking my hair behind my ear while our tongues danced, sliding against one another expressing everything that needed to be said without forming words.

His hands flowed down my body, over my breasts until he could reach the hem of my cami. I straddled his hips, painfully aware of the thin layers of cloth between us, rubbing myself up and down his hard length.

"Oh, Jesus, Hayley…"

"I want you."

"No condom."

I groaned and whimpered, and he lifted my top off over my head and I raised my arms so he could do it. He sat up, arms around me, crushing us together below the waistline. His mouth taking one of my nipples into his mouth. I half moaned, half gasped. A throaty thing that sounded like some goddess of passion and not me.

His hands delved below the waistband of the sleep shorts, squeezing my ass and I seriously, *seriously*, thought I was going to die if I didn't get him inside me in some kind of way.

"Off, I need these off and I'm gonna need you to sit on my face."

"What?" I asked laughing.

"I'm not kidding, get it all off and let me lick that pussy."

I wasn't a complete stranger to oral sex, I'd just never heard it phrased that way before. I kneeled up and pushed the sleep shorts down, sitting my bare ass onto the mattress to get them off the rest of the way. Blue skimmed them down my legs and let them drop, and before I could get back to my knees, had his boxers shoved down far enough that his cock sprang free.

"Turn around," he ordered and I did, staying up on my knees; he slid down so his face was between my thighs. He pulled me down and licked a long, wet line from my clit to my opening where he plunged his tongue inside.

"Oh, God!" I cried and put my hands down to the bed between his knees. I adjusted myself accordingly and took the head of his dick, salty with his pre-cum, into my mouth.

He worked me, and I worked him, and we did the next best thing by making love to each other with our mouths. I sucked and licked along his length and he spread me with his hands, lapping at every exposed bit of me.

I loved it. It felt amazing lying draped the length of his body while his lips and tongue wrought magic. I moaned around him in my mouth and he sucked in a breath, which is how I discovered that the added vibrations pleased him. I hadn't thought of that before, but then again, none of my other lovers caused me to moan like that with them in my mouth so I guess there was that.

I was careful, taking him deep into my throat without gagging. If I concentrated and held my jaw just so, I wouldn't choke, but it was easier said than done with how he drove me to distraction. He slid a finger then two inside me, but didn't thrust them back and forth, or in and out. Rather it was as if he were looking for something and I jerked, twitching when he found it.

I pulled him from my mouth with a soft pop and groaned, and he exploited that place inside me and my clit with his tongue and all I could do was massage him with my hand, jerking him off while the pleasure built, and built, and built.

I cried out, body jolting against my will as pleasure swept through me in ever increasing crashing waves. He was so much better at this than I was…

"Oh, God, Blue!"

He held me to his chest with an arm around me and worked me until I begged for him to stop and all I could do was lay limp and panting.

I came back to myself and resumed working on him until I could achieve the very same reaction from him, and it was so worth it to do so.

I so needed to buy and keep some condoms up here to avoid this problem in the future; however, as a work-around, this hadn't ended badly for us. Unfortunately, there was still plenty of time for that to happen, the whole ending badly part, and it could be as soon as the next day. It all depended on Duracell.

That was a scary thought.

20

D uracell...

It was an ambush, but I had to hand it to them, it was pretty much perfectly choreographed and executed. Actually, I had to hand it to Blue. He's the only one that knew that Hayley getting her way and me looking any kind of penitent would be the only thing to save me from having my ass beat. The club caught wind of how I treated her and there was no telling what they'd do but Hayley was a hell of a lot more likable than me so...

Still, it wasn't my fault she'd gotten all butt-hurt the night before when I'd told her to get the sappy shit elsewhere. That that was Blue's dog and pony show, not mine. I kind of figured I was in for it when I'd gone to Blue's room for round two and neither of them had been there.

Blue had sent me some angry fucking text messages last night which I'd gotten when I got back to my room after discovering they weren't in his and those led to me standing here sucking it up and finally taking one for the team. I mean, he was right, it'd been a while since I had.

"Why do I have to say it? You see it in my eyes, you feel it in my kiss, what does it matter if I say it out loud or not?" I argued, pouring on the charm.

She sighed, her shoulders dropping, eyes full of wounded emotion. "Because sometimes we just need to hear it."

By 'we' I assumed she meant women in general and so I contemplated her, mulling it over for a full minute before I sighed and gave in. "Fine, I'm sorry, okay?"

She didn't look like she believed me, and Blue knew I was full of shit, but that wasn't the part that mattered. What mattered was *making* her believe, making her feel loved or cherished and while I couldn't give her that, I could give her my respect. It was downright fucking ballsy of her to call me out like that. I'd killed motherfuckers for less.

She looked up at me and I could see something else in her eyes, that even though she didn't believe… she had the willingness to believe. I was totally capable of lying to her and if the compromise was going to get me out of another uncomfortable ambush like this one, I could get on board.

"I mean it, Hayley… I didn't think about it and it was an asshole thing for me to do. I fucking hate apologizing, even when I know I was wrong but that's not an excuse. Not when it comes to you. I'm sorry, I mean it."

If I chewed that fucking crow any harder, I'd fucking choke to death on it. She nodded finally and let me kiss her again and God, I hoped this was the end of it but knowing me, and knowing Blue… probably not, dammit.

"Thank you," she murmured.

"Blue told me about your past, but I guess it's just not the same as hearing it and seeing it for myself," I said. I wasn't about to take the full blame here. She could eat some of this, too.

She didn't look happy, but she handled it with grace by nodding and saying, "You're right, I'm sorry… I have a really hard time talking about it but that's really no excuse. I should have communicated with you."

I nodded. "That's all this is, I think… a miscommunication." The fuck it was, but whatever. Haley getting on board and believing it would save my ass this time, but it wasn't a card I could always play.

"I can agree with that," she said gently and I hugged her a little tighter, rubbing her back which seemed to please Blue, so it looked like I'd figured out the winning combination. With the way they both looked, it didn't seem like they got a fuck of a lot of sleep the night before, so I went with it and declared, "I think we just need a lazy Saturday."

"Yeah?" she asked and I nodded.

"Why don't we all just crawl back in bed and get some more sleep, then maybe watch a couple of movies or something. It's cold as fuck out there anyway and there really ain't shit else to do."

Hayley smiled up at me and nodded. "I like that idea. Blue?"

"Sounds great, actually."

"I'll even let you pick the movies."

Hayley laughed and said, "You might be surprised."

"Yeah?"

"Yeah, I like action movies."

"No, shit?"

"I'm a daddy's girl, what can I say?"

Hallelujah for one thing. At least I wouldn't be sitting there with my fucking dick in my hand, completely bored off my ass watching some trashy chick flick.

21

B**lue...**
"You know that she's not stupid, right?" I asked him and he looked up at me. I shut the door and crossed my arms, sighing.

We'd just kissed Hayley goodbye and sent her back to her place for the night so that she could spend the next day working on her window. I'd seen the drawing she'd come up with and it was stellar. She'd started to cut and piece the glass together, too, and I envied her talent.

"Whatever, she bought it."

"No, she didn't Cell; you said it, but you need to show it."

"Man, what do you want me to do?" he demanded and he was getting a bit hot.

"Would it have killed you to fucking hold her for ten goddamned minutes after you fucked her last night!? For fucks sakes, man, she's human like the rest of us out here and needs more human interaction."

"That's what you're for!"

"I thought you wanted this. I thought you wanted a woman for us. One that would help you carry off being more normal. If you want anything, you have to work for it, you know that!" I snarled.

He glared at me, nostrils flaring, a muscle ticking in his jaw. "You too far gone on her?" he demanded.

"You're goddamn right I am," I growled.

"Seriously, you'd throw down with me over pussy?"

"No, Cell, I'd throw down with you over *Hayley*, and the fact you can't see the fucking difference here tells me that you might just be too far gone inside your own fuckin' head to *ever* blend in."

I opened the door and went out, slamming it shut behind me. I stormed up the hall to my own room and went in, shutting and locking the door behind me, fucking missing her and wishing this would fucking work. If Cell could just stop being a dick for one goddamn minute and grab on to what was right in front of him, even his miserable fucking ass could be happy.

I dropped onto the edge of my bed and picked up my phone off the bedside table. I checked the text messages, waiting for Hayley's message that she'd gotten home okay. A little pissed I couldn't keep her with me.

I couldn't get enough of her. Lying on the couch with her draped over my chest watching James Bond flicks all day had been heaven. Having my best friend and my other lover there watching with us and seemingly actually enjoying *himself* had been even better. I still couldn't let what he'd done go, though. Something needed to be said and I'd said my piece.

Like always, it would be up to Cell on whether he acted on it.

My phone pinged in my hand and I looked at it.

Little One: Home Safe. Miss u.

I smiled and laid back on the bed, missing her keenly.

Me: Miss u too.

Little One: Come to Thanksgiving with me and Dad.

Me: What about Cell?

Little One: He's ur best friend.

Me: You sure?

Little One: Yes. I want to spend the holiday with the ones I love.

Me: I'll talk to Cell

Little One: Thank u

Me: U bet.

22

H ayley...

I was nervous. Glad that it was Thursday, glad that any moment Blue and Cell would be riding up to my back door, but terribly, terribly nervous. *What if dinner didn't turn out? What if my dad caught on I was seeing the both of them and not just Blue? What if Cell was a raging dill weed?* My mind just kept on with *what if, what if, what if,* as I moved around the kitchen, fixing appetizers to set on the table.

Thanksgiving was the one day a year that my dad was barred from the kitchen. It was his day to relax, watch football to his heart's content and for me to get my hands dirty. It'd been my mom's day to cook, and for the three years between fifteen and eighteen, we'd had Thanksgiving in a restaurant. The Thanksgiving after my eighteenth birthday, though, I insisted on doing it all myself from my mother's recipes *with no help from my dad.*

I set a tray onto the dining room table with carrot sticks, baby corn, celery, marinated mushrooms, and two kinds of olives. She used to always have trays of good stuff to munch on while we waited on the bird. I smiled at the back of my dad's head as he lounged in his recliner and cried 'come on!' at the TV.

That first Thanksgiving I'd cooked without help had pretty much been a disaster. I hadn't pulled the bag of innards out of the bird and the stuffing? We just won't talk about how big of a train wreck it all ended up being. We ended up in a restaurant that year too, and my dad? The next year it had been a team effort; he had trained me right and it'd been my show ever since.

I went back into the kitchen and washed up some of the things that I had used so far. The house was old, without a dishwasher, and with no real way to put a dishwasher in it, so in this house we were the dishwashers. I put the pots and utensils in the drain board and just as I finished drying my hands and went to pick the first thing up to dry it, I heard motorcycles rumbling down the street in front of the house.

"That yer friends, pumpkin?" my dad called from the recliner.

"I think so," I called back. I listened to them rumble down the drive and smiled. "I know so," I called, and my dad huffed a laugh without turning around.

I went to the back door after the bikes were turned off and opened it up to Blue coming up the back steps, a light of excitement in his eyes.

"Hey, Little One," he murmured and bent down to give me a kiss. A quick, chaste press of lips. I stepped aside and he went into the house and Cell stopped in front of me.

"Hey, darlin'," he said and winked, bending to give me a friendly peck on the cheek. His eyes, however, told a different story. One that made me blush.

He handed me a bottle of wine and said, "We didn't want to come empty-handed."

"Oh, thank you!"

He slipped past me into the house and I shut the door on the cold swirling into the house. Blue was shaking my dad's hand who was up out of the recliner. Cell stepped up and shook his hand after Blue and I went and set the bottle on the table.

"Sure appreciate you letting me come along with Blue."

"Aw, well, no one should spend Thanksgiving alone," my dad said. I smiled over at them and let them talk, wandering back into the kitchen to finish what I started, keeping an ear out and shamelessly eavesdropping.

"You boys like football?" my dad asked.

"I'm more pro ball than college ball, myself," Cell answered.

"Aw, yeah?"

"Yeah, favorite team is the Pats."

"Oh, well, we can't all be perfect," my dad said dryly.

A light touch at my lower back startled me and I looked up into Blue's smiling eyes. He asked me, "Can I help?" and I wasn't about to turn down his offer.

"Sure, dry these and I'll get started on the salad."

He plucked the dishtowel from my hands and picked up the next plate while I went to the fridge and pulled out the ingredients I would need and for a time it was the picture of domestic bliss. Blue helped me in the kitchen while Cell and my dad watched football, and everything was perfect.

When dinner was ready, we all sat down at the table. Grace was said as was custom at my mother's table, and even though she was gone, my father and I had carried that particular tradition on. It wasn't until about five or six bites of food that my father lobbed a grenade into the conversation.

"So, Joe... Paul... just curious, but have either of you done any time?"

I nearly choked on my bite of turkey. "Oh, my God, Dad! Who *asks* that!?"

"A man should know just who's keeping his daughter's company," my dad said defensively.

"Yes," Blue answered quietly and didn't look proud, Cell on the other hand...

"We went in together for the same stupid shit," Cell said. He looked almost angry, affronted that my dad would even bring it up and my heart sank.

"And what stupid shit would that be?" My father sounded less than impressed but a little angry himself. I set down my fork and put my face in my hands, flaming with embarrassment.

"Illegal weapons charge, first offense," Blue said honestly.

"How long?"

"Five years each," Cell answered. "We did our time, paid our debt, now we just want to be left alone, go do our jobs, and come home."

"Hayley, did you know about this?"

"Yes," I answered and shook my head, ready to cry.

"Well," my dad said unhappily, "thank you for being honest with me."

"I know you don't like it sir —"

"Of course, I don't like it," my dad snapped. "She's my little girl, my only child. Would you like it if you were sitting here instead of there?"

"Probably not," Cell admitted.

"Dad, stop!" I cried. "Oh, my God! I'm not twelve."

"You're my daughter, Hayley. I have a right to worry when a couple of Sacred Hearts come through my door for dinner."

"They're nice people, Dad."

"That's not our reputation, though," Blue said softly.

My dad frowned and said, "What he said."

I rolled my eyes. "Jesus, Dad, what would Mom say?" That made him frown harder. He shook his head and sighed.

"I apologize," he said to the two men. "I'm out of line. Hayley's right, just when it comes to my little girl's safety, I get a little crazy. She's right, though. My wife would be all kinds of mad if she saw me treating guests this way."

"Believe me, sir… Your daughter couldn't be safer with us. I care about her very much and anyone that would try to hurt her would have a lot to answer for," Blue said.

"We'd collect on that debt, believe me." Cell echoed the sentiment and his voice was as chilly as the winter wind outside.

I bowed my head feeling equal parts ashamed and loved and Blue reached over under the table beside me and gathered up my hand, giving it a squeeze. I sighed and held back the tears, still having to sniff. My dad's face crumbled a little bit and I asked, "Can we please pretend this conversation never happened and just have a nice dinner?"

"Sure."

"Yeah."

"You bet."

"Thank you."

The mood was heavier and quite a bit more sullen than it had been before my dad's outburst. I understood it, but it didn't make me feel any less awful for Blue or Cell. After dinner, Cell and Blue helped me clear plates. Cell stood with his hands braced against one of the counters, leaning back into it while I packed up some food for each of them to take and Blue helped me do the dishes.

"Well that was awkward," Cell said with the ghost of a smile on his lips. One that didn't or couldn't reach his eyes.

"I am so sorry," I murmured.

"Not your fault, Little One."

I nodded and Cell said, "Seriously, he's just a dad, being a dad." I looked up at him sharply and saw just the tail end of something passing between him and Blue. My heart swelled for the both of them that they would worry about my feelings after having been so heartily offended by my father.

My dad stepped into the kitchen and threw his empty bottle away. He got into the fridge and pulled one out twisting off the top and held it out first to Cell then to Blue. Both of them politely declining.

"Look, I'm really sorry," he said chagrined, now that he'd had time to think about it.

"Don't be," Blue said back. "We understand."

My dad nodded and rubbed the back of his neck and I set one of the final dishes into the rack.

"I'd really like to show the guys the bookstore window. I'm nearly finished now."

"Yeah, sure," my dad said.

Cell went up and shook his hand and Blue followed suit.

"You guys have a good night," my dad said, and they nodded and the knot of tension between my shoulders and dread in the pit of my stomach loosened.

I led them out the back door and across to my studio, ushering them in before closing the door tightly behind us. Cell was the first to grasp me and pull me into his arms, crushing me to him, his mouth over mine. He kissed me fiercely, pressing so hard I resisted slightly out of unease and maybe a little fear at how intense he was.

He pulled his mouth from mine and said honestly, "Your daddy pissed me off, can't say I'm sorry about wanting to defile his little girl in all the best ways possible."

I blushed deeply and laughed nervously. "Can't say that doesn't sound appealing," I said truthfully, "but not tonight."

"Damn, can't blame a guy for trying," he said with a smile and I smiled a bit ruefully in return.

He passed me to Blue who showed all the gentleness that Cell couldn't with his temper up like it was. Blue, though, held me close and kissed me sweet, massaging the nape of my neck with sure fingers.

"So, let's see this thing," Cell said and I sighed a bit.

"It's not a 'thing', it's a window."

I led them over to my work table and showed them the mostly complete window. Cell let out a low whistle. It was the first time he'd ever been in my workspace and I had to admit my nervousness. Like I said, he let out that low whistle and said, "You did all this?"

"Mm-hm."

"It's nice work, how do you do it, though?" I smiled, genuinely pleased he would ask.

"Well, first you draw the design…"

I spent the better part of an hour explaining the intricacies of making one of my designs, of tracing the space meant for any glass piece onto plain white computer paper and using the same old glue sticks we used as kids to glue it to a piece of the colored glass you desired. I showed him how to use the scoring tool, and how to snap the piece off. I showed the proper way to tape the edges with fine copper tape, and how to smooth the edges down perfectly, and then I showed him how to paint the flux and tack-weld the piece in place with solder.

"Then you solder along the entire length of the join and ta-da. Rinse and repeat; slide the next sheet of paper under the glass and trace along the edge and the rest of the design and go to the next until it's done."

"You got more patience than me for this kind of thing. This is totally more Blue's speed."

Blue smiled at me and I smiled at him, saying lightly, "That's okay, I'm just glad you let me show you."

"Sure thing, sweet thing." He winked at me and I laughed, and the mood was much lighter than it had been before. It wasn't too long after that they had to go and that was disappointing. I always hated watching them leave.

When I went back inside, the living room was dark, the kitchen light the only light left on – my dad had gone to bed – likely to avoid the uncomfortable conversation about the uncomfortable conversation and I couldn't say I was sorry about it. I was honestly tired and more than a bit emotionally drained. Totally ready for bed, myself.

The diner may have been closed today, but it would be open tomorrow and it was sure to be a long, dragging day with few customers thanks to the post-holiday shopping madness.

At least it was Friday, though.

23

B lue…

Christmas had come and gone, the New Year had come in with some serious partying and even though it was only February, it felt like spring was pretty much just around the corner. All in all, my life was pretty fucking perfect lately. Today was no exception. We'd spent almost all day together, shopping a little, seriously affectionate and finally had ended up back in my room for an hour or more of lovemaking.

Now, Hayley lay against my chest, and I cuddled her close. Cell had gone off on his own earlier in the day and hadn't come back yet. I don't think that Hayley was too terribly disappointed about it, and I felt like we'd turned a corner in our relationship where we were all more comfortable just being… Like the tack welds had set and the line of solder holding us together in a stronger bond was being laid.

We hadn't had sex, the three of us together yet, but I was thinking we were close to clearing that last hurdle. It felt like a big one.

Thanksgiving had been interesting, and we'd avoided her dad for the most part. She wouldn't say anything about it, but I was pretty sure they'd had a fight. The outcome was that she was still with us, so I would have to say that meant she'd won.

Tired of thinking about it, and marveling at how we were still managing to pull this off after so long, I decided it was time for less thought and some more action.

"Mm," I growled and turned her on her back, wedging one of my knees between hers and nudging her thighs apart.

She laughed, a joyous sound and asked, "Still not enough?" as I nuzzled the side of her neck.

"Never enough."

I licked along the side of her neck and nipped lightly, tracing my lips along the delicate slope of her shoulder, down her chest, pausing to pay particular attention to her nipple. I sucked the delicate nub into my mouth and rolled it, capturing it between my teeth in a light grip. She arched, her fingers twining into my hair as she gave a throaty moan, eyelashes fluttering with the sensation as she closed her eyes and relished the sensation.

I loved how responsive she was to my touch. Every movement honest, organic, and letting me know just what she liked and didn't like.

I moved down her body even more, light touches of my lips against her warm, soft skin punctuated with the occasional taste of her. A light, unexpected flick of my tongue that left her gasping or giggling, unless I placed it against a known ticklish spot. Then she would jerk in my grasp and squeal, a delighted sound that I don't think I would ever hear enough of.

Those gasps and squeals turned into passionate and throaty moans the closer I got to my goal. I trailed light fingertips down her skin, tracing where my lips had been until I reached the apex of her thighs. I went down on her, gladly, pressing my middle finger up inside her and coaxing her body into writhing for me.

She watched me with heavy-lidded eyes, passion and naked want radiating from her and she was so beautiful to me in that moment that it hurt. A very physical pain as my heart squeezed down tight in my chest as if gripped in a fist. Only, I would give anything to make that pain a permanent part of me because it was just that damn good.

I put my mouth to her most sensitive parts and lapped at her, teasing her clit with strokes of my tongue, and teasing her G-spot with strokes of my fingers. She gripped the sheets at her hips with her fists and would have arched off the bed completely if it weren't for my arm barring across her hips, pressing her down into the bed; holding her there so that I could torture her as sweetly as she tortured me with that look in her eyes.

I loved the way she was looking at me, down the length of her writhing body, between the valley of her breasts, chest heaving as she tightened down around my fingers in that way that told me she was close, so very close. She threw back her head with a sharp, impassioned cry and jerked wildly as her nerves overloaded and she came hard around my fingers and against my mouth.

I let up, knowing how sensitive she got, and knowing that a certain amount of a lack of control tended to frighten her. Unlike Cell, I pushed Hayley's limits slowly. I didn't want to burn her out or overwhelm her to the point she felt she couldn't handle us anymore. Never mind that she hadn't handled us together yet.

I wasn't sure why. It just hadn't come up yet.

I kneeled up between her legs, her whole body limp as she floated in the euphoria of her afterglow. I reached for a condom, my dick impossibly hard, and tore open the little foil packet. She watched me, chest heaving with deep, quick, breaths.

"You okay?" I asked with a smile, knowing the answer already, even as I rolled the condom on. She watched, and the look in her eyes always entertained me. Something about the act of putting the condom on myself always got her, always made her go still and the look in her eyes made me feel like a man on top of the world. Like I was the hottest thing she'd ever seen.

I tipped forward and braced a hand on the mattress over her shoulder. The other hand I was using to guide myself inside her.

God, she felt so good. So wet, I glided inside with very little effort. Her hips jolted slightly as they always did when I first pushed inside her, and I just kept going until I was flush against her body with mine; in as deep as I could go.

She looked up at me, raw with emotion and I smiled, bringing up my other arm and lowering myself over her until our bodies touched before I drew back and thrust forward again. She sighed, her eyes slipping closed and she just *melted* beneath me. It was the sweetest and hottest thing I'd ever had a woman do and I loved it. I loved even more when she arched a little to put our bodies back in contact. I loved it even more than that when her hand gripped my ass, nails digging slightly into my flesh as she pulled me back inside her, her other hand warm on my shoulder.

I loved her and making love to her was the greatest privilege I'd ever known.

"Blue," she whimpered, and I closed my eyes, relishing the sound of my name on her lips.

"I love you," I murmured and covered her mouth before she could reply, fearing her response and not wanting to ruin this perfect moment any further than I feared I may have just done.

Her arms went around me and she pulled me down tight against her, her legs wrapping around my hips, pulling me all the way in and holding to me so tightly, I couldn't pull out if I wanted to.

She kissed me back with such fervor, I felt my spine go liquid with relief at the weight that'd been lifted from my spirit. She loved me, too, and just when I didn't think life could get any better, the door to my room burst open and Cell called out, "Player three has arrived!"

Hayley jumped, squealing and burying her face in the side of my neck, laughing when she realized it was her other lover... *our* other lover.

"Mind if I join you?" he asked, shutting the door behind him and shirking off his jacket and cut.

"Lose the clothes first," Hayley said dryly, and I thrust into her, glad to hear it. She sucked in a sharp breath and I kissed her, a tingling enveloping my back as Cell swept his gaze over it.

"Well alright then," I heard him say, then I heard the tongue of his belt loosen out of its buckle. I kept it up with Hayley, working my way in and out of her wet and ready body while Cell got himself ready to join us. He walked up, nude and perfect and stopped by Hayley's head, already semi-hard. I pushed up to my knees and worked in and out of her, but no longer caging her with my body, she was free to do more, which she did, by reaching out and stroking Cell with her hand.

He picked up a condom and got up onto the bed beside her. She turned her head for him, and he slid his cock into her waiting mouth. He smiled at her and slid himself back and forth over her tongue, between her petal pink lips, carefully. Finding that partnership and rhythm that allowed her to catch breaths as he backed off. Hayley's face radiated perfect calm and perfect trust while Cell's maintained control.

More relief washed over me, while I worked to please her even as she worked to please him. A task that was growing a little more difficult as his erection grew. Finally, Cell tipped his head back and let out a shuddering breath saying, "God, baby, yes... that's enough. That's enough, now."

He pulled back and ripped open the condom with his teeth, watching her face as he rolled it down his thick length. He put a hand on my shoulder and got off the bed, coming around behind me. Hayley looked up curiously at the both of us, but Cell shoved me forward, back over her and I put my hands to either side of her head, above her shoulders.

"It's okay," I murmured as he grabbed the lube and got onto the bed behind me. Hayley's eyes widened and I closed my eyes, even as she stroked the side of my face.

God, I wanted this. I wanted this so bad... I wanted them both, to know her body and his and be the bridge between them. Cell pressed against my asshole and I shuddered. I cradled Hayley close and had myself all the way in her while Cell took his time, drawing this out, torturing me, knowing how much I craved the sensation of having him inside me while I was inside her.

"Dammit," I muttered and laughed nervously. Hayley smiled and laughed a little too, nervous and a bit on edge, all of this outside of her wheelhouse, but if I'd learned anything about our girl, it was that she would try anything at least once. If she didn't like it, she wouldn't do it again, but if she did...

I bowed my head, pressing my forehead between her breasts as Cell thrust into me. I about died when she scratched her nails lightly over my scalp and tightened her pussy down around me. She seemed determined to make this good for me and that screamed volumes about just how much she loved me.

I was all the way inside her, Cell doing most of the work for the three of us, his rough thrusting pushing me that little bit extra into her body, her back arching, her gasps coming in ragged pants, the three of us riding it out on a cloud of euphoria, losing ourselves completely in the sensations of each other. The course of our pants and gasps, the sound of our heavy breathing just serving to turn us all on that much more, raising us up impossibly high. She came first, her body flaring around mine, gripping me then letting go, tossing me to the four winds of my own orgasm even as I heard Cell cry out, distantly. The power of that moment explosive, mind blown right along with our bodies as all three of us came essentially in unison.

Hayley pulled me down on top of her as I went limp; languid with relief and overridden with pleasure so hard that I didn't think I would be able to move for days. Cell pulled out of my body and sat back on his knees so as not to crush us, his uneven panting and harsh bark of a laugh telling me two things.

One, it had been just as good for him as it'd been for us, and two, he wasn't done yet. I was okay with both of those. Of course, it'd be interesting for all three of us what tomorrow would bring.

24

H ayley...
   I lay, skin slightly dewed with sweat and watched Cell's face over Blue's shoulder, the memory of Blue's face as he'd both made love to me while Cell had been inside him is one that would forever be burned to memory. In fact, I think that it would be one of my favorite memories I would ever have to keep and to cherish. I don't think I had ever or would ever see Blue that happy again.

"Do me a favor?" I asked them both and Cell laughed a little.

"After that? Anything, just name it," he said panting.

"Kiss each other... for me... I want to watch."

Cell and Blue exchanged a look and Blue gave an awkward one-shoul-dered shrug. Cell reached out and pulled Blue's back against his front and said, "I'm no fucking faggot, but she asked nicely, and I'm in a good mood."

He put his hand beneath Blue's chin and pressed his head back into his shoulder, bowing his head and covering Blue's mouth with his own.

Blue seemed surprised, his gray eyes going wide before he relaxed against Cell, eyes closing and let the kiss settle and become as natural as breathing.

It was so hot to see I felt my body throb with an aching want. Cell pulled back and pushed Blue off him. Blue caught himself with a hand to the bed and looked at me, a raw emotion I had no name for in his eyes.

"Right, out of the way, dude. You've had your fun." Blue got up and stretched his legs, pulling the sagging condom off his cock and throwing it into the trash by the bed. Cell handed his own condom off to Blue and crawled up my body to lay his mouth onto mine.

I cradled his face between my hands and kissed him as deeply as he kissed me. Not even thinking about anything else but the feel of his hard body against mine. My mind couldn't hold on to anything the way he kissed me, and I moaned into his mouth as he slid himself into my sopping pussy.

He smiled against my lips, thrusting himself deep, reaching the end of me, and thrusting harder, just that little bit more until my body twitched around his. It was his favorite thing to do since he'd discovered he could make my body do it.

"Oh, I'm going to put you into a blissed-out fucking coma," he whispered against my lips. I smiled against his mouth and kissed him again and he drove into me, wrapping his arms around my back and rolled, taking me with him. I yelped and laughed, suddenly finding myself on top.

He let me go and I straightened, moaning. I loved being on top with Cell, his cock just fit right, touching all the right places inside me. I trailed fingertips down his chest while he gripped my hips, thumbs caressing back and forth as he watched me move.

"C'mere, beautiful, kiss me." I bent at the waist and kissed him as he'd asked and felt the bed dip as Blue got back up on it behind me.

Cell's arms went around me, his hips taking over as he held me to his chest, flexing up into my body even as Blue began to kiss my lower back. I jumped and yelped when he bit my butt and his hand crashed down onto the other side, turning the yelp into another moan. Then his tongue touched me, and I jumped again at the foreign sensation.

Cell chuckled darkly and told Blue, "Get the lube and work her up to it."

"Up to what?" I asked dumbly and both of them had a bit of a laugh at that.

"Just relax," Cell ordered.

I relaxed into him as he made slow, controlled, and lazy thrusts up into me, his hand tangling in the back of my hair, massaging the back of my scalp as he pressed me down into his chest. Blue continued to tease me with his tongue and I heard the light plastic crack of him flipping the lid to the lubricant bottle open. I felt myself flare around Cell's dick, my pussy throbbing in anticipation.

I'd enjoyed everything that either of them had ever done to my body and I'd been working up the courage to ask about this. About having both of them inside of me at the same time, but I hadn't been able to work up the courage to talk about it yet.

It was strange, that doing things I was just fine. Brave and adventurous, but ask me to talk about it? My palms got sweaty and my face got all flushed and the panic and what felt like embarrassment set in.

Blue teased my asshole with a lubricated fingertip, and I tried hard to relax. Cell caressed down my back and kneaded tense muscles where he found them while Blue worked a finger in and out of me. The sensation was amazing, so different with having Cell in me, too.

I closed my eyes and felt myself go limp. It felt good. Both of them felt so good I almost couldn't stand it. I closed my eyes and held still and let them do what they wanted. They never failed to disappoint with the sensations they wrought, so why not?

"You like that?" Cell asked softly, in that voice that was made for sin.

"Yeah." My own voice sounded breathy with want and Blue slowly worked another finger into my ass, stretching me and making me ready. I could feel between me and Cell, the wetness slicking my inner thighs. I was so ready for this. I so wanted this. I ground against him, whimpering and both of them chuckled, Cell darkly and Blue lightly. Both of them so different from one another yet both opposite sides of the same coin.

If it was one thing I'd learned from the both of them; there was a fine art to anal sex. The more turned on you were, the better it felt, but that your body would tell you its limits. Right now, between the two of them, my body was primed and desperate for just that little bit *more*, and I wanted it so badly. I just wasn't sure how this was going to feel with Cell buried so deep in my pussy, although, to be honest? I was glad it was Blue at my back and not Cell. Duracell wasn't as patient as Blue, and were their roles reversed, I didn't think this would be nearly as pleasurable. Not to mention, Cell's cock was much thicker, so Blue at my back made the idea of this much less frightening and much more appealing.

Nerves were starting to make an appearance as I overthought things, just in time for Blue to remove his fingers and press the head of his dick at the tight ring of my ass. I tried to relax and at first, it was too much, I felt too full, but I didn't want to give up completely. Not until I knew beyond anything that I wouldn't like it or that I absolutely couldn't stand it.

The pressure grew, and just when I was about to tap out, cry that I couldn't do it, the orgasm hit me. I'd had orgasms from the anal sex that I'd had with them before but this? This was beyond incredible. I could feel myself expanding and contracting around Cell, but it was a distant thing. It was as if every muscle in my body had turned to liquid and that liquid moved like mercury, full of the shimmering golden glow of all things good.

185

I think I lost myself in them, but when I came back, it was to Cell almost lovingly cradling me against his chest while Blue smoothed his hands over every bit of the exposed skin of my back, both of them softening in my body, just as spent as I was.

"That," I gasped, "was intense."

"I think she likes it," Cell said laughing and Blue laughed, too. It was infectious, and pretty soon all three of us were a laughing, blissed-out heap of sweaty, tangled bodies. That was okay, though. It felt just so damned exquisite.

25

D uracell…

"Spill, why are you *really* in such a good mood?" Blue demanded and I chuckled. Yeah, he knew me too well.

"Why do you care? That was some good fuckin' and we sent her home happy."

He narrowed his eyes looking me over and then his eyebrows shot up straight into his hairline.

"You're fuckin' high, aren't you?" he demanded.

I didn't respond, just gave a half smile and put my hands behind my head, lying back in the bed. He'd walked Hayley out to her cage and had taken his sweet time getting back, while me? I'd had no desire to fuckin' move. I was just layin' here and feeling great.

"Maybe," I conceded with a cheshire grin.

"Where'd you get it and what is it?" he demanded.

"One of the hookers at *Sugars*. She had some coke and felt like sharing. What the fuck was I gonna do? Turn her down?" My grin widened at the look of angry disgust on Blue's face. "Don't be a bitch," I told him.

He bowed his head and shook it. "I swear to Christ, you *better* have wrapped it up."

"With the hooker? Fuck yes. I may be reckless but fuck that shit. Somethin's gonna kill me, it'd better be quick." I closed my eyes and relaxed, floating on cloud nine and sort of already coming down from the coke. The sex had been great and the mood I was in was pretty good, leave it to Blue to bring me fuckin' down.

"I hate it when you talk like that," he said and I opened one eye.

"Okay, Mom."

He hung his head and shook it. "I just can't with you sometimes," he said with a defeated sigh and he went over to his dresser, going through drawers and pulling things out, stacking them up.

"Where the fuck you going?"

"To take a shower, but more importantly... Away from you."

I barked a laugh at his sullen 'little boy Blue' routine and he shut the door on it. Fuck him, anyway. I did what I wanted, he knew that and Hayley was learning it. I'd had a good fuckin' day for all that I didn't get to blow any shit up or put the hurt on anyone. Sure, I'd pissed the hooker off doing the coke off her tits and walking off like I had. She'd wanted the 'D', but I hadn't given it to her. I'd been more interested in coming back here and getting my rocks off with the people I knew were clean.

Blue was right, it was kind of convenient having a bitch between us.

I hadn't lied either. I had every intention of living fast and leaving behind an ugly corpse, but I sure as fuck wasn't going to go out because of some terminal fucking disease I got from a goddamned hooker. Life itself was terminal as it was. Only one disease at a time.

I got my ass up before he got out of the shower and threw on some clothes. I wasn't interested in listening to his fucking bullshit when he was done cleaning up. I also wasn't interested in sharing any space with him while he was being a moody prick, so instead, I took myself to the locker room showers down at the opposite end of the barracks.

I was jazzed, and felt like doing something still, so I figured I'd clean up and hit the bar for some darts. Let Blue fucking sulk, he'd come around later, he always did.

26

B^{lue...}
"Son of a bitch," I muttered.

"Yeah, I'm not happy about it either," she said. We were out back of the club, a fire going in the firepit. It was cooler than what was comfortable now that the sun had set, but the fire beat that shit back and my jacket and cut laying draped over Hayley as she lounged on the bench, her head on my thigh, was keeping me plenty warm enough by getting me fucking hot.

She was gorgeous in the flickering firelight and my cock was already straining in my jeans. It'd been a few weeks since Cell's mini-coke bender, and he was sitting across from us, swinging on his own bench, drinking a beer.

"Guess we'll get our fun in where we can," he said and sounded even less happy about the current turn of events than I did.

"I don't think it will take long to figure it out. I mean, they've all quit on a Friday or Saturday night, so there's that. I think my dad has the right idea. Melody is more than capable of handling day shift as an acting manager, and we really need to get to the root of the problem with the night waitresses."

"Going twenty-four hours is working out enough, then?" I asked.

"Yeah, we were surprised at how much money we're making. Dad says he wishes we'd done it a long time ago."

"We could see about getting on a night crew," Cell mused, "but I really fucking hate that shit."

"No, don't do that. It should only be for a few weeks," Hayley said.

"Guess we'll just have to come in for dinner instead of lunch," I said and she rolled her head back on my thigh so she could look up at me. Her smile said it all, radiating love and light. It was amazing having Hayley look at me that way.

"Well, you two do whatever you're gonna do. I'm going to bed. Come on back to my room tonight."

"Feeling cuddly?" Hayley asked.

"No, just not feeling like I'd hate having you guys in my bed."

"Horny then," she said and smiled a little wistfully. I knew that look, I'd worn it on my own face countless times when it came to Cell. Wishing for the affection he just wasn't capable of giving me.

He looked around and secure there weren't any other brothers out here lurking or whatever, bent down and kissed me. I froze for half a second and closed my eyes, letting him. It was something he did for Hayley because when he did, it got her hot and willing to do things his way a little more than usual.

He bent down to her next and kissed her deeply, drawing back just enough to give her one of his more pragmatic looks.

"If I'm out, wake me up with a blowjob. Bonus points if Blue is loosening you up while you do it."

"You are so bad," she whispered, blushing. I smiled at the both of them and Cell grinned at her.

"I love it when you tell me just what I like to hear," he said and straightened up.

"Love you," she called after him softly and he barked a laugh.

"Whatever," he called back over his shoulder, and Hayley rolled her eyes. She looked up at me and sighed.

"You believe me when I tell you, right?"

"Yeah, and it feels better than I ever could have imagined it would."

"What?" She frowned and I chuckled.

"Being loved by you."

"Oh." Her expression softened and I let my hand drift from her ribs, down the front of her body, beneath my coat. It was warm under there, and even warmer when I slipped it under her shirt and down the front of her pants. I rubbed her lightly over her panties and her eyes closed, her breath rushing out in a contented sigh. I pulled back enough to get under her panties and slipped my fingers between her pussy lips, finding her gathering arousal and bringing it up over her clit.

Her eyes closed, her lips parted, she held stalk still. When I tripped her trigger, her legs would twitch slightly, and she'd let out this gorgeous little breathy sound that drove me crazy. I smiled and played with our woman's pussy out under the scattershot of stars and pretty much felt true happiness.

"You are so bad," she moaned, her voice thick with lust and desire.

"Me? I thought I was a saint."

She laughed and laughed at that, finally calming down enough to say, "Compared to Cell, you are."

"He still scare you?" I asked her.

"I think I would be a little crazy or have no sense of self-preservation if he didn't."

"I think you're right." Silence stretched between us, the only sounds filling the night the crackle of the fire and the emerging insect life and frogs. Occasionally, the chains holding the bench would rattle when her legs twitched and that made me smile.

"I do, you know…" she said suddenly, and I looked back down at her, taking a drink of my warming beer.

"Hm?" I asked as I swallowed the mouthful and took another.

"Love him. I mean, not like I love you… I feel like I have more of a connection with you, but I *do* love him… I don't really know how to explain it, or why."

"You don't have to explain it," I said. "I know exactly what you mean."

We stared into the fire for ages, just comfortably soaking up each other's company as I teased her lightly and rocked us back and forth lightly on the swing. I finished my beer and set the dead soldier aside as the stars lazed their way across the sky above us.

Hayley sucked in a deep breath and shuddered as if coming awake and said, "I can't handle you teasing me like this anymore. I need you."

"Just me, or do you need us?" I asked, curious. She didn't answer right away and when she did, it held falsehood.

"I need both of you."

"Then to Cell's room we go."

She sat up and I sucked her essence off my fingers. Her lips parted, and her eyes grew wide and I winked at her.

"Think we could stop at yours first and have a moment?"

I smiled wide and said, "Whatever you want; whatever you need."

27

H ayley...

My father and I were thoroughly confused. We'd worked the night shift at the diner for a couple of weeks, now, and we hadn't seen or had anything happen. I was leaning against one of the stainless appliances talking about it with him while he flipped a couple of burgers for the tired travelers out in the dining room.

"I'd really hate to think it's one of the employees," he was telling me.

I felt my mouth set into a grim line. "I don't think it's Julio, Dad. I think whatever it is, it has Julio just as scared."

"I reckon you're right, pumpkin. I tried to ask him about it, and he wouldn't make eye contact. I tried to get the last couple of waitresses to talk but they wouldn't return my calls. I have no idea what's going on and it's driving me nuts." I shrugged and let out a gusty sigh as the bell chimed over the door.

"You're not the only one, Daddy."

"Can't go back to days until something happens."

"I know."

I backed out of the kitchen and turned to greet the people that'd come in with a smile. My face didn't falter one whit, but my heart sank when I saw who it was. There were four of them, all of them male and all of them in designer jeans and expensive brand-name shoes. All of them had polo shirts or rugby shirts except the one who was just in a tee. They didn't wait for me to seat them either. They just took what booth they wanted, which was fine, but didn't exactly bode well for the rest of the coming interactions when the sign read 'please wait to be seated.'

I brought over menus and handed them out with a friendly, "Hi, guys."

They all laughed, faces flushed and eyes sparkling with too much to drink. It wasn't quite quitting time for the bars, but when I reached across to lay out silverware, the smell of alcohol radiated off of the lot of them as if they'd showered in it rather than drank it.

I knew the type. Rich kids that wanted to come down here and slum it around us poor folk. It happened, and it rarely ended well for us poor folk.

"I'll be right back to get your drink orders," I said and the one on the end of the bench, closest to me to the right side of the booth looked up at me with a cocky grin that would have done something to me once upon a time, but now? Next to Duracell? It was a pale comparison.

"I think we know what we want, don't we, boys?"

They let up a rowdy "Yeah!" and whooped and hollered some, and I pasted on a smile, whipping my pad and pen out of my apron pocket.

"Okay, what'll it be?"

"Jack Daniels on the rocks would be nice," the one on the left at the back of the booth against the wall said. He had longish hair, chin length, and a broad set to his shoulders beneath his wide-striped white and royal blue rugby shirt.

I smiled and said apologetically, "Sorry, boys. We don't serve alcohol. Closest thing I could get you is a Shirley Temple. We have the cherry juice and 7-Up."

Three of them laughed, the one closest to me on the right, the one with the short blond hair, bright blue eyes, and a red polo with the collar popped... his expression went as cold as winter ice.

"You making fun of us?" he asked.

"No," I said frowning. "I was just joking."

"Coke, lots of ice," he said. I nodded and wrote it down.

"Coke," another said.

"I'll take a water."

"Got orange soda?"

"We surely do," I answered the boy in the green polo, as green as the Crayola crayon. "I'll get those out here and give you some time with the menus."

I went behind the counter and drew the sodas and water from the fountain, put them on a round tray and brought them out. I set them out in front of everyone and pulled straws from my apron pocket, handing them out.

"What's your name?" Red polo asked.

"Hayley," I answered, thinking surely a name couldn't be that big a deal and to be honest, being reticent would likely aggravate him. I just had a bad feeling about him. The kind of feeling all women and girls are taught to listen to. His shirt one giant physical red flag to match all the ones raised in my head.

"You're a pretty girl, Hayley." I blushed faintly as I did with every compliment that came my way.

"Thank you," I murmured and then asked, "Do you know what you want to order?"

The boys placed their orders and I wrote everything down carefully, also afraid of what the reaction would be if I got something wrong. The fact that they were all in here like they owned my father's diner was off-putting to say the least. The fact that they were loud and rowdy another.

Tension rode the air, thick enough to slice with a knife and I wished that I knew what to do about it, but they hadn't done anything. I just *knew* when someone wasn't being sincere, or nice, and the one in the red polo was clearly the ringleader of this little circus.

I served them their food and they talked and laughed, but red polo's eyes followed me wherever I went in the dining room. Traveling up my legs, lingering on my ass, and staring pretty unabashedly at my tits when I went over to ask how their food was. I froze when he took liberties and put his hand on my waist as he talked to me.

"Why don't you leave with us?" he suggested. "We could show you a good time tonight, take you home in the morning, might even have the maid make you some breakfast. See how the other half lives."

I pushed his hand off my hip way more politely than he deserved and said, "Thank you for the offer, but I have a boyfriend. I don't think he would appreciate it."

I turned to walk away, and he grabbed my wrist. I startled, dropping the pitcher of water I'd brought to refill the one guy's glass and it hit the edge of the table, ice water dumping from the knee down along my left leg and soaking into my chucks.

Off balance from trying to avoid the water, he pulled me down into his lap, his hand gripping the top of my thigh.

"Stop!" I said. "Let me go, please."

"I don't want to let you go, and somehow, I don't think you want me to let you go either." He ran his hand up my leg and cupped my pussy through my tights and panties. I froze in absolute shock, the door swinging open.

"I said *let me go,*" I said strongly and squirmed in his lap trying to get away from his groping hand.

A loud whistle split the air and I whipped my head around. Cell stared down at us and murder was in his eyes. "You've got less than two seconds to get your damn hands off our girl," he grated and continued to give them a hard look.

I reached out and he took my hand and pulled me past him, flinging me at Blue.

I crashed gratefully into Blue's arms and he pressed my face into his chest, his arms going protectively around me.

"Don't kill them, but hurt them," Blue said devoid of any discernable emotion, and Cell shot back, "I do what I want, little boy Blue."

Everything was happening so fast; the next thing I knew, someone was screaming, then the screaming was muffled. I went to turn my head but Blue pressed it tight against his chest, resting his chin on the top of my head, keeping me from looking.

I wanted to look, I needed to see, but Blue wouldn't let me and that just made me want to look more.

"Shh, it's alright my little one, I've got you now."

I let him hold me and held back to him tightly, but I wanted to know so I fought his hold and turned back so that I could see Cell, afraid for him. I mean, there were four of them and only one of him and my Blue…

28

B lue...

   We pulled up at the diner and had no idea what we would be walking into. I was really glad it was a Friday night and we'd decided to grab a bite and see our girl rather than stick around after church.

I was the first through the door and I froze, Hayley struggling in some prep school motherfucker's arms that couldn't have been more than nineteen or twenty by the looks of him but was more than likely over the age of twenty-one by the smell of him and his buddies. Cell crashed into the back of me and I took a halting step forward and looked back at him.

His eyes had gone that flat dead brown that meant grievous bodily harm was in someone's future and I didn't even bother to yank on his leash. He whistled sharply to break up the party and looked at the four at the table.

"You've got less than two seconds to get your damn hands off our girl," he grated and gave them a thousand-yard stare that meant bad things were about to happen.

I could count on one hand and have fingers left over the number of times I'd seen that look and somebody didn't die.

"Don't kill them, but hurt them," I commented dryly, and Cell shot back, "I do what I want, little boy Blue."

He grabbed Hayley by the hand and flung her past him into the safety of my arms. Cell was a fast motherfucker, and as he'd pulled her past him, he'd used the other hand to pick up a fork off the table. The rich mutt that'd had his hand up our girl's skirt made a fatal mistake then. He put his hand flat on the table to get up from his seated position. Cell, savage fucker that he is, capitalized on the moment and crucified the kid's hand, slamming the fork tines through the back of his hand into the top of the Formica table.

Hayley, face tear-stained and body trembling in my own, jumped and struggled to turn her head in Cell's direction but I held her fast, murmuring into her hair that it was alright. Cell had this shit under control. There were only four of them.

As soon as the kid screamed, Cell leaned in and clapped a hand over his mouth. He put his face less than an inch from the kid's and said, "I said less than two seconds motherfucker, your time was up."

The kid wasn't so tough anymore, and the boys with him were positively ashen. One of them losing his dinner right there at the table at the sight of the blood leaking out of his leader's hand.

"The rest of you might want to get the fuck out," Cell said, voice low and controlled. "Now!" he barked.

The one behind red polo was the only smart one out of the four of them. He stood up, vaulted the back of the booth over into the next one, and fell all over himself to get the fuck out of there.

"I'm gonna teach you boys a valuable lesson."

"Oh yeah? What's that?" the built one in a blue and white rugby shirt demanded. He was a match for Cell in size but not in experience, or cunning.

"Never touch another man's property."

Cell smashed his forehead into the kid with the red polo and the kid dropped like a fucking stone. Hayley shrieked, and I pulled her back, away from the fight, just as a kid in a green polo threw a punch at Cell's head.

Cell leaned to the side, the kid's fist sailed by, and Cell lobbed a knee right into the kid's nads. The kid crumbled and the one that might actually cause Cell a problem caught Cell right in the mouth. I shook my head. He shouldn't have done that, and the reason why was apparent. Cell's head snapped to the side and Cell brought it back. I couldn't see Cell's face, but I didn't need to. I knew the rictus grin he had going on. I also knew that it was probably bloody and therefore even more terrifying.

This kid was dumb like an ox but strong like a bull. He and Cell threw down, but Cell still made short work of him. It was a just and fair asswhoopin' by Duracell's standards. He was in control tonight and didn't even come close to losing it. He stopped all on his own with no need for me to interfere… that's how I knew.

When the cops burst through the diner doors, he automatically dropped to his knees, lacing his fingers behind his head. Hayley screamed out and pushed off of me, and I let her go. She fell to her knees in front of him as the cops started to cuff him up and clung to him, her arms around his neck.

The cops backed off confused and looked at me and it was Hayley's dad who spoke up from the kitchen.

"No, officers, you've got the wrong guy. He's the one that stopped them from hurting my little girl." Jake stabbed a finger at the kid in the red polo. "That little bastard sexually assaulted my daughter, these men stopped them."

I stood, powerless for this part of things, adrenaline raging through my system, and made eye contact with Cell who was smirking at me over Hayley's shoulder. He turned his head and kissed her temple and said, "It's okay, darlin'. Go with Blue, let him look after you."

And he was right. Cell did the heavy lifting, I did the rational explaining and emotional clean up… it was us; how we worked, and I was ready to do my part in things. I shook myself as if coming awake and put myself into action, kneeling behind Hayley and pulling her back against me.

She was scared and shaking. The adrenaline wearing off, her system crashing; her eyes leaking tears she couldn't control causing her makeup to run in muddy tracks down her cheeks.

"Take her home, bro," Cell said grimly, while Hayley's dad stood to one side, talking in earnest with one of the sheriff's deputies.

"Alright, come over here and sit until we get this sorted out." The deputy who'd put Cell into cuffs, led him over to the lunch counter and helped get him seated onto one of the stools.

"Ma'am, can I ask you some questions?"

Hayley looked up at the deputy from where she'd been staring at Cell and nodded, finally, once his words sank in.

"Can you tell me what happened here?"

Hayley sniffed and nodded slowly. "I served them and then that one," she pointed at the dude in the red polo with the fork sticking out of the back of his hand, "he grabbed me and pulled me down into his lap." Her face crumbled and she scrunched it in an effort not to cry. She took a deep breath and couldn't keep from breaking down, but pushed out in a warbled voice, "He stuck his hand up my skirt, and grabbed me by the vagina… That's when my boyfriend came in and stopped him from doing anything else."

"You the boyfriend?" he asked me, and I opened my mouth, but Hayley clung to me and stopped me with her own voice.

"They both are. Judge me if you want, but he was just trying to protect me!"

"I see," the deputy said, and his mouth turned down at the corners.

"And what did you do?" he asked me.

"I just kept Hayley out of the way."

"Uh huh, so you're telling me that one," he pointed at Cell, "did all the damage?"

"Wouldn't you if it were your wife or daughter?" I asked evenly.

The deputy looked at Hayley who was huddled miserably in my arms and back at Cell whose face was painted in a thick layer of seething hatred as he bored holes in the rich kid with his gaze. He looked back over his shoulder at Hayley's dad and said, "Jake, where were you?"

"Kitchen, and I came out as soon as I heard my little girl scream. Paul just got to her before I could, and it's a damn good thing, too. I would've killed the little bastard. Since he had them, I called you."

The deputy raised a hand to cut Jake off and made several notes in his notepad. More deputies had arrived and were standing around waiting for any cues from their coworkers on who was getting locked up.

"Ma'am, you want to press assault charges?"

"Absolutely," Hayley said.

"Alright, hook that one up, take him to the hospital," he said indicating red polo.

"Unfortunately, I'm going to have to take your boyfriend in, too."

"What? Why? He stopped him from hurting me then that one attacked my boyfriend!"

"Their buddy says that's not how it happened, and until we get this cleared up, it's best if all of them come down to the station."

"Take it easy, baby. Blue, get her the fuck out of here and take her home. Call Dragon and see if he can't get me a lawyer."

"You're sure you want to do that?" one of the other deputies called to Cell.

"Fuck yeah, only thing I don't trust more than pigs is fuckin' rich little twats. I ain't stupid, I know my rights – lawyer!"

"Right." The deputy talking to us sighed. "Get him the fuck out of here."

Another deputy, a woman with long, light brown hair in a ponytail went up to Cell and heaved on his arm. He stood up and let her march him out the door and into the night. Hayley burst into a fresh round of tears and I held her tight, shushing her and reassuring her it would be alright when on the inside, I felt just as bleak. I fucking hated that Cell was going on the inside without me, even though I knew the inside in this case wasn't like the inside last time.

These were just a bunch of rich little fucks, and probably would get off scot-fucking-free. Cell on the other hand was an ex-con and was probably looking at felony assault, not to mention a second strike with this. *Goddammit...*

"Jake," I said and he looked over to me. I dipped my chin to indicate Hayley and he nodded.

"Take her home. I'll close up and clean up here... and thanks, the both of you."

I nodded and looked to the deputy. "You can go. If we need anything else, we'll call you. It'd be nice if you'd come down in the morning and file official statements and complaints. Might help your... friend."

"Thanks," I muttered and took Hayley out front.

I helped her into the passenger seat of her cage and got into the driver's seat. She handed me the keys from her apron pocket and huddled miserably, gripping my free hand that wasn't on the wheel the whole way back to her place.

I guess we knew why girls had been quitting left and right, I guess we also knew why they wouldn't talk about it – fear and money were both pretty fucking powerful motivators.

29

H ayley...

He took me home, held my hand, and waited until I was safe in a warm bath in my studio's bathroom before he stepped out into the studio itself and made his phone calls. It was awkward, listening to him. I could tell he wasn't comfortable speaking. While I couldn't make out what he was saying, the cadence of his voice was halting with one-word answers punctuated with long swaths of his boot heels clonking back and forth along the polished concrete as he paced.

Finally, there was a long silence where I imagined him letting out a gusty sigh, his head back as far as it would go as he tried to work through easing the tension riding his posture. When he came back into the bathroom, it was without his jacket and cut, and without his phone. He sat down on the closed lid of the toilet and reached out, chasing a stray lock of my hair behind my ear where it'd escaped my bun.

"How you doing?" he asked and I sniffed.

"Scared."

"They can't hurt you now, Little One."

"No, not for me," I said scrubbing my face with damp hands, "for Cell."

He nodded in understanding and sighed. "I get you. Cell's gonna be fine, though. He'll be arraigned in the morning, and bail won't be a problem."

"What if there's a trial? I mean, he didn't do anything!"

Blue shook his head. "There won't be. This'll all be plead out. It's how it works. With luck, it'll be a misdemeanor and some community service, no jail time."

"You really think so?" I asked, desperate to believe him. He smiled but it wasn't terribly convincing.

"Yeah, I really do."

He pulled the washcloth down from the towel bar and dipped it into the water, raising it to my shoulders and swiping it gently across my back where it was exposed above the waterline, warming me as I hugged my knees and shivered, but not from any actual cold.

"Will you stay with me tonight?" I asked.

"You know I will."

I nodded and let him console me the way that only Blue could, with gentle touches and soft kisses along my skin, kneading tense muscles with just the right amount of pressure until they gave up all their secrets. He let me stay in the bath until my fingers were pruned and the water had grown tepid and I was still reluctant to get out.

I liked the closeness of the tub and bathroom. I felt shattered, and it was like the close space held the broken pieces together while Blue worked to fuse them into a whole that was more beautiful than it had been before... like I did with my glass and my windows.

"I love you, and I'm sorry this happened to you," he murmured while I stood in ankle deep water, the only sounds in the small space the water draining and his hands rubbing me briskly through the towel, drying my skin.

"I love you, too… and I'm sorry it happened to you, too. That Cell is in jail… I feel like it's all my fault." Blue shook his head and pulled me tight against his chest, kissing the top of my hair.

"Not your fault. Not at all, Not Cell's fault either. I told you, if he liked you, you'd never be safer. That's what I meant."

"It was terrifying, seeing him like that."

"Yeah."

There was silence between us, but then again, there was really nothing to say. I put my arms around Blue and held tightly to him, taking shelter against his hard body and he was right – I felt safe. Safe from any kind of harm coming from any direction and that was an empowering feeling.

I looked up at him and felt a measure of calm return to me and he asked me, "Are you tired?"

I nodded. "I really am."

"You sound surprised."

"I sort of am… I mean, I feel like I should be wired and wide awake."

He chuckled. "Wait until you actually lay down."

"You want to sleep here or in the house?"

He paused as if really thinking it through before finally saying, "I'd love to see your room but what about your dad?"

"I think he'd prefer knowing I was in the house, but I completely understand if you'd be more comfortable out here."

"I'll go wherever you want to go, Little One. After the night you've had, it's all about you."

I smiled up at him and led him out of the bathroom. He went over and grabbed his jacket and cut, following me as I quickly stepped across the backyard to the steps up into the house. I was wrapped only in a towel, and it was late enough at night that I didn't worry about the neighbors. He followed me close behind and up into the house, holding my hand as we both ghosted up the stairs and into my room. I shut the door behind us, and he hung his jacket and cut on the doorknob.

"I feel like a teenager," he confessed and I smiled.

"Me, too." I dropped the towel and reached for him and he came willingly, dipping his head to capture my mouth with his own, his warm hands moving over my cooler skin.

He came with me to the bed, shedding his clothing a piece at a time, making love to me slowly, with care and consideration and it was just what I needed. To know he still loved me, to know that my body was mine and, in some ways, his, to do with what we please because *I* chose it to be that way.

Blue was careful and slow, and for once, I wished he were Cell. Rougher, more demanding; it's what I craved which was also frightening and confusing after what had just happened to me.

"What's wrong?" Blue asked, mid stroke and I knew he would understand, and that I could tell him, so I did. I could trust Blue not to make fun of me, get angry or disgusted with me. He was the most nonjudgmental person I knew and my faith in him was maintained when he pulled out of me and said, "Get on your knees," in a rough growl I don't think I'd ever heard come from him.

I got onto my knees and leaned way down low to the mattress, gripping the sheets in my fists and biting my lower lip, craving him, needing him, and he gave me just what I needed. He lined himself up and slammed into me, bottoming out against my cervix with that sharp, sweet pain.

"Oh, yes, harder!" I begged and he gave me what I wanted. My bedroom echoing with the fervor of our sex, the sharp reports of flesh hitting flesh, the force with which he did it setting a bass tempo of thumping, a deeper sound beneath the sharper slapping.

God, it wasn't enough. I *wanted* it to hurt, I *needed* it deeper, harder, faster and I whined without words my frustration.

This was Blue, though. Blue who was far more in tune with the subtle nuances of a person than Cell ever was, and so he knew… he saw it and heard it and delivered, grabbing me by my arms above my elbows and hauling back on them, jerking my back into a bowed arch that was severe but not uncomfortable. Still…

Oh. My. God.

He touched places inside of me that I didn't even know I had. Each long stroke of his body into mine awakening sensations I never even dreamed were possible. My nipples tightened, sparkles invading the edges of my vision, as pleasure flowed through me warm and inviting, raising me up on a cloud of euphoria.

The fall was amazing.

I undulated with the crashing waves of my orgasm but that part of me felt far away… my body that is. The part of me that mattered, that undefinable thing that made a person who they were, plummeted as from a great height and kept falling, warm winds whipping past until I fell completely, madly and as deeply in love with Blue as anyone possibly could.

Anyone who could connect with another person like this, so meaningfully, so deeply, was a treasure that was to be held onto and coveted. I felt myself locked into them. The piece that seemingly fit between them and made them whole because I had both known and understood for a long time, there was no Blue without Duracell and there was no

Duracell without Blue. It's just how they were. It just was what it was and there wasn't any changing it.

Duracell coming to my defense, protecting me like he had, sacrificing himself like he had... going to jail, perhaps even worse for me just told me that I was right where I was supposed to be and it killed a part of me that he wasn't with us right now, that he wasn't the one giving me the punishing sex that I craved.

I had entered into this arrangement knowing that I would love Blue and figuring that if anything was going to happen, it was that I was simply going to have to put up with or tolerate Cell in order to be with Blue until something changed.

I never in a million years expected to collapse into my bed, Blue lying on top of me, inside of me, and miss Cell as keenly as I did now. I never expected to feel this swell of longing and love for the cruder, more violent man... but I did. I choked up hard and felt myself sob with how much I wanted him here with us.

Blue pushed himself up and touched my back asking me uncertainly, "Hayley, what is it?"

"I miss him, I want him here with us and I'm so very afraid of what's going to happen to him... he didn't do anything wrong. He was just protecting me, and now..."

Blue gathered me to his chest and made a soothing sound, kissing every bit of me that his lips could reach.

"I know, my little one... I miss him, too. I'm afraid for him, too, but it's good this way. Having one of us at least, here to look after you."

I nodded. "But who will look after him in that awful place?"

Blue was silent then and I looked up into his solemn gray eyes; at the worry radiating from them. I realized I'd just voiced his greatest fear and asked helplessly, "What do we do?"

"The only thing we can do. Wait until morning, get him out as soon as we can. Try not to get too worked up. Cell took care of himself long before I ever showed up, then took care of us both. He'll be okay for one night. Tomorrow, we can try and take care of him but that's never really been how he works."

"How do you take care of a man who doesn't want to be taken care of?" I asked, genuinely curious.

"Make yourself available to meet whatever need he's got when he gets out of there."

I nodded and swallowed hard. With his unpredictable nature, that seemed to be a tall order, especially after the savagery I'd seen him show just hours ago.

"He loves you, as much as he's capable of it, Hayley," Blue said and I cuddled into his arms. "He really sucks at showing it, but I swear to you, he does. He would have taken those boys out regardless for their actions but not because it was the right thing to do, more because he loves a good fight. The fact that he took them apart as hard as he did and with that level of heat means he was pissed they touched you."

"Will I ever understand him?" I asked.

"Probably about as much as I do, which isn't as much as you'd think."

"I can pretty much forget ever hearing it from him, can't I?"

"What? That he loves you?"

"Yeah."

He held me tighter and said, "Yeah... but that's what you've got me for."

It was surprisingly a lot more comforting than I think Blue realized. I needed him and his softness. I needed that reminder that I was loved, and Blue made me feel that. I held to him tightly and he eased us down, so that we were more comfortable and for sleep, pulling the blankets and quilts on my bed up over us.

"I love that you love us," he murmured against my ear just as I was on that first edge of sleep.

I loved that, too. I loved that I took the chance, faced down the risk, and dared to love them both… they completed me.

30

D uracell...

　　"Man, this is fucking bullshit. He sexually assaults my fuckin' girl and I'm the one that's gonna end up locked up for a year?" My lawyer looked at me from across the table and blinked slowly.

"Maybe you didn't hear me, but what you are facing if you take this to trial is a class B felony. First degree assault is *serious,* Mr. Glenn. Pleading it down to a class D is a gift from God."

"It was a motherfucking *fork,*" I argued.

"A fork with which you did grievous bodily harm! You could have killed that boy with that fork, and as it is, his hand will never be the same."

"Good."

My lawyer pinched the bridge of his nose and shook his head.

"I strongly urge you to accept the deal."

"And take a second strike? Fuck no." I got up from the table.

"Mr. Glenn! What do you want me to tell the prosecutor?" he called after me.

"No fuckin' dice! See him in court!" I called over my shoulder and left the fuckwit's office.

It'd been two weeks since what had gone down with Hayley at Jake's diner, and she'd bounced back pretty good. I didn't regret for one minute what I'd done, but then again, I wasn't in the business of regret. It was a pretty fucking useless emotion when you stopped to think about it. I got on my bike out front of the lawyer's office, pissed that I'd had to take a day off of work for this shit.

A long hard ride was calling my fuckin' name and maybe, just maybe a long hard fuck after would help get rid of my pissed-off mood. These fuckin' charges weren't going to go away. Not even if I killed the little bastards, so I had to either accept the plea or go to trial. I could think of a couple of ways that could go down. Jake, Hayley, and Blue were definitely on my side, it was the rich little bastard's butt buddies that were the problem.

I fired up the Harley and left a line of rubber down the road as I left out of there. I hit the highway at full speed headed back for the club, but even full speed wasn't enough, so I did what I always did when I sought wind therapy; I twisted the throttle that much more.

I passed any number of cages using the left passing lane until some dipshit started to slow down with me coming up on him. I ducked around him and saw it too late. There wasn't any stopping it, there wasn't any slowing down or slamming on the brakes. I knew when my ticket had been punched and I saw it in that flash of silver as the car turned in front of me.

I slammed into the passenger side front fender and was airborne, just like that. I resigned myself, and it felt like a fucking millennium before I came down. I'd done a full goddamned flip and landed on my back, skidding along the pavement, my head snapping back and connecting even as I *heard* shit in my body go snap, crackle, and pop.

The wind was knocked clean out of me and I stared at the blazing blue sky, the sun bright and suddenly fierce, my sunglasses missing. I lay there, unable to move, trying like hell to drag in a breath, mouth flooded with the taste of copper as tires squealed and shouting went up.

I couldn't turn my head. I wanted to. I wanted to push it back more, but my brain bucket against the ground was tipping my chin into my chest. I finally got that fucking breath and shit was bad, shit was really bad. It *ground* into my lungs, and the fact the pain wasn't there told me this was it.

I always wondered if it hurt to die, and I guess I was getting my answer.

A woman kneeled beside me, tears streaming down her face which was white with panic as she cried, "I'm so sorry! I didn't see you. Oh, my God, I'm so sorry!"

Sorry wasn't going to save my ass, but it sure was going to save the courts a gang of money prosecuting it.

I thought about Blue.

I thought about Hayley.

I fucking knew regret then. I knew anger, too, as I fought to breathe, dragging in breath after breath.

I looked at the woman that'd hit me and I raged on the inside though I doubt she could see it. I could make her feel it though…

"Should… have looked… twice. I had someone… to… go… home… to…"

Shock and devastation spread out through her eyes and I smiled. The last thought I had before the world went black was the taste of my little boy Blue's lips and the silky wet heat of Hayley wrapped around my dick.

Fuck.

I would miss them.

31

B lue...

I stood in the hall at Doc's hospital, numb. They'd brought Cell here they said. Dragon had gotten the call because it was club doctrine that we all put him as our emergency contact of the emergency feature of our cellphones... because of this... precisely because of this.

The rest of the club waited in the ER waiting room behind me as I paced up and down the hall. When the doctor came out, pulling that fucking scrub cap off his head like every bad fucking movie's rendition of this scenario played out... I knew... I just fucking knew, and it broke me.

"I'm so sorry," he said addressing the lot of us. I didn't really hear anything he had to say after that. I was too busy staring at the ceiling while my eyes fucking watered, trying to remember what it was to breathe and I couldn't.

The automatic doors whooshed open behind me, and I turned around. Hayley and Mel came through the doors and Hayley stopped, mid-step at the look on my face.

I stared at her, committing every line and curve, the deep well of her brown eyes glassy with tears and didn't want to be the one... the one to break it to her, to crush every dream she had of the three of us while every single one I had burned inside me to the motherfucking ground.

But this was us... and as us, it had to be me.

I shook my head, once left, once right and I watched her fall. I watched her crumble right in front of my eyes. Her legs going out from under her, the tears spilling down her cheeks as she screamed, the most painful sound I'd ever heard. The echo of what it sounded like as my own heart cracked in two.

Melody tried to stabilize my little one. Going to her knees beside her, and I knew I should go. That I should be the one... but I couldn't. I couldn't hold her up while I was spiraling out of control all on my own, spinning in a fucking freefall, about to crash and erupt into flames myself.

I turned so I didn't have to look and started walking. I had to get away. I needed to regroup. I needed to figure my shit out. I needed to find Duracell and ask him what to do but I couldn't. I wouldn't ever be able to, ever again.

I don't remember what I did after that. It was impossible to know. All I knew was that I felt sick. Terribly, terribly ill. I shook with it, I rolled off the bed onto my hands and knees so thirsty.

I turned my head and my vision swam and things vaguely came back to me. The awful look on Hayley's face. Leaving the hospital. The bar. The bitch I fucked in the back of *Sugars* and the coke I did off her tits... the alcohol.

A bender from hell... that's what this is. You're coming off a bender from hell.

Still, Cell was gone and he wasn't coming back. My being in his room didn't change that. Not a goddamned thing was different. *Cell was*

*gone and he wasn't coming back because there ain't no coming back...
once you're dead, there ain't no coming back.*

I screamed my rage and pain to the empty room wordlessly and punched the carpet. It felt good, so I did it again. Knuckles bruising, the rug burning them, I punched the floor again and again and again the pain making me feel *alive*.

But Cell wasn't because he was dead, and there ain't no coming back... not from that.

The door opened and Dani stood in it, a glass of water in one hand. She looked down on me, pity clouding her bright blue eyes, dulling their sparkle, and I looked away. I put a bleeding hand out to her in a bid to ward her off and keep her away, but she ignored me.

She stepped into the room and shut the door behind her. She kneeled next to me and pushed the cool glass against my palm. I suddenly remembered how thirsty I was and sat up, shoving the water into my face, drinking greedily, some of it dripping onto my shirt, but I didn't care. I threw the glass against the wall and it shattered. Dani jumped and sat back on her heels and I felt bad about that. I felt horrible about that, actually.

Dani didn't deserve to be scared... not of me.

I put a hand on her shoulder, and she wrapped both of her slim hands around my forearm like a hug. I needed a hug... I needed... *I needed...*

I keeled over onto my side, my head in her lap and pulled my knees to my chest. I was lost... Cell's little boy Blue only without Cell there to watch my ass and protect me. I didn't know what to do. I missed him. I loved him... I didn't know what to do.

Dani petted my head and whispered, "Shh, I know... I know... You don't have to."

"I don't know what to do," I repeated and only then realized that I kept repeating it like some kind of a mantra.

"I don't know what to do... I don't know what to do... *I don't know what to do...*"

32

H ayley...
I didn't know what to do.

For myself or for him... The look of raw pain in his eyes in the hospital corridor told me everything I needed to know, and I just folded like his paper creations, only instead of something beautiful, I was left as nothing more than a crumpled sobbing mess on the hospital floor.

I looked up when Dragon took my hands and helped me to my feet. Blue was gone... just like that... gone. *Just like Cell? God, please don't let it be just like Cell... don't let me lose them both.*

"I know, 'salright, chica. We got you." I stood shaking and nauseous and took the comfort provided to me by the surrounding club members, dying inside like I'd lost an important part of me... and I had. We both had, except I felt like, in that instant, I'd lost them both.

"I don't know what to do," I said mournfully, and Dragon hugged me tight.

"Ain't gotta do nothing, honey, that's what we're for."

I wanted to believe him, and it turned out that he was right... I didn't have to do anything like plan the funeral, or cook for anyone, or handle any of that stuff. I just had to show up, which I did, and hope against hope that Blue...

I didn't see Blue. He didn't come to me. He didn't call or answer the phone. He didn't answer my texts either.

I knew he was hurting, and I was hurting too, but I needed to tell him. I'd needed to tell them both, but I couldn't. Not now... but one day stretched into two, then two into four and then it was the wake and I was at the club with all of these people and all I wanted to do was die myself, but I couldn't.

Not with the life growing inside of me.

"Have you seen him?" I asked numbly.

Melody was sitting on one side of me, and Dani took a seat on the other. She put a hand on my back and rubbed useless circles, her face full of sympathy as I stared at Duracell's prone form in his casket.

He looked like he was asleep, and I hated that, because it was all wrong because even in sleep, he was tense, and his face held that wicked edge of danger and he didn't look like that lying there... he looked *gone*... because he was, and I would never see him again. I would never feel him again, and I would never tell him that he had a fifty-fifty chance that he was going to be a father and that killed me more than anything.

No one knew. Not even my dad. I wouldn't tell anyone until I could tell Blue or Cell and I'd never had the chance... I'd only taken the test and found out two days before...

I'm going to be a single parent. He's abandoned you... my mind whispered, and I faltered, the tears pouring from my eyes, body shaking with the sobs I tried so hard to suppress but couldn't.

Melody and Dani both hugged me and tried to console me, but I needed Blue.

"Nobody's heard from him, but it's Blue... his whole world revolved around Cell, until you," Dani said kindly.

Everett came near with her brand-new baby boy in her arms, standing near and delivering the message...

"He's here, he just walked in."

I looked up hopeful, but the look on her face, it wasn't a good one. If anything, it was downright tempestuous. I stood up and looked past her at Blue... but he wasn't *my* Blue.

His hair was unkempt, and he wore the same clothes that he'd had on in the hospital four days earlier. His eyes were red rimmed but whether it was from a lack of sleep or drugs, I couldn't tell, and it *did* look like he was on something.

I felt my shoulders drop and I shook my head.

I couldn't... I couldn't tell him, not when he was like this. I *wouldn't* tell him. Not if this was how it was going to be.

I pressed my hands to my stomach and made a hard decision right then and there. I would do this alone. I couldn't and wouldn't expose a baby, *my* baby to Blue. Not when he was like this... drunk, strung out. I loved him, I loved him with everything that I was, and I didn't want to lose him, but the way he looked at me, seeing me without even really seeing *me* told me that this was a lost cause... at least for now.

"Hayley?" he asked, his voice dreamlike and far away.

I closed my eyes, took a moment, and just *breathed.*

"Melody," I said, voice hollow, "do you think Archer could take me home?"

"Yeah, honey... two seconds."

Dani looked at me with deep empathy and stood with me.

"Don't worry, this isn't the end," she said and I sniffed hard. I so desperately wanted to believe her, but looking at Blue, the way he was now... I wanted to help him. I didn't want to give up and I didn't want to walk away. I wanted to go to him and weather the storm with him but... *but the baby*...

Two of his brothers, Trigger and Reaver stood in front of him, protecting me from him so I could make a clean run for it and I realized that Blue was dangerous like this. Unpredictable, and scary, like Cell had been sober.

Archer was standing near me and grasped my elbow gently. I looked up at him and he asked with kindness in his eyes, "You want you should say one last goodbye?"

He jerked his head in the direction of Cell's open casket and I nodded. He let me go and I went to the glossy black box that held my lover's body, fresh tears falling. I smoothed my hands back and forth over the satin and heard Blue, growing more agitated behind me.

"I love you," I whispered, and bent, lightly pressing my lips against Cell's cold and waxy ones. One last goodbye.

"Hayley!" Blue cried.

I let Archer lead me away, to the back door and Blue shouted at my back, "I folded them, but they were his words!"

I swallowed hard and marched out, the sounds of a scuffle breaking out behind me. I needed to wait until he was sober. I needed to wait... I needed to wait but I needed him now. I needed him to put his arms around me and I needed him to hold me, but Blue just wasn't *there* right now.

I didn't know who that was.

"It'll be okay. Not the first time it's happened. We'll keep him here, let him finish out his fuckin' bender, and when he's sobered up and himself again, he'll come a crawlin'. I've seen it a thousand times."

"I don't know that I can do this," I said honestly.

"You ain't gotta do shit except breathe, baby girl. Blue ain't himself. You ain't yourself, and no one expects either one of you to be – not after something like this. I know it hurts like hell, but it'll get better. Just let the club do what it's supposed to do. Let it look after y'all until you can look after each other." I turned to look at who'd spoken and found Dragon standing outside the back door. I hadn't even known he'd followed us out.

"He's gonna need you, just as surely as you're gonna need him, especially with that." He pointed and I looked down to realize I'd pressed my hands protectively to my stomach again.

Tears tracked down my face and I nodded, looking back up. Archer took a step back and was smiling, a ghost of a thing.

"Well ain't that some shit?"

I sniffed and shrugged. "Judge me if you want, but I don't know whose it is."

"Who cares." Archer shrugged. "It's a baby, a life, and that's precious."

"Ain't our place to judge, sweetheart. Arch, you go on and get Ms. Hayley home… you an' Mel look after her. She's family now."

I let Archer lead me away and for the first time since this nightmare began… I felt hope and like I was on solid ground again. Blue's words echoed in my head for the entire drive back to my house and I went straight for my studio and my loft. I kicked off my heels inside the door and went straight for the ladder, hauling myself up into the loft.

I paused, heart thundering in my chest and reached out for the first folded bit of beautiful hanging from my ceiling and plucked it from its fishing line. With shaking fingers, I carefully picked it apart and when

I unfolded it all the way, I turned it over to the blank side of the receipt... except it was just as Blue had said... it wasn't blank.

"I'm getting to adore the way you walk across this place. I can't help but watch you, coming or going. I know that's probably creepy as fuck, but I don't care. Call us..."

The lines ended in Duracell's phone number. I stood there trembling, reading the lines over and over again before the slip of paper fell from my fingertips and I reached for the next... desperate to read what he'd said. The words like an echo, almost making me believe he was still here.

33

B**lue…**
Dani set a steaming black mug with the club's logo down in front of me and I reached out with shaking hands to grab it. The tape holding the IV Doc had running into the inside of one of my elbows pulled and I winced.

It was just fluids, and I think some antibiotics seeing as I'd more than likely had unprotected sex somewhere on my coke and booze fueled misadventure somewhere. I'd be getting a full panel and I'd have to come clean with Hayley about it – that is, if she even wanted to ever see me again.

I took a slug of the straight black coffee in the mug and winced. Dani took the seat across from me and looked me over, worried, but with that neutral look that said she was trying very hard to hide what she was really feeling and thinking.

"Whatever it is, just tell me," I said miserably.

"Just know I say this with love, but you *really* are an asshole this time."

"I know."

"I want to chew you out."

"Please do."

"You sure about that?"

"Yes."

"You *really* sure?"

I contemplated her for a moment, one dark brow elegantly raised, and Shelly dropped into the seat next to Dani's.

"Too late, I'm on it," she said to her then looked at me and said, "Just what the fuck were you thinking?" I grunted and slid my eyes to the side and to the floor.

"That's just it, I wasn't."

"No, you weren't and who do you think got to suffer for it?"

"Shells, go find yer ol' man. Dani, you too."

Oh shit.

The girls wordlessly got up and disappeared and I sat waiting. There was the click of a zippo cap and the familiar *fwoosh!* of it lighting up. The cap clicked shut and it was the ominous echo of boot heels against concrete as Dragon circled around and came into view.

"You look like hell," he said and I nodded.

I didn't say anything. I mean, what was there to say?

My president sighed and said, "Yer gonna have to find yer voice this time. Ain't no one left to speak for yah."

I gripped the coffee mug between my fingers until the nail beds turned white and sucked in a breath. The dig had hurt. It hurt like hell, but he was right... Cell was gone.

"I'm on my own." I hadn't meant for it to come out like that... out loud, but it had, and Dragon huffed a derisive laugh.

"Is that what you really think, boy?"

I looked up sharply and he narrowed his eyes, dropping into the seat Dani had vacated and kicking back. He ashed his cigarette into my coffee and I relinquished the cup. He slid it closer and burned a hole in me with his gaze.

"I asked you a question," he said and I swallowed hard, shaking my head. He raised his eyebrows and I sucked in a deep breath, the air, tainted by his cigarette smoke, gave me the courage to respond. He smoked the same brand as Cell.

"I didn't think so until just now," I said honestly and he gave a nod.

"Good answer, and yer right on both accounts. Yer not alone, that's what being a member of this club is. Cell may be gone, but you've still got the rest of us. You know... your brothers, who I might add, have been lookin' after yer girl for you while we've been waitin' around for you to pull yer head out yer ass."

"I don't even know what day it is," I said honestly.

"Funeral was six days ago, and while you've been wallowing in your own self-pity? Your woman's been handling it all on her own." I met Dragon's disapproving gaze and he heaved a heavy sigh.

"She okay?" I asked.

"What d'you think?"

I wanted to ask him to cut me a break, but I was well aware I didn't deserve one. I sighed and swiped a hand over my face and told the truth, "I don't know what to do."

"Man the fuck up. Take a fuckin' shower, clean yourself up and go see if you got a relationship left with that girl to save." He eyed me up and down and added, "No matter what the outcome, stay out of the fuckin'

230

bottle for a while. Seriously, surprise yer fuckin' liver and drink some fuckin' water."

"Yes, sir."

Dragon sighed heavy and said, "You need to tread lightly when it comes to that girl, she's stronger than you know, and she's got some shit to fight for. Don't expect it to be an easy row to hoe. She dumps yer ass, you've fuckin' earned it. Just know that even if shit goes south between you an' her, the club's gonna be there for her. We know she was with both of you, but we're treatin' her like the ol' lady of a fallen brother. She'll be looked after the rest of her days. Always has a place to go."

I nodded, tears collecting in my eyes. I was grateful for that. The club didn't have to do that. Not when neither Cell, nor I, had claimed her as our property. I wanted to, now… I just may not have a choice in the matter.

"Go on, git. Take that fuckin' thing with you. I suspect you'll feel more like yerself once yer cleaned up."

I nodded. "Thank you."

"Don't thank me. All the shit we've done so far has been for yer woman."

I searched Dragon's face and saw nothing but tough love there. He may have said it was for Hayley, but it'd been just as much for me, too. I sucked in a deep breath, in through my nose and out through my mouth and got my ass up, gripping the IV stand I was hooked up to and rolling it toward the back door so I could go do what I was told.

The IV bag was damn near empty and I still didn't have to piss. I wasn't exactly a hot mess anymore, thanks to the care of my brothers and best friend… I guess I was just more like a giant steaming pile.

I sure felt that way, anyway.

34

H ayley...
Three days after Duracell's wake, two days after we'd buried him, and still no Blue. My father had forbidden me to work; Melody was picking up my day shifts and the girl that'd been on days with her while I'd worked nights had gone to night shift.

I'd been through every single bit of origami hanging from my ceiling and had lain among the drifts of scraps of paper for over a day, hugging that damn stuffed unicorn from the Harvest Festival that Duracell had won me; wallowing in my misery until my morning sickness had forced me from my bed and down my loft's ladder.

I was trying to force myself to eat but wasn't hungry. I wanted to do everything right by the baby, but I felt frozen. Scared to death of telling anyone. I hadn't even told my father.

It was late and I was sitting in front of my latest project. An abstract, classic Victorian stained-glass round window that was meant for no one in particular. I typically sold pieces like these on consignment at a local antique and gift shop but the joy in my work had left me.

I was oscillating wildly between bouts of tears, rage, and pain and I hated it, but I didn't dare start taking the anti-depressants again. I'd started forgetting to take them when I'd been with Cell and Blue... hadn't taken them at all since before Christmas and now... now I couldn't take them. Now, I had to be strong on my own and you know? I could do that.

I closed my eyes and tried to take a deep breath around the crushing weight of grief that'd taken residence on my chest and the rage bubbled to the surface. The helplessness, the powerlessness rising hot and fierce with it and I snapped. I swept the window off my worktable and let it crash to the floor, screaming wordlessly into the dim light of my studio in the only way I had left to *just let it out.*

It was cold comfort. All of it. It also left a giant mess for me to clean up.

I got up from the stool I was sitting on and stepped right on a piece of glass, screaming "Dammit!" to the high ceiling.

"Stupid, Hayley!" I berated myself. "How could you be so *stupid*!?"

I didn't know if I meant the glass, or if I meant falling in love with them... I guess it could mean either or both at this point.

I sat back up on the stool and carefully pulled the broken shard out of my foot, staring at the red coated glass as blood pattered to the concrete. So red, like heart's blood...

I closed my eyes and looked at all of the broken shards as another thick drop landed on another shard of glass and took a deep breath and let it out.

I knew, not what I *wanted* to do, but what I *needed* to do...

35

B^{lue…}

I still had a job. I couldn't fucking believe that one… but I did. Maybe because losing two of us had been pretty damaging or crippling. Who the fuck knew? All I knew was that I went back to work to see if I could get my job back and the foreman had grunted and said I'd never lost it and welcome back from my fuckin' vacation.

When I'd stood there dumbfounded, he'd told me how many hours of vacation I had left and to get to it before he changed his mind.

I went back to the club, cleaned up, and now I was on Jake and Hayley's doorstep, my heart pounding in my chest, terrified that I wouldn't even be allowed to see her. He opened the door at my knock and grunted.

"What do you want?"

"I was hoping to see Hayley."

"What if she doesn't want to see you?" he demanded, and he had every right to be pissed.

"Then I'll leave her be, but I would really like to hear that from her if it's alright."

He looked me over and sighed, nodding. He opened the door wider and let me in the house, shutting it behind us.

"She's in her studio."

"Thank you."

"Don't thank me. If it were up to me, I'd've shut that door right in your damn face, but it ain't up to me and I'm scared for my little girl again."

"What do you mean?" I asked.

He sighed and said, "She's gone quiet again. Won't even talk to me, barely even comes in the damn house. Just stays out there all day and all night. I can't get her to take her pills, I can't get her to talk, or go out, and I don't want her coming back to work… not yet. I don't know what to do,"

"Let me try?"

He harrumphed, "Not sure what that'll do; you dropped her like a bad habit. She not only lost that friend of yers, she lost you, too – at least as far as I'm concerned. Leaves me asking myself what yer gonna do when the going gets tough in other ways."

"That's fair," I agreed, nodding.

"You hurt my little girl," he accused. "Can't say I'm ever gonna let you come back from that. Not after how many times she's been hurt before."

I tried not to let my irritation with people get to me, I mean, *I lost my best friend, my lover and love, too*. Losing Cell had hurt me bone deep.

Losing Cell had hurt Hayley, too. Losing you, what do you think that did? my traitorous mind whispered.

"You better go on, before I change my mind," Jake said, and I nodded and went through the house and out back. The lights were on inside her studio, the crickets chirping lazily out here, my heart picking up and keeping pace with them as I crossed to her studio door.

I opened it up on silent hinges and stopped cold, staring at her in a white high-low dress, her bare feet poised on the bottom rung of her stool as she bent over her work, a curl of smoke rising from the solder she laid.

She called over her shoulder, "Dad, in or out please. I don't want moths coming in."

I stepped in and shut the door, clearing my throat. She looked up, blowing her bangs out of her eyes, her braid slipping over her shoulder to lay along her back and she froze.

"What are you doing here?" she asked, and it wasn't unfriendly, but it wasn't friendly either... if anything, it was cautious.

"Came to see you."

She bowed her head and switched off her soldering iron, setting it aside. She got to her feet and I eyed a bandage around one and took a step forward.

"What happened?"

"It's old... like three days old. I stepped on a piece of glass."

"How did that happen? You're usually so careful."

"It just... did..."

She hugged herself and I took another cautious step forward. She didn't retreat but she didn't step to meet me, either.

"Seriously, Blue, what do you want?" she asked softly.

I halted three strides from her and sighed. "To beg forgiveness... to see if you still want me... a lot of things I don't really deserve."

"You're right," she swallowed hard, "you don't."

Ouch.

"Hayley, I'm so sorry…"

"Me, too," she said simply, her eyes welling. She sniffed and they spilled over and my heart broke all over again, only this time it was for her.

"Fuck, what have I done?" I uttered and she looked at me sharply.

"I loved him, too… I mean, not like *you* obviously, but I did… and I love you, but I couldn't be around you. Not when you were like that, not when you weren't *safe*."

I'd scared her, and that made me feel like shit. She smoothed her hands down the front of her body and it made me ache for her.

"Where *were* you?" she demanded.

I cleared the lump out of my throat and sighed. "I can't really tell you, mostly because I don't really know… at least I don't remember, not all of it."

"Well, what *do* you remember?"

I barked a derisive laugh. "Nothing good, Little One."

She closed her eyes and swallowed hard, and I echoed the sentiment.

"Well, tell me what you *do* remember," she ordered, and I rolled my lips together.

"I'm afraid if I do, you really won't want me around anymore."

"Well, that's the risk, the price you pay, for abandoning your girlfriend when your mutual boyfriend dies."

That was a fair point, even if I had never considered Cell my *boyfriend*, it was closer to the truth than it wasn't; so, I couldn't quibble semantics on the issue.

I sighed heavily and said, "You'd better sit back down."

She sank onto her stool and I watched her heart sink as she did it. I bowed my head and worked up the courage to tell her what I could remember, fully expecting this to be the last time I ever saw her.

"I don't expect you to forgive me for any of the shit I did when I was drunk and coked out. Hell, I don't expect you to forgive me for *being* drunk and coked out."

"Just... tell me..."

I told her, and memorized every line of her face, as stoic and shut down as it was as I did it because the more neutral her expression became, the more certain I became that I would never be seeing her again.

No woman in their right mind *should* forgive me for abandoning them in one of their darkest hours... not only abandoning her but cheating on her to boot. It didn't matter how out of my mind I'd been.

Hayley had dropped her eyes and stared at a fixed point on the floor for a really long time. Finally, she raised her eyes to mine and said, "You're right, I don't know if I can ever forgive you for this... but I have to try."

"Why?" I asked frowning, confused at her phrasing.

"Because I'm pregnant."

I didn't know it was possible to feel both elated and devastated at the same time. I was torn between wanting to drop right on my ass right then and there and start rocking back and forth, and wanting to go to her and kiss her and pick her up and swing her around cheering. I held still, though, and didn't do either of those things until I got some kind of a measure of how *she* felt about it.

Her eyes bored into mine, tears sliding down her face until I ached to be able to wipe them away. I took a halting step forward; the urge was so strong but her next words halted me.

"I don't know if it's yours, or if it's Cell's… I just know that I can and will be a single parent if I have to."

I shook my head vehemently. "You're not going to be a single parent, my little one. Even if it's Cell's, it's mine… even if I can't make it up to you, you put my name on the birth certificate and I'll pay. That's *our* child," and I could tell she knew exactly what I meant by *our* child.

She shook with sobs and stuffed her hand against her mouth, taking a deep breath in through her nose and trying and failing to hold it together. I knew the feeling, my own eyes hot and glassy with my own unshed tears at the enormity of what was in front of us.

"I don't know what to do," she moaned, and it broke my heart hearing my words come from her lips, knowing the pain I'd dealt her with my absence and my actions.

"You don't have to do anything right now, baby. I do. I need to figure out how to fix what I broke."

"Blue…" Her voice held such an infinite amount of pain, it broke me to hear it.

"Just tell me what you need, baby, just tell me what you want me to do and I'll do it."

She looked at me plaintively and shuddering said, "Stay with me."

36

H ayley…
  "Stay with me."

I felt weak for saying it, but I was scared. I was terrified of having a child alone. Scared of losing both Cell *and* Blue at once, but mostly I was scared of living the rest of my life with the deep regret of not having at least tried – of having my child ask me to tell them about their father, of having to explain to them why he wasn't there and a part of their lives.

There was far more at stake here than just me, or Blue, and I couldn't deny that even though these last ten days had been soul-rending, I was still deeply in love with the man standing in front of me.

None of it meant that I would be a doormat, however. All of it meant that I would likely be judged as being one by outside parties.

He strode toward me to grab me, to hold me and I wanted that so badly, but I held up a hand, afraid if I let him touch me now, my resolve would crumble completely.

"This does not, by any means, mean that we're somehow fixed, or okay," I said and he shook his head.

"I know that."

His arms around me felt so good when he put them around me, and I couldn't help my arms going around him, holding him back... Weakened, I sobbed, and he held me so tight as if afraid if he let go, he would lose me forever.

I was still on the fence as to if he would.

"I'm so sorry," he said into my hair and while I believed him, I couldn't forgive him. Not yet.

"I miss him so much," I whined, and I felt him tremble as he fought tears of his own, which it was just us here... just him and just me, and I wished that he wouldn't just stand there stoic and pretend to be strong for me. I wished that he would just hurt like I hurt, I just wished that he would hurt *with me,* so I didn't have to do it all alone.

I couldn't hold back anymore. I said so. I told him everything because like it or not, he was the only one who understood and the dam broke.

I sat at my worktable, Blue stood with me, and we both cried over the loss of our lover, our safety.

37

Blue...
"You took them down..."

I was surprised at how much it hurt to see it, all these bits of empty fishing line hanging down above us as we lay on the bed in her loft. We were just talking. I wasn't about to press my luck, no matter how much I wanted the feel of her soft skin against mine.

She rolled her head along her pillow and looked at me startled. "Don't you remember?"

I shook my head and thought hard, finally having to admit defeat. I looked at her and she searched my face, deciding I wasn't lying, and took pity on me.

"At Cell's wake, you told me that you folded them, but the words were his."

"I did?"

"Yeah."

I swallowed hard and said, "They were good words."

"Yeah. I wish I'd known about them."

"I don't remember saying that... maybe it was because you needed to know then?" I said hopeful. Hell, I'd grasp at anything to make her feel even a little bit better.

"Maybe..."

She sounded so solemn another piece of my heart broke off and fell away. I sniffed and said, "I'm so fucking lost without him. He was always in control, the man with the plan, and I was good with that. I think I needed it, you know?"

She was quiet for a time and said, "Maybe it's time to come up with some plans of your own."

I threaded my fingers through hers where our hands lay between us and absently brought her hand to my lips, brushing a kiss along the back. She inhaled sharply and while I was glad she was still attracted to me, the conflict I heard in that sound told me just how far I had to crawl to earn back any of her favor.

I'd crawl a thousand miles through broken glass if it made a difference.

"I don't know that I want a 'me' without *you* if I can help it," I said honestly and she stayed silent. I closed my eyes and let out a frustrated breath. "That didn't come out right. That wasn't supposed to be some creepy threat of suicide should we not work out. I just meant to say, I didn't want to make up plans for just me. I'd rather we make plans together, for *us*."

More silence, then a soft rush of her breath and, "What do you think those plans would have been if Cell were still here?"

"I honestly don't know..." and I didn't.

"What would you have wanted?"

I swallowed hard and told her the absolute truth, "I would have wanted to move the hell out of the club, for one. I would have loved to have gotten a house for the three of us. Made a home, whatever the fuck that would have looked like. Cell wasn't exactly the domestic type, you know?"

"That's putting it mildly," she said with a slightly bitter laugh.

"What about you?" I asked.

"What about me?"

"What did you dream your life would be like?"

"I always dreamed I would meet a man and fall in love. That he would love me back, fiercely and patiently. I always dreamed we would get married, maybe travel… and that when the time was right, maybe have kids. It wasn't a deal breaker, though."

"Travel, huh?"

"Mm, yeah. No place exotic, mind you. Just around… maybe New England, maybe Florida. Maybe even the west coast, just somewhere *different* from here."

"Sounds nice."

"Yeah." I felt her hand drift over her stomach.

"And now?"

"I don't know."

"Come on, you have to have thought of at least something."

"I have to keep working, obviously, and I need to tell my dad. Other than that, I hadn't gotten very far. I mean, I don't have money for a home of my own. I have no idea how my father will react other than he won't be happy. I always pictured myself married before pregnant… I never wanted it any other way."

"You're going to be okay, you know that right?" I kissed the back of her hand again and felt her shake her head.

"No, I don't know that, and that's what scares me."

"That's fair, that's fair."

More silence, and I couldn't tell you how grateful I was that it was a comfortable one. I took a breath, then stopped, then decided, to fuck with it, and went for it.

"So let's make a plan. Doesn't have to be grand, just something to hold on to. One step, one day at a time."

I turned to face her, and she rolled her head on her neck to face me. She searched my face and dipped her chin; I couldn't tell if it was in agreement or if it was to tell me to go on, so I split lanes.

"We both have to work, and I know I've set us back a long, long, ways, but, Hayley... date me again. Same as before. Let me pick you up on Friday or Saturday. Let's go do things and figure this shit out just you and me this time. As things progress, let me take you to the doctor and go to whatever classes with you... I mean, that's a reasonable starting point, right?"

She nodded, and said, "It sounds reasonable."

"Okay."

I was going to make this up to her. I didn't know how, I didn't have the first clue how, but in her and in the baby she carried, I had everything to live for and as much as I felt overwhelmed and shit, I knew that we weren't, either of us, really alone. That I had the backing of the club for all I'd been shitty to them, too.

It was as if I needed to relearn how to live my life and the guilt that came with thinking that way was pretty immense. I mean, the way I said it made it sound like I was some kind of prisoner of Cell's or some shit...

Maybe in some ways I had been?

I lay in the dark beside Hayley, fingers entwined with hers, my thumb swiping back and forth over the silky skin along the back of it. I stared sightlessly at the raw wood beams of her ceiling, thinking for God knows how long, but when I looked back at her again, her eyes were closed, her breathing even and deep.

I stared at her sleeping face for what seemed like forever until the golden glow of morning lit her studio's windows.

38

H̲ayley…

The roar of a motorcycle outside startled me awake. I opened my eyes and jerked my head back and away from whatever was in my face. I picked up the folded paper lily and the flat note beside it.

No words in this one. I swear to you, I'm going to make this up to you. I'll pick you up on Friday for a date, if you'll let me. Just text me… Maybe I'll see you for lunch tomorrow…

Blue

I got up and carefully hung the lone flower off of one of the empty bits of fishing line and sighed. Rebuilding this relationship was going to take a lot more than origami flowers, but I would be foolish not to try. Still, I had to stick to my guns… he only had one chance to be faithful, to do this, and I couldn't let him off easily.

I gave the unicorn with the rainbow mane a squeeze before I went down the ladder out of my loft. I used the bathroom before drifting over to my table and the broken bits of black, crimson, and a more muted red lying on it. I didn't have a map for this piece. Nothing on paper… just bits and pieces of random broken glass and a clear idea of what I was doing. As if building this window was the physical representation of mending my broken heart.

"Hayley…"

I looked back over my shoulder at my dad in my studio doorway and sighed, "Hi, Daddy."

He came into the room and over to my table hugging me and looking over what I was making. He didn't come out here as a general rule, so his appearance here was out of sorts.

"Saw that Joe just left," he said and didn't sound exactly happy about that. I closed my eyes and sighed, sitting back.

"Nothing happened… we just talked."

"And?"

"And he has a long way to go with me before anything could happen."

"I don't like it, Hayley. Hurt you once, shame on them, hurt you twice…"

"Shame on me, I know… but you never not once screwed up with Mom?"

"Not like that, no, but I see what you're saying, and I made my mistakes, sure."

I shifted uncomfortably and said my piece. "I don't know if what I'm doing is right, but in my heart, I know it's not wrong… and I know you're going to be disappointed with me, but…"

"Pregnant?" he asked, and I looked up sharply.

"How did you know?"

"You always were really bad at keeping secrets," he said. "And you're right… I am disappointed, I'd have liked to have seen you married off and in a stable relationship with a man who respected you and who's not a felon."

I bowed my head and nodded. It did sound awful when he said it like that and deep down I was beginning to feel awful about myself. He didn't exactly help when he sighed out harshly and said, "I thought I raised you better than this."

Tears sprang to my eyes and I squeezed them shut. They spilled over and I just gripped the edge of my stool to either side and hunched my shoulders.

"I'm so sorry," I whined, but I knew it probably didn't mean anything.

"You're my only daughter, Hayley... old enough, now to make your own decisions, but I ain't got to like them... I just have to live with 'em."

I nodded and he sighed out harshly asking, "Do you even know which one it belongs to?"

"Does it matter?" I asked, suddenly indignant. "As long as it's loved and has two parents, does it really matter? I mean, will you, its only grandfather, love it any less?"

He jerked back a little as if he'd been slapped and I stood my ground on this one saying, "Because if it matters that much to you, I need to find another job and will work on finding someplace else to live. I was raised in a house of love and I won't accept anything less for my baby."

My dad sighed and said, "You're gonna be fierce, just like your momma."

"You're damn right I am."

He smiled and he shook his head. "You made your point, and no, I'm not gonna love it any less, baby. I love you, and it's a part of you, so I'm gonna love it just fine... I'm just not sure about this guy."

Which was totally ironic, to be honest. If you really thought about it, Cell had always been the questionable one of the two, Blue always the more dependable. Which is the only reason why I was even willing to give him a second chance... because I knew just how far out of sorts Duracell's dying had made my poor Blue.

Still, that wasn't an excuse for Blue's behavior... there was no excuse for that.

My dad and I talked until he absolutely had to go and get to the diner. I told him I was coming back to work the next day and he asked me if I was sure. I'd nodded, mostly because I knew raising a child was expensive and I needed to start saving for the impending medical bills, for regular doctor's visits, and for giving birth.

The rinky-dink insurance plan that was all my father and I could afford only covered so much and there were still copays and other things to be covered. I also had to convert one of the upstairs rooms to a nursery. My father giving me what was the guest room.

I'd thanked him, and he'd told me not to mention it, but it broke my heart that our relationship was so strained. That things didn't feel the same and probably never would.

For having his support and the support of Blue and his club, I never felt so alone in my life before.

"But I'm not alone, not exactly, am I?" I asked out loud of my little bean, not even sure it was to a stage it could hear me or what have you, but I'd like to think that it could feel something and if it were to feel anything? I wanted it to feel loved and wanted.

I turned back to the project in front of me, well aware that if I were to go back to work come morning that I should work on it as long as possible today. Still, first I would need breakfast and so I drifted across to the house to fix something to eat.

39

B lue...

I picked up cones, stacking them, walking alongside the pickup and heaving them up into the bed while another guy, Chip, stood in the bed and arranged them neatly.

"You doin' alright, man?" he called down to me and I looked up and nodded.

"Yeah," I grunted back, remembering at the last minute that I didn't have anyone to speak for me anymore and that I needed to make more of an effort to do it.

"Got any plans for lunch? Me and a bunch of the guys were gonna hit Jake's diner. Ain't that the place you used to go to everyday with Cell?"

"Yeah, my girlfriend works there... I actually planned on it. Today is her first day back to work."

"Why don't we all go?"

I nodded, we were actually wrapped up early today, the job completed until we hit the next one tomorrow. I was suddenly looking at a free afternoon.

"How many of us?" I asked.

"Six or seven," he called back, and I heaved up and handed him the next stack.

"Sure, let me call ahead and let her know to expect that many. She might have to move some tables."

"Sure!"

Chip knocked on the window and Sean who was driving turned around. Chip gave him a big thumbs up and Sean gave one back before getting on the radio.

"That's all of us boss," crackled out of the one at my hip and I remembered…

The end of each job, the boss tended to treat all the guys to lunch either that day or the next. Cell and I had only gone once or twice, preferring to keep to ourselves. I guessed that was still an option for me but why? I didn't have anything else to do. That and I was pretty sure the guys had picked Jake's to get me to go with 'em so I wouldn't be on my own. It was a nice gesture and I would have been going anyway, so why the hell not?

I shot a text to Hayley letting her know what was up and we kept on until all our cones and signage was cleaned up.

Several of the guys rode together in their cages but I was on the bike. I didn't think twice about mounting up and putting my knees in the breeze, but I spared a thought to Hayley and how she might feel about my riding after Cell. I feared a fight might be brewing there, because I couldn't, and wouldn't, give up my bike or the club – not if it was all I was going to have left.

It was everything to hold myself together as it was, lately. Not just for Hayley and the baby, but for me, too. I didn't want to end up locked up, and I was well aware I somehow dodged that bullet while on my bender. I was also well aware I'd dodged ending up like Cell.

Just thinking about what that would've done to Hayley, losing us both within days of each other, I felt sick with guilt. My gorge rising and bile burning the back of my throat. I pulled in at the diner and backed my bike by the door in that space that wasn't a parking space at all but was perfect for around three bikes next to each other and freed up the rest of the marked-out spots for cages.

The rest of the guys on the road crew I worked parked a minute later, a couple of the trucks having to find street parking, the lot pretty full. It was busy at the diner today, and I checked my phone. Hayley had just given me a one letter answer to my text about two minutes after I'd sent it. A simple 'K.'

I got off the bike and went up to the diner's door, pulling it open and holding it for Chip, who held it for the boss, who held it for Sean and right on down the line. I was surprised to find my heart thundered in my chest and I was nervous as hell about seeing her. About whether my presence would be welcome or not.

Jake looked out from the kitchen and his face was entirely unfriendly. A booth had a table and chairs moved up to it and was set up for seven, a 'reserved' card on it and I looked around for Hayley.

"Table's for you." Mel thrust her chin in the direction of the setup with her chin as she breezed by with a pot of coffee in one hand and a tray balanced on the other, making her way across the dining room to her section.

"Thanks, Mel," I said and she gave me a megawatt smile, likely over the fact that I'd spoken to her.

We all sat down, and Hayley came out from the back and the direction of the restrooms, drying her hands on a paper towel. She threw it away in the trash behind the counter and came over to our table, expression guarded, slipping her pad and pen out of her apron.

"What can I get you guys to drink?" she asked lightly, and the guys put in their drink orders. She didn't bother to take mine. I always drank just water, and water is what she brought us first, bringing me an extra-large glass.

She moved as she did before, quietly and withdrawn and it killed me that I was responsible. That Cell and I had brought her so far and that I had set her right back to square one... hell, further back than even that.

I had a lot to answer for and I would crawl on my belly through broken glass if it would make any of it better. I didn't think it would, though, and I didn't know what to do.

The guys laughed and tried to draw me into conversation and I pretty much found the whole thing to be excruciating, but I knew they all meant well, so I did my best to just go with it. When lunch was over, the pie most of the guys had ordered for dessert devoured, and the bill laid down at our boss's side I perked up a bit.

"Can I have that?" I asked.

"What?"

"The receipt paper."

My boss frowned, but his curiosity got the better of him and he passed it down. I stared at it for a long minute before I folded it down into a square and folded the excess back and forth. I folded the square carefully into a tiny paper crane and with a pen from the inside of my cut, wrote 'no words' on the discarded scrap of excess.

"Thanks," I muttered and left the crane and the note beside it on the corner of the table.

I looked over the rest of the guys who were looking at me like I was crazy, and I got up muttering, "I'll see you guys tomorrow."

I watched through the diner's window as Hayley returned and picked up the small folded offering and the discarded scrap of paper. She looked over and I nodded, and the pain unmistakable in her eyes, the longing and wistfulness clear in her expression, she inclined her head gently back.

Chip said something to her, and she bowed her head, slipping the bits of paper into her apron pocket and taking the boss's money.

I rode back to the club, frozen down to my soul despite the warm weather.

When I got there, I went around back and straight to the outbuilding. I found Dani right where she always was, Red-Thirteen in his corner by the door, a book in his hands. He gave me a questioning look and I nodded, and he smiled at me; a sad smile full of understanding.

"Babe," he called out and Dani looked up and back over her shoulder. He got up and went out past me giving me some privacy with my best friend but his woman and I couldn't express how grateful I was for that.

"What is it?" Dani asked and I dropped into the seat Thirteen had vacated.

"I don't know how to fix this thing with Hayley, but I want to... I want to so bad and it's killing me inside."

Dani's true-blue eyes grew sympathetic and she turned to set down what she was working on. She looked over her tools and with a sigh said, "I honestly don't know how to begin to fix something that big either, Blue. The fact she's even willing to give you a second chance shows just how much she loves you and that she understands."

I nodded. "I figured that."

Dani sighed and said, "I'm almost done with this piece, you want me to help you make something for her?"

A.J. DOWNEY

I looked up and gave a wan smile. "I don't think a piece of jewelry will fix anything, but it couldn't hurt."

She smiled and asked, "What does she like?"

I thought about it and finally said, "I fold paper into things."

"Origami?"

"Yeah. Something that I picked up doing in prison. It's calming to do it, you know? Meditative almost."

"I can work with that."

"You can?"

"Yeah. It won't be super easy, but I have an idea."

She waved me over and I got up, curious about what she had in mind. I blinked and looked her over and said, "You're a genius."

"Tell me something I don't know," she said with a smile. "It's not going to be easy though. I mean, it's not pliable, you're going to have to work at it."

"No, I get it, and I have to work at a lot of things." I rolled my lips together. "Dani, she's pregnant." Her eyes and smile lit up but one look at my face and her enthusiasm cooled. I shook my head and said, "No, I'm happy, believe me I'm happy. I'm just *scared*. Horribly fucking scared."

"No, I get that, and Blue that's totally *normal,* I'd imagine. I mean, why don't you talk to Dray, and Ghost, and Archer? Dragon even. I imagine they all will have some kind of wisdom about this. They're all fathers. They've all been where you are."

I nodded and she turned back around, picking up what she was working on, turning it this way and that under her magnifying light. She got absorbed in working on the piece pretty quickly and I just sat and watched her for a time until Thirteen came back – at which point I got up to give him his seat back.

256

"Come back tomorrow afternoon," Dani said. "I should have something for you by then.

"Thanks," I muttered and went back to my room to grab some clean shit so I could take a shower and wash the day, short as it'd been, off.

I felt a little stir crazy, with too much time to think being by myself. I wanted to give Hayley the time she needed and so I showered, went to the weight room in the main clubhouse and worked myself ragged and went back and showered again.

I did all manner of menial tasks just so I would have something to do. Filling up the rest of the day with laundry, cleaning up around my room, fixing a healthy dinner for me and the guys around the club only to finish it with a bottle of Jack and staring at the ceiling of my room. A lit cigarette, one of Cell's brand, burning down in an ashtray like some kind of morbid incense.

I picked up the key from around my neck, the one that Dani had given me and closed my eyes. Cell had been buried with the matching leather cuff that bore the key plate.

Afternoon dipped into dusk and dusk deepened into night and I just sipped the Jack and stared at the ceiling. Eventually, the exhaustion caught up and I passed the fuck out, but the dreams were uneasy.

40

Hayley...

Friday came and it was nearly eight o'clock. I stared at myself in the mirror and swallowed hard. It was supposed to be mine and Blue's first date. Well, the first one since, you know...

I was in one of my favorite summer dresses while I could still wear them. The weather in the low eighties today, spring as sprung as it was going to get and moving right on into summer. My stomach was still deceptively flat, and I realized I had no idea how any of this pregnancy stuff worked; like when I was going to start to show, or when the morning sickness was supposed to stop.

I heard his motorcycle pull up and went out the back door to meet him. He swung a leg over and turned around, stopping and taking me in. His face was tired and carefully closed off, and I fidgeted nervously, waiting for him to say something.

"You look beautiful," he said and I managed a brave smile.

"You look tired..." God, I didn't know why I said that, but it was true. It was so very true. He looked *exhausted.*

"Working hard, picking up some overtime, trying to sock some extra money away for the baby."

I nodded. "Me too. Saving up every bit I can, actually."

"You're not doing any of this alone," he said, and it sounded like a vow or promise.

I took a step and then another down the back steps and asked, "So what did you have in mind for tonight?"

"Um, first…" He went to one of his saddlebags and undid it, pulling out a bouquet of flowers and turning back. He came to me with the hydrangeas and handed them to me and I smiled, the stems wrapped with string and a tag. I admired the carefully folded paper blossoms and turned the tag over to read it.

No words except 'I love you'

I felt my heart twist in on itself with such an extreme longing to go to him and have him put his arms around me and tell me that all of this was just some terrible dream, but it wasn't. Still, I didn't care to punish him, or us, any more than we'd already been punished by fate and who knows, even by God himself. I just couldn't stand the thought of either of us hurting one another anymore and so I looked up at him with tears staining my lashes and told him the truth…

"I love you, too."

He came to me carefully and put his arms around me, drawing me against his chest and said, "Shh, don't cry. You'll ruin all that careful makeup."

I uttered a broken laugh and cried anyway, saying in a broken little girl voice, "It's waterproof."

He held me lightly and breathed deeply, and it was as if he was trying to commit the feel of me in his arms to memory. As if this was the last time he would hold me like this, and though I didn't think he was completely forgiven, I didn't think we were quite as broken as we'd been the moment before.

"Let me put these in my studio and we can go," I told him and he nodded, reluctantly letting me go.

I set the flowers on my work table and returned to him and he said, "You want we should take your cage?" I nodded, not quite ready to face a ride on the bike so soon after Cell's accident.

"Let me drive so you can fix your face."

"You never said where we were going."

"I figured the good ol' classic of dinner and a movie."

I nodded. "Sounds good."

"I thought we could both use something a little fun," he said, holding the door open for me and I got into the passenger seat of my own car. He closed the door and jogged around and got in on the other side.

"You going to leave me hanging?" I asked with a faint smile, curiosity getting the better of me.

He threaded his fingers through mine and raised the back of my hand to his lips and said, "You'll see."

He took me to a *Texas Roadhouse*. When he pulled into the parking lot, I had to laugh and he smiled shyly and said, "I told you, fun."

It was fun and the food was good, the topic of conversation quickly steering in the direction of our baby.

"I have to ask; how do you want to do that?"

"What do you mean?" I asked carefully, spearing some more of my salad onto my fork.

"Do I need to get us a place?"

I shook my head and he stared at me, waiting me out. I finished chewing and said, "My dad is letting me clear out one of the upstairs rooms so that I can build it into a nursery."

Blue nodded and didn't look happy but what could either of us say. He sighed heavily and said, "I'll come by and help you with it… you know, paint and stuff."

"I won't know for a while if it's a boy or a girl, although if you're in a hurry, I suppose we could choose gender-neutral colors, like green or yellow."

He shook his head. "That shit's for pussies."

"I don't know about that."

He smiled and sounded just like Duracell, or something that Duracell would say when he said, "I do. A boy is a boy and a girl is a girl. I don't much like fucking with that and giving kids screwed up ideas."

I looked at him pointedly and said, "Next thing you'll be telling me is I belong barefoot and pregnant in the kitchen."

"You're already pregnant, but no, that's not what I mean. What I mean is, there's nothing wrong with blue versus pink and there's nothing wrong with a girl hunting, shooting, or doing whatever the fuck she wants. Boys are boys, girls are girls, activities and colors and shit aren't gender specific, they never have been." He shrugged. "People just made 'em that way."

I could see his point and knew what he was saying, and the view was mighty progressive for these parts… he was just really bad at explaining it.

"Melody wants to hold a baby shower."

"You should let her. The club and ol' ladies love to do shit like that, and they can be a pain in the ass if they don't get to…" it was his turn to look pointedly at me. "And I'm not just saying that to save my own ass, I'm telling you so that you can save your own because it won't be me that they pout and whine to until they all get their way. You just inherited a whole bunch of siblings. You'll get used to it."

I changed the subject, slightly uncomfortable with where this was going, still wounded and preferring my isolated bubble right now. The one where I chose who could and could not come in.

"So, what movie were you taking me to go see?"

He took me to a romance, something sweet that left my face slick and salty, and I have to say I melted a little, my resolve to stay angry, to not forgive him, weakening but still steadfast. *Just because I understood why, didn't mean that it was okay...* but I had to keep telling myself that.

He took me home and stopped me outside my studio door.

"I have to go, my little one." His voice was strained and filled with regret and I looked up at him.

"Why?"

"Because if I don't, I'm going to stay and I'm trying to win you back, not get pushy and drive you away further."

"Oh."

I wondered if he was going to kiss me, but he didn't. Instead he pulled a fine golden chain out of nowhere and said, "Lift your hair for me."

I did and he reached for me. I turned around so that he could clasp it behind my neck, and felt it fall against my skin. He kneaded my shoulders and before I could drop my hair to protect the nape of my neck against the cooler evening temperature, his lips fell warm in a single, simple, chaste kiss.

I sucked in a breath, hair standing on end and delicious shivers cascading along my back, setting my whole body awash in light, pleasurable tingles. I'd never felt anything like it.

"I love you, Hayley," he murmured by my ear and then he was gone.

I turned around to watch the back of him, the brightly colored patch on his cut fading into the dark as he made strides down the driveway along the side of my house to his bike, he left parked at the curb out front.

I unlocked my studio door and went straight into the bathroom, flipping on the light. I stared into the mirror at the glinting bit of gold at the hollow of my throat. A perfectly folded paper crane, except not paper at all... somehow, he'd folded it out of a thin sheet of gold and attached a loop.

Tears, hot, fierce, and immediate, welled in my eyes and I let my breath out in a shuddering hitch, bracing myself against the sink basin as the enormity of just how much Blue loved me, overwhelmed me.

I ended up slipping to the linoleum floor where I sat and just cried my eyes out, swearing it would be the last time. I needed to sit down with him, make a plan, and figure things out.

41

B lue...

"I want to ask Hayley to marry me." I braced myself for a punch in the face, but Jake just stared at me. "I know I fucked up, but I love her and with the baby... I know it's important to you and to her that marriage happens before a baby. I'm totally cool if she decides later down the line to divorce my fucking ass or whatever, but I never meant for any of this to happen this way. I always meant for Hayley to stay an honest woman."

Jake leaned back in his chair and crossed his arms and asked the inevitable question meant to hurt, "What if the kid ain't yours? What if it's Paul's?"

"Doesn't matter the genetics involved, even if Hayley says no, that kid is mine and I'm man enough to take care of it, pay for it, provide for the mother of my child – whatever needs to happen."

"Oh yeah?"

"Yeah, because that's what men do." I gritted my teeth and Hayley's father gave me a look like *really motherfucker?* I nodded. "Yeah, really. They own their shit when they fuck up and I'm not going to pretend I didn't when Cell died, but –"

"But it fucked you up but good, didn't it?" he asked, and I was surprised that there wasn't any judgment in his tone. I nodded carefully. I think the only one to really get just how much it'd destroyed me was Dani… and maybe Dragon, but Dragon had a soft spot for women and Hayley was always going to be Jake's little girl, so I didn't bother to even try to use it as a defense for my actions when it came to her.

It didn't look like I was going to have to, though…

"Not sure what to make of you loving another man like that. I personally find it to be distasteful in the eyes of God, at least that's what I've always been taught."

I bowed my head and shook it. "It didn't start that way, at all… but it did end up that way that I loved him, but his being a dude didn't have anything to do with that. I don't look twice at any other dudes. It was just something about *him* specifically. It's not the kind of thing I thought I would ever find again in anyone else."

"Until you met my daughter, am I right?"

"Yes, sir."

"I want to hate you," he said frankly, and I nodded again.

"I get that. I even understand it, but what I don't understand is why you say it like that. That you *want* to hate me. It totally implies that you don't."

"Oh, I'm angry with you. Pretty fiercely, too… but no, I don't hate you. I can't hate anyone who did the good that you boys did for my Hayley. She was a different girl when she was with y'all. Happy… outgoing again. I didn't know how you'ns was gonna do it, but I figured love would find a way."

It had, just not the way any of us had expected. I rubbed the back of my neck and said, "I can't imagine loving anyone else the way I love her. I want to do everything right, but I can't help but feel I'm doing everything wrong."

"Hell," he said with a note of irony, "that's just part of life, son. This shit doesn't come with an instruction manual." He took a pull from the neck of his beer bottle and let out a long-suffering sigh.

The bar we were in was still pretty quiet, it being only the afternoon and in the middle of the week. He'd met me here, at my request, to talk about Hayley as soon as he'd gotten off work at the diner.

"Does that mean...?" I asked.

"That I give you permission to marry my little girl? I'm not happy about it entirely, but yeah. I give you the go ahead to ask, but if she tells you to fuck right off?"

"I fuck right off and pay my child support," I agreed.

"Men make mistakes. Lord knows I have. I spent a stint in the county jail for being a drunk and slappin' Hayley's momma around once, before Hayley was born. Eileen never should'a forgave my ass but by some grace o' God she did and I not once raised my hand to her again. Hayley doesn't know."

"She won't hear it from me."

"She's already forgiven you, you know. I know my girl. She's the forgiving type. She just has to convince herself that she's done it."

I almost cried right then and there with relief.

"So, future son-in-law... Just how you planning on asking her and when are you moving in? Seems to me shit's a changing and I sure as fuck ain't letting my baby girl move out or into that club of yours."

"The club's a nice place to visit, sir, but I am sure sick of living there."

He barked a laugh and it was like a thousand-pound weight had been lifted off my shoulders for a hot minute. It was quickly replaced with the nagging doubts and fears of *'what if she said no?'* which I couldn't let that happen, but I also couldn't spring it on her right the fuck now, either.

We were doing okay, had been on a couple of dates, and at the last one had even kissed goodbye. It'd taken everything in me to keep it civil, to not just pull her body against mine and carry her to the nearest bed.

I sighed and figured I'd need to ask the girls for help in planning this wedding. It was important for her to be married before kids and for some reason, it was important to me that she not be showing yet in the wedding photos. That I get just one night of pretending that she was just mine because when that kid came? It would be 'us' again, only a whole different kind of 'us' and believe me, I was good with that, I was totally good with that, but I would love to have something to look back on, you know? A short between time when it wasn't Blue, Hayley, and Cell or Blue, Hayley, and baby but just Blue and Hayley.

When I left the bar, I called Dani. When it came to this type of shit, the girls had it down pat. Besides, I needed to talk to Dani, anyway. I needed a ring.

When I walked through the front door of the club into the barroom, I stopped cold.

"What the fuck did you do? Phone tree that shit?" I asked.

The ol' lady collective laughed and blinked. All of them were fuckin' here. From Mel, to Maren, Red, and Em. Sunshine and Doll both sitting there with stacks of notebooks and, I shit you not, swatches of fabric.

First words out of Shelly's mouth were, "First off, what is our budget?"

I blinked. "Cheap... like really cheap. I'm broke with a baby on the way."

I forgot that Dani knew how to keep a secret because the next thing I knew I was drowning in girly squeals that would have had Cell screaming at 'em all to shut the fuck up. I didn't though. I kind of appreciated that they were all sharing in the joy because as fucked up as life had gotten without Cell in it, I needed every bit of joy I could come across and I was hoarding the hell out of them.

By the time all was said and done, we had a plan. It wasn't super pretty, a justice of the peace wedding, but the girls had a fine reception planned and I think, one that Hayley would like.

The only reason I knew Hayley would like it is because once upon a time when it'd been me, her, and Cell, we'd talked about it. About her dream wedding, and her dream reception and they'd both surprised me.

She wanted low-key. She didn't want big or fancy. She didn't want a dress that made her look like some kind of a cartoon princess, she wanted to *feel* like a princess, but the rest of it all? It didn't matter to her. She was perfectly fine with a Justice of the Peace courthouse wedding and a backyard barbecue reception as long as she was happy.

If anything, I was the girl of the relationship when it came to the wedding issue. I figured that we could meet half way. A courthouse wedding followed by a reception that was half barbecue and half what Melody and Archer had… just not here at the club.

"This is going to be so easy," Hayden declared.

"In the time it takes you to tie the knot at the courthouse we could have this shit set up where you want it for the reception," Everett agreed.

"I'll go to the courthouse with you guys. Stand with Hayley and her dad to throw suspicion," Mel offered.

"I'll be on your side with Dragon and probably Dray," Dani said and smiled at me. "No way that you're getting *married* and I'm not going to be there."

"The club can have things set up and ready and that will save a *ton* of money," Shelly said.

"Details, now," Red chimed in. "What do you want for flowers?"

I smiled and felt some more weight come off. I sincerely hoped she didn't hate me for this.

42

H ayley…

I turned from the counter in the middle of a horrendous lunch rush to the bell above the door chiming. I looked up, the words 'be right with you' dying on my lips when I spotted Blue and several of his coworkers.

"Two seconds and I'll get a table cleared," I said and he nodded, a strange look in his soft gray eyes. I bussed a booth carefully, went to the counter and pulled menus but when I turned around, Blue was on his knees and the diner had gone quiet.

"What are you doing?" I asked, and he raised his eyes to mine, a small gray velvet box appearing in his hands.

"Blue?"

I felt my face burn, a matching one taking up residence in my chest as my heart just *stopped*.

He opened the box and there, resting neatly inside was a paper orchid, a band of green electrical tape forming a ring.

"Marry me, please… I'm begging you," he said, and I swallowed hard, tears collecting in my eyes.

I stared at him hard, past the perfect ring in its perfect little box, and silently asked him if this was what he really wanted… searching his face to make absolutely sure that this was real and not just because I was pregnant or because of any other reason but the simple fact he loved me and wanted me.

"You know this is forever, right?" I asked breathlessly.

"Is that a yes?" he asked.

I nodded dumbly and said, "That's a yes."

The diner erupted in cheers, whistles, and applause. He leaped up and wrapped his arms around me crushing me to him like I'd wanted him to, despite remaining stubbornly in limbo with my anger and forgiveness. I flung my arms around his shoulders and buried my face in the side of his neck breathing him in, dying for more. Wanting and needing him like never before.

He put me down and kissed me like he was a drowning man and my kiss was the only thing that would provide him air, and I knew the feeling.

"Go on and get out of here, you two!" my dad called from the kitchen and Blue called back, "Would love to, sir, but I have to get back to work myself."

A man behind Blue said, "Aw, fuck off with that shit! Go on and get out of here with your girl."

Blue laughed and I stared at him, begging him silently to take me anywhere but here. He nodded and said, "I'll follow you home."

My hands shook as I turned the wheel into my driveway. I kept staring at the ring on my finger, a match for the first one he'd ever made me, the night he'd slipped it on my finger and had told me, *I see you.*

I parked my car and he pulled up on the bike, shutting it off and heeling down the kickstand. I got out into the warm sunshine and sighed.

I hated that he rode after what happened to Cell, but I couldn't and wouldn't ever begrudge him doing it. I couldn't. It was too much a part of him. He came to me and leaned down, one hand on my lower back the other on my lower stomach. He kissed me, and I melted into it.

"I love you," he said against my lips.

"Show me," I murmured and went to kiss him again.

He drew back, however slightly and said, "The next time I make love to you, it will be as my wife."

"Then we'd better hurry up and get married."

He chuckled lightly. "How does a date with the Justice of the Peace sound?"

"When?"

"Next week."

"You're on."

"Okay, then."

I backed off, and took his hand and said, "Come here, I want to show you something."

He followed me to my studio door where I unlocked it and left the door standing open to the warm weather outside. I led him to my worktable and said, "I finished it last night."

He stopped and looked down at it, eyes roaming the bits of melded glass, from smoke to crimson, blues, reds, fiery oranges and blacks. He turned to me and asked, "What made you do this?"

I looked down at the large window with the Sacred Hearts' logo done in bits of scrapped glass and shrugged. "It was for Cell… to remember him."

"Little One, it's beautiful."

"Do you think that they'll want it?" I asked. "I mean, I made it the dimensions of that front window, the one with the flag in it… I just thought if you didn't want people looking in the front window that this might be a better way to do it."

His eyes traveled over the bits of stained glass and metal and he brought out his cell phone, snapping pictures of it. He frowned at his phone and asked, "Turn on the overhead light?"

I went to it and flipped the switch and he nodded. "There we go." He took several more pictures and fiddled on his phone.

"Who are you sending them to?"

"Dragon."

I was nervous and a moment later he looked up from his phone. "He says he can have it transported today."

"It still needs a frame," I protested and Blue grinned.

"We've got a guy for that."

"Oh." It *would* be nice to get it out of here today so that I could start something else, now that it was done. I nodded. "Sure, send them the address, tell them to bring the guy and the wood, it really should be framed for stability before it moves."

"You've got it, beautiful."

I was shy and nervous about the men who showed up coming into my studio. I recognized them all. Dragon, Rush, Reaver, and Trigger. Dragon and Trigger showed up in a pickup truck full of timber and boards in the back and when Rush and Reaver got off of their bikes they were the ones to ask, "We building a framework for the back of the truck to transport this thing?"

I nodded. "It would be best."

"Let's see it."

"This way…"

Reaver came up and hugged me and said, "Congratulations and welcome to the family."

I smiled and nodded, blushing fiercely and Trigger laughed. Dragon grumbled, "Quit stealing my thunder, Reaver." He came over and hugged me next.

"Thank you," I murmured lightly, and he said, "I can't believe you did all this."

"I needed to do something… I just wonder if he would have liked it."

Reaver was the one to answer me, which surprised me. "He would have thought it was cool," he said and the look on his face, distant, wintery, a match for the look I'd caught on Cell's face time and time again, I had to believe him.

"I'm kind of dying to see this thing, now," Rush stated and I took them over to my work table.

Trigger let out a low, low, whistle of appreciation. "That's something," he said.

It was just like the flag that hung in the window, only a full sized to spec for the window that was at the club. I'd asked Melody to have Archer measure it and he had, and never even once had pried about what I needed the measurements for. The logo would glow with fire and look alive from the inside. I'd used nearly opaque black glass for the surround and for the logo itself, I'd used the most richly tinted but transparent glass I could.

For the barbed wire wrapping around the heart, I'd used solder to make between glass pieces and the most impressive part about it all? I'd freehanded it entirely with no base image. I hadn't needed one. I'd looked at that patch so often, stared at it so many times I didn't need to.

"I used black as a background rather than white because…" I choked up a little.

"You ain't got to explain," Dragon said kindly.

"I've got an idea or two," Rush said, sucking his teeth and I looked at him curiously. "In fact, I got a lot of ideas."

"Oh, Lord," Trigger said and gave a gusty sigh.

"You sell this stuff?" Reaver asked.

"I have some pieces in an antique shop downtown that are on consignment."

"Should give her the middle space at the club," Rush said.

"Between you and Dani?"

Rush nodded his head. "My stuff is moving out of there as soon as we finish the outbuilding for it on the farm."

I wasn't following anything they were saying so I just kind of politely stood by while Rush measured the window and wrote things down on a notepad. He twisted his head back and forth and I said, "If it helps, I have the brackets right here."

"That does help, yes!"

The rest of the day was spent watching these men, unfamiliar with working with stained glass specifically, but capable around wood and window installation, work to safely get a rack built in the back of the truck and the window itself framed out. My dad even helped when he got home, and I was surprised to find that he seemed happier than he had been for a while to just have people around and something to *do*.

"Afraid we're gonna run out of daylight before we can get this in back at the club," Dragon said.

"I didn't think we were gonna *install* it today," Reaver called.

"Red-Thirteen already has the old window demoed out. He's waiting on us."

"Really?" I blurted, surprised.

"Damn straight. This beauty is going in and staying in."

I was surprised, shocked and amazed that it would matter to them as much as me. Dragon smiled and huffed a bit of a laugh and said, "Let's get going, boys, or we're going to have to set up the floodlights.

I looked at Blue, who smiled at me like I was the sun, and I felt my shoulders drop, as if a weight was taken from them.

They really knew how to make a girl feel like she belonged.

43

Blue...

We had to apply for a marriage license and apparently that shit took a little more time than we wanted, but that was okay. It gave the girls and yeah, even the guys, enough time to really plan the surprise reception. It also gave Everett the time to pull strings and get in touch with the one major concession that I wanted.

We were offering the three-man band a lot of money to play at our reception. Yeah, the guys from the Harvest Festival and our first solo date. I wanted to remind my little one of all the good things about our relationship. I wanted her to be happy and I figured that would do it.

We were out back of the club, chillin' around the firepit. Hayley was lying on her side along the bench, head on the top of my thigh, staring into the flames. I'd been prepared this time, had picked up a light, fuzzy and cuddly throw from a local discount store to keep her and the baby warm.

"What about, Ezekiel?" Thirteen asked and Hayley laughed.

We were trying to come up with a boy's name and a girl's name for the baby and it'd sort of devolved into the worst names ever to name your baby.

"That one's actually not bad," I said and Thirteen looked at me from across the fire where he and Dani lounged on the hanging bench opposite of ours.

"Really?"

"I knew a Zeke once," I told them. "He was a good kid… kept me out of trouble when we were both coming up together. My dad, he was a drunk. Zeke and his family would give me a place to crash when my dad ran afoul of the bottle."

"Where is he now?" Hayley asked, voice a little far away as she was pretty much hypnotized by the flames.

"Died. Joined a gang, took a bullet when we were fourteen that paralyzed him, took eight more years but the bullet migrated and eventually finished the job."

"Damn," Reaver said and shook his head. Hayden looked grim in his lap, and he looked up at her. "No worries, Doll, I don't have any hardware still floating around like that."

She sniffed and her eyes welled up and she nodded. "I know."

Reaver sighed and I echoed the sentiment. It'd been a real long time, fuck, pushing three years since he'd been shot, and Hayden still hadn't let it go. I didn't think she ever would.

"What about Gertrude, or Eunice?" Data asked and there was a bunch of aww's and hell no's.

"Baby, not an old lady!" I laughed.

"What? Those old ladies were babies once."

"You hear about that celebrity that named her kid Audio Science?"

"No!" Hayley cried. "Absolutely not naming my kid, boy or girl, something that doesn't even sound like a name."

"I always thought Sailor would be a cute name for a little girl," Hayden said and Reaver laughed.

Hayden gave him a withering look and he said, "Oh, shit! You were serious," which made the rest of us laugh, even Hayden.

"You're such an asshole sometimes," she said between giggles.

"Just don't name her 'Tulip' or some other flower name that's just fucking stupid," Trigger said.

"Flower names aren't stupid!" Sunshine argued.

"Well yeah, not a flower name like 'Rose' but could you imagine calling your kid Tulip, or Hyacinth or some shit?"

"Sounds like a dog's name."

More laughter. Hayley rolled her head to look up at me and I looked down into her beautiful face. She rolled her eyes and I grinned, bending at the most awkward angle ever to peck her on the tip of her nose.

"Why does this have to be so hard?" she complained.

"You should do what Shelly did," Ghost called walking up.

"Where is Shelly, man?" Trig called back.

"Home with a sick kid; she told me to save myself."

"Oh. What did she do?"

"Picked the top three names she wanted for Harmony, went out the back door and screamed each one of them ten times at the top of her lungs."

"Why?" Reaver asked, making a weird face.

"I asked her that. She said if she was gonna end up screaming it for the rest of her life that she might as well get to trying them out now. The one that was easiest or that she didn't mind screaming was the one she stuck with."

"Oh, my God, that totally sounds like something she would do!" Hayden fell out laughing and a bunch of us joined in.

Hayley pushed herself up. "It's a good thing that we have time to figure it out," she said, stretching.

"Ready for bed?" I asked her softly and she nodded.

"K, come on."

I stood and set my half empty beer aside and held my hand down to her. She got up and I called out, "Night all."

"Night!" they called back.

We went tiredly across the grass and into the barracks. I let her into my room, and she turned sharply. I put my arms around her to keep from completely crashing into her. She looked up at me, all seriousness in her eyes and on her face and said, "Kiss me."

I bent carefully and played my lips across hers and it was the sweetest thing. I closed my eyes and rested my forehead on hers and whispered, "I meant it about waiting for the wedding."

She chuckled lightly and said, "I understand you feel the need to punish yourself, but do you really need to punish me, too?"

I laughed, a surprised thing that I broke off quick so I could ask, "That really the way you feel about it?"

"Maybe..."

"Don't be coy, not about this."

She nodded, and her face grew solemn. "I want you. I miss your hands on me."

"I can't remember all that I did." I swallowed hard. "Doc says it could take six months to a year for certain things to show up in my blood-work, so…"

"So, wear a condom."

"You're sure?"

"Yes."

Fuck. I couldn't say no. I couldn't. It was killing me not being with her. I wanted her, I needed her so damn bad. I bowed my head and kissed her again and let my jacket and cut slide off my shoulders and into my hands. I swung the door shut behind me and hung it on the hook before I turned my attentions to getting her naked.

We moved slow, one piece of clothing at a time. Kissing, exploring, taking our time with each other and it was new and different – as if we were discovering each other for the first time. We stood in the quiet dark of my room, skin to skin, the cool air-conditioned air pushing us closer together for warmth and I couldn't say I regretted that one bit. If anything, it made me want to crank that bitch up higher.

She kissed me as if she were poisoned and my lips held the antidote. I knew the feeling and I returned every bit of her desire and enthu-siasm tenfold. I walked her over to the bed and reached into the drawer beside it for a condom. She took a step back to watch me roll it on and I loved how her dark eyes *glowed* with her arousal, how her lips parted, her long dark hair tumbling around her face and it was a miracle I didn't come just from that expression on her face alone.

The fact that she was so turned on pushed me right up to the very edge. I went to her, lifting her bodily and flinging her back onto the bed. She yipped in surprise and laughed. I followed her, caging her body with mine, showering her in kisses, light little touches of my lips all over her chest – paying particular attention to any spot that had her arching into me – licking and sucking my way down her body.

"Blue, please," she begged, her voice sultry and full of passion and I raised myself up, making eye contact, showing her rather than telling her, just how much I loved her. Just how much I adored her.

Her breath came in a passionate cadence, and I loved it. I worked my way back up her body, lying over the top of her, keeping her warm from the chill of the room and slipped inside of her, slowly, agonizingly slowly, using up every bit of self-control I had not to take her with the frenzy I wanted to. There would be plenty of time for rough sex later, right now, we both needed love and to support each other.

She bowed beneath me, her back arching off the bed, her pussy gripping me rhythmically and I gritted my teeth, trying not to go myself. I needed to draw at least two more orgasms from her before I could take any pleasure myself. She deserved that peace, she deserved to feel good after all of this bad, all of this pain and misery. Some of it caused by me, some of it caused by the gaping hole that Cell had left behind.

"Oh, God, Hayley," I moaned as she twined her arms and legs both around me.

"Blue..."

I loved the sound of my name on her lips. I loved her just so goddamned much.

44

H ayley…

Slow, so beautifully slow and so full of meaning, love and light, I couldn't even stand it. I adored Blue and the care he'd shown me the first time we'd made love since… Well, since. It was what was going through my mind as I stood, hand in hand with him in front of the judge marrying us.

Dragon, Dani, and Thirteen stood behind him, and I could feel my father, Melody, and Archer at my back as we exchanged vows. My hands trembled and shook with the magnitude of the moment as I slid the gold band Dani handed me onto his finger, his eyes alight with all things love, hope, and desire.

"Mr. Barry?" the Judge asked and Blue slid first a simple gold band and then a proper engagement ring onto my finger.

The judge's voice was a wordless buzz in my ears as he finished what he had to say and Blue's smile grew wider. I felt my own echo his and my heart swelled and we kissed. The first time we ever would as husband and wife.

A couple of cheers, a smattering of broken applause, and happy tears leaked from the corners of my eyes.

I just couldn't stop kissing him.

I never *wanted* to stop kissing him.

"Alright you two," the judge said with a wink, "I do have some more people that would like to get married today."

Laughter in the courtroom, and Blue pulled me into the shelter of his arms and turned us away from the judge, taking the manila envelope with our marriage documents inside from the clerk.

"Congratulations," she said.

"Well now, we need to get back to the house," my dad said. "Finish getting your stuff moved in."

I laughed and said, "Dad, all he really has are clothes… we can't do anything about the rest for now." Blue and I had agreed that his bed needed to come but we weren't sure how it would fit in my room. There was still so much up in the air and undecided and I was going just a little bit insane trying to keep track of and implement all of the changes happening all at once.

"We'll figure everything out," Blue murmured. "We have everything we could want, or need, and the rest? We'll figure it out and let the chips fall where they may."

He was right. We'd already survived some of the worst things that could happen to a couple. Anything else would be so small by comparison.

My dad drove us home, and when we pulled up, it was to a line of motorcycles backed up to the curb in front of our house. I blinked and asked, "What is going on?"

"Surprise," Blue said from the backseat of my dad's Explorer. I twisted around in my seat and blinked at him, his smile smug even as fiddle music lazed through the open car window from our backyard.

As soon as my father pulled up to the curb past the motorcycles, Blue leaped out of the back and opened my door for me. The way he did it screamed that I would likely never have to open a door for myself in his presence again and I thought, *How sweet that he does it.* It was, too. It spoke of a man who was desperately trying to be all that a man should be, but I knew that the only real role models that he'd had growing up for what that was, was how men behaved on television and figuring out from his dad's behavior exactly what it was *not* to do.

He took my hands and steadied me as I stepped out of the truck in my heels onto the grass and made sure I was safe getting onto the sidewalk. I smoothed down the front of my summer dress. It was more than a little bit country and I loved it. White eyelet material and form fitting around the bust with just enough give to the front to hide the small pooch that was just barely starting to show.

It had taken a while to get an appointment to get married, some kind of a backlog with the courts, so here it was, June but here we were... married and apparently having a party?

Blue led me around the side of the house down the gravel of the drive to the backyard which was indeed set up for a reception. I laughed as everyone turned and yelled, "Surprise!" and covered my mouth with my hands as I flamed in a giant blush.

My dad pulled off his suit jacket and loosened his tie and I took in our fully transformed backyard.

A barbecue pit was in full swing at the back of the house with food piled high. Rush had put up a little gazebo for shade near the lilac bushes my mother had so loved. There was a table for two under it facing out over several freshly built picnic tables, all of them decorated with flower arrangements that I could see from here weren't flowers at all but carefully folded and hand-crafted paper flowers done by Blue.

Two aluminum troughs filled with ice, beers, wine, water and soda flanked the back steps and Blue went and got me a bottle of chilled water before coming back to me as I just took everything in.

In the main part of the drive, a tent had been erected and a dance floor put down over the gravel. To one side a small stage and on it? The band from our first date.

I couldn't help myself... I started to cry.

Laughter and a whole bunch of 'aww!' caught my ears as Blue pulled me against his chest and rubbed my back murmuring, "I love you and I wanted your day, the one we talked about, to be perfect."

"I love you all so much!" I cried and there was applause. The singer for the band put his lips to the microphone and started to sing, and I spent a good portion of my time having person after person come to me and shake my hand congratulating me.

Melody came up and I hugged her tightly. She had her camera around her neck and had been taking photos at the courthouse for us and said, "I'd love to get photos of you and Blue at your table."

I stood with Blue who had done what I asked and had stayed in the attire I most loved him in. His jacket and cut over a clean white, form-fitting tee tucked into his best jeans with his motorcycle boots on his feet.

Melody took pictures of us from every angle doing everything and I loved her for it, never in a million years being able to afford a professional photographer.

"Blue," I murmured at one point, "I don't know how we're going to pay for all of this!"

"Hush yer mouth," Dragon said from behind me and I startled. "There ain't nothing *to* pay for, darlin' girl. This is the club's gift to y'all."

"I don't understand."

"Sunshine and Trig paid for the band, and Rush built all of the tables and the like which will get used back at the club. The food came from everybody. The cake from Mandy and Everett, the rings from Dani and Thirteen. Setup was all the club and anyone that didn't have a hand in the reception, their wedding gift is whatever we need done work-wise for the nursery," Blue explained.

"You're family now, sweetheart, and in this family, not no one wants fer anything," Dragon said.

I swallowed hard, choking up and sniffed.

"Aw, come on now, don't do that!" he said and I laughed a little.

"Why not? It's my party and I'll cry if I want to."

Blue and Dragon both let out surprised laughs at that, Dragon's booming out far more than expected causing me to jump.

"I say it's time for you two to have your first dance!" Dray called out and there was a lot of raucous cheering at that.

"I'd like that," I murmured and Blue smiled at me.

"Yeah?"

"Yeah."

45

B^{lue…}

Taking Hayley into my arms for our first dance was just as magic as it'd been taking her into my arms for the very first time all those months ago at the Harvest Festival. The band started something slow for us, a lazy, easy, slide of the bow across the fiddle's strings and I stepped, taking her lazily around the dance floor, Melody snapping away with her camera.

I tried really hard not to think about anybody watching us and instead, focused on Hayley's upturned face, her lovely brown eyes following every line, every plane, and every angle of my face as if the answer to existence itself could be found there. It took me a minute to realize that for her, maybe it had… that maybe it was for her just like it was for me.

"I love you," she whispered up to me and I stilled, bowing my head and kissing her gently in what, unbeknownst to me, would become my absolute favorite photo of our wedding day.

I saw it then, as I would for years to come, on her face as I drew back. The same kind of peace I felt every time I looked at her or heard her voice. We resumed dancing; I held her close and let the music carry us around the floor and soon there were other couples around us. Beautiful, happy, a light in the dark for both Hayley and me.

"I wish we could afford a honeymoon," she murmured quietly.

"We'll take one on our first anniversary," I promised her.

We were both holding onto every penny for the baby, to make sure he or she wouldn't want for anything. We had a pretty grim outlook on the bills associated with a pregnancy, but it was a good thing she'd thought of all that, otherwise we could have really been in financial trouble.

My girl was smart as well as beautiful, and I was so very damn lucky that she was forgiving, and I silently vowed to her and myself, she would never have the occasion to need to exercise that forgiveness on me in that way ever again.

"You're my life now, Hayley. I promise to take care of you and our family... I promise to be our safety," I murmured and kissed the top of her head and she cuddled close to me.

"It's a strange little life we're building," she said. "And I love it... even though it's not how we planned or would have done things, I love it, anyway."

I smiled, a content and happy man, and we danced until after sunset, stopping only for wedding cake and to see guests off as they left.

Her dad came up to us and said, "Well, it's your wedding night and I know you aren't going anywhere, but for tonight the house is all yours. Dragon's offered to put me up for the night so you two can have a little privacy and I'm going to take him up on it."

"Dad! You don't have to do that." Hayley tried to argue but he and I exchanged a pointed look. I stuck out my hand and he shook it, heartily.

"Thank you, Jake."

He huffed a laugh and said, "Don't 'cha mean Dad?"

"The word 'dad' has some rough meaning where I come from so if it's all the same, I'd rather not go there yet," I said.

He nodded and said, "My ol' man was a bastard, too. It's why I moved the hell out of Ohio and came down here in the first place. Why I never let him see Hayley."

"I didn't know that," Hayley said softly.

"He died when you were ten. It's not something your mom and I talked about. He wasn't a good person to be around." Hayley nodded but I could tell she wasn't happy by the revelation. "Anyhow, that's a conversation for another day. Try not to think about it too much."

Her dad leaned down and hugged her tight. She hugged him back and said, "I love you, Daddy. I'm so sorry if I've disappointed you."

He huffed a laugh and said, "Never in any way that's really counted, baby girl. You are all that is good and right in my world. I couldn't be prouder of you, if I wanted to."

Hayley sniffed and came off her tiptoes. Jake looked at me and nodded saying, "I'm glad you get that."

"I do get that. She's too good for me."

"Ha! She's too good for all of us."

Hayley wiped at her eyes and said, "Okay, knock it off you two!"

Jake and I chuckled and he walked away, down the drive calling over his shoulder, "Don't either of you dare try to clean any of this shit up tonight."

"He's right, got a cleanup crew of some of the guys and the ol' ladies coming over as soon as the hangovers are bearable," Dragon said, coming up behind us and wandering around so he could face us and talk to us.

"Thanks for everything, Pres."

"It's what we do," he said with a shrug.

Hayley went forward and hugged him, and he chuckled and hugged her back. "Aw, hell," he said grinning.

"Thank you so much for everything." She echoed my sentiment and Dragon tipped her chin.

"Yer a good girl," he said with a nod. "You two do everything I would do tonight, y' hear?"

"Yes, sir."

We watched him trail up the side of the house along the driveway whistling and Hayley looked around the yard.

"Nope, I know that look," I declared.

She laughed lightly as I bodily steered her in the direction of the back door.

"Okay, okay!" she cried.

"Out of sight, out of mind," I said.

"So what next?" she asked.

"Next, I get you out of that dress and do to you what I've been dying to do all day."

"Oh really?"

"Yeah, really."

I walked her up the back steps and into the back door, taking her directly across the kitchen to the stairs of the second floor. She didn't resist me, in fact, if I didn't know any better, I'd say she was just as eager as I was to get out of these clothes to slip into each other.

We went into her – excuse me, *our* bedroom and I have to say, I loved this woman. She was neat, organized, and fastidiously clean like me.

Everything in its place, bed made every morning, room so perfect it looked like it belonged in a magazine spread and that no one actually lived in it, which was sort of the case, honestly. I mean, she slept more in her studio loft than up here anymore but that was okay – at least until the baby came.

"You look like your mind is going a mile a minute," she said, fingertips touching either side of my face.

"I'm nervous," I realized with a start.

She laughed and asked, "How could you be? It's not like this is our first time…"

"Yeah, but it is… I mean, you're my wife."

She smiled and closed her eyes like what I'd said was the sweetest music she'd ever heard.

"Say that again."

"What? That you're my wife?"

She let out the most contented and happy sigh that it felt like liquid gold ran through my veins. Warmth suffused me inside and out and I felt my spirits lift.

"My wife," I whispered gently and lowered my mouth to hers, my hands smoothing over the light, crisp cotton of her dress, drawing her into my arms. She kissed me and it was everything I had ever ached for. A kiss that said I belonged but made me *feel* it down to my bones.

A kiss that told me, *I love you, I want you,* and most importantly, *I need you.*

I hadn't realized how important it was for me to be needed until I thought I wasn't. So many things got turned upside down and inside out when we'd lost Cell and I was just now beginning to realize for myself that Hayley wasn't a bridge between me and him, she had been a bridge *out* and *away* from him…

One that I'd needed for a long time.

I held her close and eased the zipper to her dress slowly down her spine. The fabric parted and she gave a little whimper of relief. I took my time, running my hands over her soft skin and kneading her lower back which was probably killing her after all day in heels.

She took a slight step back, breaking the kiss and let the dress fall and pool at her feet. It was one of the most erotic things I'd ever seen, all that perfect white cotton whispering down and revealing her soft smooth skin. I felt my already hot and hard cock throb behind my zipper by way of response and there was only one thing for me to do.

I reached for her and pulled her against me again and kissed her, just holding her body against mine, soaking up her warmth through my clothes until I could go to my knees in front of her. I smoothed my hands over every inch of her skin that I could, pressing my lips wherever I felt like it. I reached up blindly behind her, her nails scratching sensually along my scalp as she ran her fingers through my hair. I unhooked her white lace bra and slid it down her arms revealing those perfect breasts and probably could have died right then and gone nowhere because this was heaven.

Her eyes glowed with desire and lust as she sucked in a breath between her slightly parted lips, swollen with my kiss and I burned this scenario into my memory forever. We could be eighty fucking years old and every time I looked at her, I would see this, right here, right now. This perfect moment frozen in time.

I sucked first one then the other nipple into my mouth and watched her while I did it. Her breaths deepening, the cadence of them speeding up as arousal swirled behind those dark eyes. Her hands gripped my shoulders as I trailed kisses down her stomach and hooked fingertips into the light elastic of her matching white lace panties.

I slid them slowly, so agonizingly slowly, down her legs, the perfume of her sex a heady thing, a fierce desire of my own walking blazing fingers down my spine. I wasn't able to resist. I buried my mouth at the apex of her thighs, and she threw back her head, the long line of her body arching above me. I steadied her, hands on her hips and slung one leg up over my shoulder.

"Oh God, Blue!" she cried.

I played my tongue back and forth over her clit and she held onto me grinding her body closer, into my assault. I loved that. I loved that so hard. I loved even more what I did next and that she trusted me to do it. I picked her up, legs over my shoulders and backed her against the nearest wall, standing with her riding my face as I teased, licked and sucked her slowly to orgasm, her fingers tangled in my short hair, gripping me as I played with her body.

I listened to her breath, her gasps and moans coming at regular intervals and sweet to the ear. I loved listening to the sounds of passion I wrought out of my partners, but out of Hayley? It was seriously some next-level erotic shit.

"Oh God, oh God, *ohGodohGodohGod*!" Her hips jerked off the wall and toward my face before slamming back against it. Her whole body writhing with a powerful orgasm and I held her, bringing her down, sliding her carefully down my body until her legs wrapped around my waist and her arms around my shoulders.

She crushed her mouth to mine and kissed me beyond passionately and I smiled against her lips. She was ready and judging by the amount of pre-cum soaking into the front of my boxers, I was past ready too.

46

Hayley…

So amazing… I couldn't believe he'd done that and now, all I wanted was the bed behind him and both of us naked and in it. I pushed at his jacket and cut and let them slide off of his shoulders and crash to the area rug over the hardwood floor.

"Shit! Hey!" He reached down immediately and picked them up, laying them off to the side on the dresser before returning to me with a nervous laugh. "That never happened, okay?"

"Oh, okay…" I laughed nervously and wondered if it was some kind of rule I didn't know about but I would ask later. Right now, he pulled his tee over his head and my mind went on the short honeymoon my body had just been on. I went to him and pressed my lips over his heart, even as he kicked out of his boots and worked at his belt.

He picked me up, hands gripping my ass, hauling me up his body, erection pressing against me, and I ached to have him inside of me. He carried me to the bed and set me down and grabbed a condom off of the bedside table.

While I longed to make love to him with no barriers between us, I *loved* watching him put one on. The look in his eyes, the eagerness with which he tore open the foil packet... It was one of the hottest things ever for me.

He rolled the condom down his length and climbed up onto the bed after me, lying down beside me. I smiled and eagerly straddled his hips, picking his cock up off his stomach and positioning it carefully, sliding down over the top. My body was wet and ready and the desire in his eyes as he watched me stoked an answering fire in my own body. I rode him, gently and carefully at first as my body grew accustomed to his presence and I found just the right place for him to touch inside.

I found it and tipped back my head and moaned. His hands on my hips, he pulled me down tight and pushed and pulled me back and forth, encouraging me to grind on him the way he knew I liked, even though it didn't stimulate him as much as *he* liked.

"Make yourself come," he ordered me lightly and I nodded and availed myself of his cock, grinding back and forth, torturing that place inside that sent sparks of pleasure up through the center of my being. Working it, exploiting it in a hedonistic display that would have had me burned as a witch two hundred years ago.

"Oh, God Hayley, that's it. That's it, fuck me, baby. Come for me," he encouraged between deep, passionate, panting breaths.

I braced my hands against his chest, and I was so close, so very close, riding that edge where everything glowed, in that place where orgasms lived, the feeling just there on the horizon. I just was missing something, needing that one little extra push and Blue gave it to me, licking the pad of his thumb and delving into the light cleft at the top of my sex where our bodies met. He rubbed back and forth, teasing my clit and I felt the change. I felt the glow intensify, the light filling my being, and just when I thought I couldn't take it anymore it burst up and out from the very center of my body, flowing in a rush down every nerve. It left my muscles expanding and contracting, so crazy, so wild, so free that I very nearly blacked out and found myself gasping, pressed against Blue's chest, one of his muscular arms around my waist, the other along my back.

One strong hand buried in the back of my hair, kneading my neck as he lazily took over, thrusting up into the wet heat of my body while I gripped the covers beneath our bodies in my fists.

My hearing came back in stages, and when it did, it was to his voice, soft, gentle, and encouraging but also soothing; his breath ruffling my hair. I pushed up and he let me go, smiling while I went for a third orgasm and worked diligently to give him his first. I found an undulating rhythm, bracing my hands on the headboard and working myself back and forth and up and down on him until his eyes slipped shut and his breath came fast.

His hands found my hips and he caressed up and down my body, gripping my breasts, teasing the nipples with forefingers and thumbs, sparking me up again; my body still felt so good from the last orgasm, but already another was beginning. Deep inside my pussy it felt heavy and warm, my body nurturing the tiny golden glow remaining into a raging fire.

"Oh, God!" I cried and leaned into his hands. He grinned and worked with me, thrusting up as I thrust down and I swallowed hard, holding onto that feeling, riding that edge for as long as I could, growing only marginally frustrated when I didn't immediately tip into that glorious fall.

I could live in that space between forever, right on the edge, one muscle spasm away from coming, body filled with love and light, but alas, it wasn't to be. Blue grunted and thrust up, even as his hands found my hips and slammed me down onto him. I felt so good that when he bottomed out, striking my cervix, rather than hurt it sent me spiraling out into the ether, as if my soul separated from my body and was cast adrift.

This time it took much longer to come back from that. This time, when I came back, my ear was pressed over Blue's heart, listening to it thunder, even as it matched the cadence of my own which pounded so hard, I could feel it's every beat reverberating against my ribs.

I pushed up, sweat dewing both of our skins and looked down at him as if seeing him for the first time. He looked back and the same expression I wore was painted on his face.

"I love you so fucking much," he gasped, and I smiled down at him and laughed, bowing down and pressing my forehead to his.

"I love you, too."

"God, I want you all over again."

He'd started to go soft inside me, but I could feel him begin to already grow hard again.

"One second," I panted and reached between us, holding the condom at the root and drawing my body off of his. I discarded the used one and grabbed a fresh one, tearing it open and rolling it on.

"On your knees, baby," he said patting a hand against my thigh and I got off of him, lowering my body to the bed, arching my back low, while he set himself up behind me. He reached under the pillow and pulled something out and I asked, "What is that?"

"Anal plug, now stay down."

I felt my nerves spark to life as he reached for the lube on the bedside table. He shoved himself back into my pussy and fucked me low and slow while he pressed a lubricated finger to my asshole. I sucked in a deep breath and closed my eyes.

"Not the same, but best I can do," he murmured and worked me up slowly into taking the plug into my ass. It felt good. A full feeling that I hadn't gotten anyway else since... well, since he and Cell had shared me.

He held the plug in place with the heel of his hand and sucked in a deep breath, striking a harder more punishing rhythm with his cock. I exhaled sharply and began to pant, gripping the covers with my fists as the pleasure began to build.

"Oh, God, Blue!"

"Yeah? Does that feel good?" he demanded.

"Yeah!"

"Good."

And it was good. Not the same, obviously, but good. I loved him so much and I loved that he would explore with me and that he loved me, and that what we shared with Cell was something to be celebrated more than mourned.

I loved that he would be a father to our child regardless of its genetics and I loved so very much that they had both taken a chance on me and had opened up my life and my world to so much more than it had been.

I loved them both and I always would, even if one were gone, he would always be a part of the both of us and by loving each other as fiercely as we did, we brought a sort of honor to our memories.

I arched low to the mattress, coming hard and long and continuous – finding a never-ending bliss in the pulse of my husband's body in mine.

EPILOGUE

Blue...

Hayley was eight months pregnant, but we still hadn't missed the Harvest Festival. We'd still danced to her favorite live music and we still rode the Ferris wheel and we still ate cotton candy, and when we got home? I still bent her over her studio work table and fucked her like she wasn't smuggling a basketball under her shirt. I couldn't help myself – pregnancy looked so damn good on her and her OB said there was absolutely nothing wrong with an active sex life while Hayley carried. In fact, she kind of encouraged it when Hayley ended up overdue.

I'd checked out just fine according to Doc, my momentary lapse in judgment while in the throes of grief firmly in the rearview, we'd dispensed with the condoms. She was already pregnant and skin on skin felt so much better, anyway.

Plus, when Hayley reached eight days past her due date, her doc had suggested sex as an option to speed things along. Said something about sperm might get things going. Considering how miserable Hayley was, just ready to have this baby out, we'd gone for it and wouldn't you know? Her water had broken this morning.

I held her hand while she went through another contraction, the way her nurse had shown me, and I figured this boy had to be Cell's because it was eighteen hours and counting and he wasn't going to make an appearance until he was damn good and ready.

"Oh, God, Blue!"

"I know, baby, but you're doing so good! You just hang in there okay? You've got this."

She screamed and the doctor checked her out and fuckin' finally declared, "Okay, Hayley, it's definitely time to push!"

The shriek my wife let out was fucking soul-rending to the point I seriously contemplated making this an only child, even if that meant I got myself snipped because Holy God… I knew making a life was painful and messy, but this shit was unreal.

She moaned and groaned and tried again and after what felt like an age, the doctor lifted a blue baby boy up and passed him immediately to a nurse.

I panicked on the inside. I mean was he supposed to be blue like that? Why wasn't he crying? What was wrong and then…

The sweetest sound that I ever heard split the air. I never knew that a newborn baby sounded like a kitten, but it did. My baby boy did.

Hayley sobbed and I held her, pressing a kiss to her sweaty forehead as the doctor worked between my wife's thighs and the nurse brought our son over. She laid him on Hayley's chest, and we exchanged a look, both of us wearing twin expressions of relief at the shock of bright red, wispy hair on his scalp.

"Hi, Damon," Hayley murmured and kissed our boy while I had to stand up, overcome with a flood of emotion that poured out my eyes whether I wanted it to or not.

"Oh, my God, you did good Little One," I said and reached out to caress our baby's head.

"I'm so happy," she declared and I looked at her, my vision swimming and said, "Me, too."

ALSO BY A.J. DOWNEY

The Sacred Hearts MC

1. Shattered & Scarred

2. Broken & Burned

3. Cracked & Crushed

4. Masked & Miserable (a novella)

5. Tattered & Torn

6. Fractured & Formidable

7. Damaged & Dangerous

8. Brother to Brother

9. Her Brother's Keeper

10. Brother In Arms

11. Between Brothers

12. A Brother's Secret

13. A Brother At My Back

14. A Brother's Salvation

The Virtues

1. Cutter's Hope

2. Marlin's Faith

3. Charity for Nothing

4. Stoker's Serenity

5. Justice for Radar

6. Lightning's Honor

Sacred Hearts MC Novella

Christmas with the Brotherhood

Indigo Knights

1. Her Thin Blue Lifeline

2. His Cold Blue Command

3. A Low Blue Flame

4. His Wild Blue Rose

5. Her Pained Blue Silence

6. A Cold Blue Call

7. Her Reluctant Blue Cavalier

8. Forged Under Fire

9. Under A Blue Moon

10. Sound of Blue Thunder

Sacred Hearts MC Pacific Northwest

1. Over the High Side

2. Wind Therapy

3. Apex of the Curve

4. Low Sided

5. Eating Asphalt

6. Hammer Down

7. Only Fool Riding

The Voodoo Bastards MC

1. Bourbon & Blood

2. Whiskey Shivers

3. Moonshine Lullabies

4. Cognac Secrets

5. Tequila Damnation

Iron Wraiths MC

1. Original Syn

2. Love & Fear

3. The Hangman's Rope

Royal Bastard MC: St. Augustine Chapter

1. Iron Hearts

Paranormal Romance (with Ryan Kells)

1. I Am The Alpha

2. Omega's Run

3. Hunter's End

Indigo City Darker (with Jared KingPacal Lain)

1. Triple Threat

2. Double Shot

Standalones

Synchronicity

ABOUT A.J. DOWNEY

A.J. Downey is a Pacific Northwest girl living in an East Tennessee world who finds inspiration from her surroundings, through the people she meets, and likely as a byproduct of way too much caffeine. She specializes in real and relatable romance stories featuring that real-life kind of love that everyone craves.

Stalker Information:

Website
www.ajdowney.com

www.ingramcontent.com/pod-product-compliance
Lightning Source LLC
Chambersburg PA
CBHW071108250626
47159CB00002B/646